Get Lost with You

Also by Sophie Sullivan

Ten Rules for Faking It

How to Love Your Neighbor

A Guide to Being Just Friends

Love, Naturally

Can't Help Falling in Love

Get Lost with You

A NOVEL

with You

Sophie Sullivan

ST. MARTIN'S GRIFFIN
NEW YORK

First published in the United States by St. Martin's Griffin, an imprint of St. Martin's Publishing Group

GET LOST WITH YOU. Copyright © 2025 by Jody Holford. All rights reserved. Printed in the United States of America. For information, address St. Martin's Publishing Group, 120 Broadway, New York, NY 10271.

www.stmartins.com

Designed by Gabriel Guma

Library of Congress Cataloging-in-Publication Data

Names: Sullivan, Sophie, 1976– author.
Title: Get lost with you : a novel / Sophie Sullivan.
Description: First edition. | New York : St. Martin's Griffin, 2025.
Identifiers: LCCN 2024041765 | ISBN 9781250875853 (trade paperback) |
    ISBN 9781250875860 (ebook)
Subjects: LCGFT: Romance fiction. | Novels.
Classification: LCC PR9199.4.H6454 G48 2025 | DDC 813/.6—
    dc23/eng/20240906
LC record available at https://lccn.loc.gov/2024041765

Our books may be purchased in bulk for promotional, educational, or business use. Please contact your local bookseller or the Macmillan Corporate and Premium Sales Department at 1-800-221-7945, extension 5442, or by email at MacmillanSpecialMarkets@macmillan.com.

First Edition: 2025

10 9 8 7 6 5 4 3 2 1

To you, the person reading this book. Thank you.

You look like the rest of my life.

—BEAU TAPLIN

One

There were only two reasons to go to a high school reunion. First, you'd reinvented yourself to the point of envy through riches, love, or some other form of success. The second, and the only reason Jillian Keller was heading into her former high school gymnasium, was to rescue her best friend who went for the first reason but was now, unsurprisingly, regretting her decision.

Jillian didn't have any horrible memories of attending Ernest Simel High, but it wasn't a place she'd ever missed either. It certainly wasn't a place, or time, she wished to go back to. Especially not on a Friday night, twelve years past graduation, to hang with people she'd never really been close to. Besides, it was Smile; every Sunday at the market was a reunion with someone.

In and out, she assured herself after locking her sunshine-yellow VW bug. Hopefully she'd go unnoticed, since she'd gotten the text to rescue her best friend just as she'd started to nudge her daughter, Ollie, over to the other side of her bed—because Ollie had recently decided Jillian shouldn't sleep alone—and tuck herself in. She didn't want to be here, and she definitely didn't want to be seen in her Get Lost hoodie and baggy sweatpants, sans makeup—not that she usually wore a ton—with her auburn hair piled on top of her head.

She heard the music even before she pulled open one of the double doors. A dark blue banner welcomed everyone. Jillian knew her way to the gym even without the arrows and signs reminding former students. Unlike her brothers, she hadn't spent much time there, other than watching them play whatever sport they were into at the time. She preferred the quiet of the library or the quad with its skylights and bench seating. The bass of the song vibrated beneath her feet, and without warning or reason, nerves tiptoed in. Something about high school. Anyone who went back felt seventeen again. She laughed at her own silliness but didn't open the gym door. Instead, she grabbed her phone from her hoodie pocket to text Lainey.

Jillian

I'm here. Let's go.

Don't make me come in there.

Come on party girl. The night is over.

The door whooshed open, unleashing the scents of too many perfumes and sprays mixed with sweat. A bundle of sequins and color tumbled out in the form of laughing women, hanging on to each other while moving as one huge, bejeweled unit.

Jillian stepped back, letting them pass, aware that her heartbeat was picking up its pace, matching the steady thump of the music. She stared at her phone, silently cursed her best friend, and sucked in a sharp breath like she was about to dive into ice-cold water.

She crossed the gym threshold and it felt like stepping back in time. Lights flashed, music blared, and familiar faces jostled past, some dancing, some laughing, some at the round tables, others holding up a section of the wall as they stared around the room with a drink in hand.

Jillian kept her head down, weaving between groups, hoping people were having too much fun to notice her. She probably should have brushed her hair. Worn something other than sweats. She didn't mind conversation and enjoyed meeting up with people, but being a single mother had a way of changing a woman's interests, not to mention her bedtime.

There were so many streamers hanging from the walls it looked like blue-and-white webs of tissue paper interspersed with balloons. People hammed it up for photos behind a large, decorated cardboard cutout frame. Anderson Keddy, a Smile local who did a little of everything, from haircuts to taxiing—and, apparently, taking pictures—waved when they saw Jill. Their shoulder-length brown hair bounced as they directed poses and snapped pictures. A guy Jillian recognized but couldn't name danced behind the DJ table, pressing buttons on the soundboard, likely controlling the light show making Jillian squint.

It wasn't until Jillian moved out of the way of a couple forgetting they were in the middle of a crowded gym and *not* a hotel room that she spotted Lainey.

Her bestie since kindergarten, when Danny "once a jerk always a jerk even if he was good-looking now" Rutherford had pushed Lainey down by the swings after making fun of her lunch. Another girl their age, Kylie Williams, had raced after him when he'd run away, dragged him back by his T-shirt, and forced him to apologize. Jilly, who'd watched the whole thing unfold from the shade where she'd been reading, came over to pick up the lunch containers that had fallen. The three girls had bonded, and despite all of them moving away, two of them moving back, and life getting in the way, they were all still close.

Lainey was no longer a wallflower, though Jillian had never seen her that way. At the moment, she was the life of the party, leading a line of dancers through the crowd like a human snake of pheromones and hair gel. Jillian could only shake her head, letting loose a deep, slightly tired belly laugh. Lainey raised her hand in the air, pretending to yank a chain while yelling "Woot, woot!"

As she passed, Jillian called out, "This does not look like you need rescuing."

Lainey craned her neck as she led the line away, grinning at Jillian. "Five more minutes, Mom."

Letting herself slink away from the crowd, she leaned against the wall to text her mom that she'd be back soon. Her parents were traveling later this summer, taking an RV trip with some friends. They were following their favorite band on part of their US tour. It made Jillian laugh to think of her parents like groupies. Her mother and her best friend, who was like an aunt to the Keller siblings, even had shirts made that read: WE GO WHERE THEY GO.

They'd come home midsummer last year after a much shorter trip. When their oldest son, Grayson, acquired the fishing lodge, they'd pitched in to get it in shape and ready to accommodate guests. It was so nice to have her whole family close. Jillian and her two older brothers, Gray and Beckett, got along very well, and both were great with Jill's daughter, Ollie. So was Beckett's girlfriend, Presley, whom he'd met at the lodge through a strange set of circumstances. She'd moved to Smile last summer, and Jill enjoyed having another woman her age around. Ollie was just thrilled to have everyone she loved within hugging distance. It'd be hard to watch her parents go, but the lodge and the siblings were in good shape, gearing up for this summer's season. Jillian's phone buzzed.

Mom

> You could always let your hair down and dance while you wait

Jillian

> I didn't come to get down, Mom. Just to pick up the Bracelet Babe

Mom

> You could use a little fun, sweetie

Jillian

> I live with a nine-year-old, you, and Dad. My life is nonstop fun.

Mom

> I take that back. What you need is a dictionary. Clearly, you don't know what the word means.

Jillian

Or I could Google it?

Her mom sent her a facepalm emoji that made Jillian laugh out loud before slipping her phone back in her pocket. When she looked up, her gaze caught on the hint of dark hair against a white collar and wide shoulders moving through the crowd.

She rubbed her hands over her biceps in an attempt to tame the strange tingling waking up all of her nerve endings. *Weird.* He looked like Levi Bright. Just the simple thought of him prompted her mouth to tip up in a smile, her heart to speed up. *Haven't thought about him in a long time.* Giving her head a slight shake, she reminded herself that she was here to grab her friend and get out, not get mired down in the past—on the dance floor or in her head. She'd lost more hours than she could count in her teenage years thinking about Levi or writing about him in her diary.

She really needed some sleep. The lodge wasn't opening for another month. They'd decided to open on the first of June so they could make sure everything was ready to operate at full capacity. This also allowed her to do a trial run of hosting an event there to see if it was feasible. It'd been Jillian's suggestion to start with a kids' overnight camp before the end of the school year, because really, were there any judges harsher than eight- and nine-year-olds?

Lainey bounced over to her, bumping her, *hard,* with her hip. Jillian straightened off the wall, stopped herself from falling.

"You lift weights with your hips or what? You could knock someone out like that."

Lainey laughed, lifting her long arms in the air and letting her gorgeous, uniquely designed bracelets slide down until they stopped at her elbows.

"These hips can do wonderful things. Come dance," Lainey said, shaking said hips.

Dressed in a body-hugging red sheath dress with little silver sparkles catching in the rays of the disco light, her friend looked stunning. Six feet tall without the three-inch heels, she had cropped hair that winged out at the ends, accentuating her sharp jaw and cradling her beautiful face. On a regular day, Jillian felt like a shrimp next to her, but tonight, dressed for comfort and bed, she also felt a bit frumpy. She pushed the thought away, blaming the sudden and uncharacteristic moment of insecurity on being in a high school.

"I need to get home. You texted, said 'save me.' I'm here."

Lainey wrapped her arms around Jill. "Like a perfect best friend."

She pulled back and Jillian caught just a hint of *something* in her gaze. Enough something to make her skin itch.

"Time to go, right?" Jillian said, taking a few steps forward.

"So, you'll never guess who's here."

Jillian looked around before sending her friend a wry smile. "Most of the 2012 graduating class?"

Lainey bit her lip, a total tell. Jillian's head whipped around, scanning the crowd. Who else would be here? That lip bite meant Lainey had boxed Jillian into something "for her own good."

It'd started in their teens when Lainey had "helpfully" arranged for Jillian to have a private goodbye with the aforementioned Levi, who left town at seventeen—to Jillian's fifteen—to pursue his culinary dreams. Of course, neither of them could have predicted that the goodbye would go down in history as one of Jillian's most embarrassing moments. Ever. In her life. Though, Lainey's "help" wasn't always bad. During a visit after Ollie was born, Lainey secretly blocked WebMD from her phone.

That had saved Jill a lot of diagnosing she shouldn't have been doing anyway. Then there was the time, when they were teenagers, Lainey pretended to hurt her ankle so Jillian would be forced to drive them onto the ferry for the first time. Or, more recently, when she'd convinced Jillian to go for an overnight girls' trip in Michigan by teasing her with a trip to Costco. Jillian braced herself for whatever her friend had in store. When Lainey continued to smile, her head tipping to the side, Jillian's skin prickled.

"What did you do? Am I going to have to bury your body or someone else's on the way home?"

Lainey put an arm around Jilly's shoulder and looked straight ahead and, like they'd choreographed it, Graham Bennett, a former colleague and friend in the loosest sense of the word, approached. As usual, he wore a soft-looking sweater that highlighted his trim, athletic build. His smile was worthy of a toothpaste commercial and his hair was definitely more styled than her own. He was good-looking, sweet, and nice. And she had absolutely zero interest in dating him. Which Lainey knew.

"Hi, Graham," Jill said, doing her best not to pat down the nest of hair on her head or appear more awkward than she probably looked.

"Jilly. I was hoping for a dance with you tonight."

Lainey had stepped to the side as soon as he joined them and was now mouthing, *Just do it* behind Graham's back.

"That's very sweet. I'm not staying, though. I'm sorry."

The way his smile dropped always made her feel bad, but pretending she had interest when she didn't would make her feel worse.

Lainey's eye roll was cut short when Graham turned and shrugged. "We tried. Nice to see you, Lainey."

Shaking her head, Lainey came back to Jilly's side as he walked away. "Why do you say no to someone who would bend over backward to make you happy?"

Jill scanned the crowd, looking for the straightest path out, and caught that same glimpse of dark hair and felt immediate awareness. How could she say yes to someone like Graham when just the thought of a man she hadn't seen in ten years made her stomach muscles tighten and flutter? Or, more importantly, when she knew she couldn't fully trust someone else until she regained her trust in herself?

"I'm perfectly happy, thank you. Can we go?"

"I don't mean happy in the overall sense of the word," Lainey explained as Jillian guided them through the sea of people.

"Of course you don't," Jill muttered. "That would be too easy."

Lainey tripped, knocking Jill off balance, as a lull drifted between songs. It had to be then that her friend added, "I mean happy in the postcoital-glow way."

Laughter ensued, but only for a second until another song muffled it. Jilly's stomach burned as she ducked her head and picked up the pace. Just what she needed: people talking about her nonexistent sex life at a high school reunion she hadn't even attended.

Lainey was repeating "sorry" as they walked and nudged, reaching a door at the side of the gym. Jillian was so focused on getting out, on people not seeing her, that she didn't know if her friend was apologizing to her or to the people they bumped into on their way.

Lainey hustled beside her, pulling at one of her arms, and made her stop. "Jill. Sweetie. Stop." She pulled Jill around to face her. "Graham's a good guy."

Jillian was on the verge of cranky, but she knew her friend just wanted good things for both of them. "Then you should date him. I'm happy with my life."

"How happy?" Lainey's grin, like her personality, was relentless.

Jillian tipped her head up to the dark sky and groaned. "Can we go? Please? Stop worrying about my dating life."

Lainey walked beside her, bumping her with her shoulder. "Can't worry about what doesn't exist. Though, maybe you're right about Graham. Maybe you're right to hold out."

Jillian huffed out a breath as they walked along the side of the school toward the front parking lot. "I'm not holding out."

Lainey gave her that look again; the one that hinted there was something she knew that Jilly didn't. Fortunately, Jillian knew better than to open another can of worms.

As they hopped into her beloved VW bug, Jillian's thoughts returned to Levi, her childhood crush. She wasn't actually holding out for anyone, but if she were . . . he'd be the one. Lainey was snoring softly before they even reached her home, but, with Jilly's help, she roused enough to get into her apartment over her shop.

Jilly didn't have a direction in mind when she left Lainey's, but her mind was swirling with a mix of the past and present, and she knew if she went home now, she wouldn't sleep. She might not have a man in her life but she could, and would, always have pie.

Two

Every town worth its name had a decent pie shop. As the night waitress at Petal's Pie Palace took her order—decaf tea, a piece of apple (a classic), peach-blueberry (her favorite), and chocolate cream (obvious reasons), Jillian told herself it was okay to indulge. She'd rather have three pieces of pie than a six-pack of beer. She might feel as gross as Lainey tomorrow as a result but it wouldn't give her a headache.

She glanced around the small shop that was basically a Smile institution, and memories of coming here as a teen drifted lazily through her brain. Petal's stayed open until the wee hours of the morning for people who needed a delicious, carb-rich snack after a late night at Brothers' Pub, Lakeview Bar (which wasn't really much of a bar at all but stayed open until two on the weekends), or unnecessary high school reunions.

The booths were a faded teal color with bubble-gum-pink flecks that, at one time, looked like confetti or sprinkles. Music played softly through the speakers but Jilly knew it came from a Bluetooth speaker rather than the antique jukebox in the corner. The place had the same sort of nostalgic vibe the breakfast diner on Middle Street, Pete's, did.

The waitress dropped off three plates of pie and asked, again, if anyone was joining her.

"Nope," Jilly said, pushing down the need to explain herself for ordering three pieces. She could eat a whole damn pie if she wanted. Being a grown-up didn't come with nearly as many perks as kids thought it did. Ordering as much dessert as she wanted was one of them.

"'Kay," the waitress said, like the one syllable was all she could handle. She was probably about seventeen or eighteen and it was late, so maybe two syllables was asking too much.

Sliding her fork into the chocolate cream first, she then let the rich flavors burst on her tongue. Was there anything better than pie at nearly one in the morning? Scooping up a bite of peach-blueberry, she smiled, knowing what Lainey's answer would be.

For all her teasing, Lainey didn't date much more than Jilly did. Though her best friend didn't have the ex-husband who turned out to be a lying, embezzling rat-snake (Ollie insisted that was the worst combination of creatures imaginable) in her past, Lainey shared Jill's wariness of leaning too heavily on anyone other than herself.

While she nibbled from each pie plate, Jilly went through her Notes app and her to-do lists. Most people in Smile wore many hats, and Jilly was no different. She'd taken a leave from her job at the accounting firm to help her oldest brother. In the end, she'd loved working at the lodge enough to not go back. She had a few businesses that she did books on the side for, including Pete's, her brother Beckett's bike shop, and Lainey's bracelet shop. But she also had other plans and here, at the pie place, in the middle of the night, when she didn't want to dwell on the past and didn't want to go home to her present, she could think about her future.

The lodge was well set up to handle events like team-building sessions, bachelor or bachelorette parties, and even weddings. She just needed to find the most cost-effective way to present the idea to Grayson. Presley, her soon-to-be sister-in-law if her brother Beckett ever got around to proposing, would help her with the marketing.

By next year, she hoped Get Lost Lodge would be the go-to place to host events in Smile, Northern Michigan, and surrounding islands.

"You want anything else?" the waitress asked, appearing like a pie-wielding ninja.

"I'm good," Jilly said, glancing up.

There were only a couple of other people in the shop but the waitress hesitated, staring at Jill, not delivering her orders.

Jill waited, wondering if the teen was okay, if maybe she needed something. Her nose scrunched up, making her nose ring look uncomfortable.

"Everything okay?" Jilly asked.

"You have pie in your hair," the waitress said, then walked past.

Jilly closed her eyes and sighed. Time to go home.

Leaving the three partially eaten pieces of pie in the fridge of her parents' home, where she'd been living temporarily for about four years now, she got ready for bed and crawled in beside a softly snoring Ollie.

Inhaling deeply, she caught the scent of vanilla bath wash and bubble-gum-scented shampoo. Ollie stirred, rolled, and nearly whapped Jilly in the nose with her hand.

Jilly caught her fingers, tucked them close to her body.

"Mom?" Ollie whispered.

"Yeah?"

"Just making sure it's you." Ollie snuggled closer.

Jilly huffed out a soft laugh. "It's my bed, honey. Of course it's me."

"I need cupcakes for tomorrow for my whole class," she whispered even as she fell back asleep, practically snoring out the last word.

Jilly sighed into the darkness. Lainey might think she was lonely, or worry about her happiness, but Jillian Keller had everything she needed, right here beside her. Except cupcakes. And she could grab those in the morning.

Three

Levi Bright had missed a lot of things about Smile, Michigan: the water, the view of the mountains and the Mackinac Bridge, his mom, and even his dad. But what he'd truly missed, more than he'd realized, was the quirkiness of the people who lived here. Unique personalities created one hell of a fun vibe in a small town. Something big cities couldn't compete with.

He'd already been ready to come home for good when his mom called saying his dad had to have surgery. Nothing major, according to her—routine gallbladder removal—but it was the final push that cemented his decision.

Leaving home at seventeen to attend culinary school in New Hampshire was a huge adventure and he'd had a lot of fun. Freedom, working toward his dream of being a chef—what more could he have asked for?

He'd performed well enough to get some prestigious offers from big-name restaurants in different cities. He'd chosen to settle into the Vermont restaurant scene with a few of his culinary school buddies. What he saw of Burlington, when he wasn't in the kitchen working his way up, was great. But it wasn't home.

He stared at the community chalkboard that took up a wall in the back of the General Store, his lips twitching at the messages, some scrawled, some printed with fine precision.

I need a dog sitter this weekend. Tipper has some bladder issues & can't handle the long car ride. Anyone? Message me: 947-555-0091

Forgot my umbrella at the park. If you found it, please return it here. Shelley.

Should Beckett propose to Presley in public?

Yes
####
|||

No
Mind your own business
—Beckett

Beckett, of the chalkboard poll, had been one of his best friends growing up. Levi definitely missed him and his brother Grayson. And of course, Jillian Keller. Their sister. If he was honest with himself, he'd only said yes to pitching in at the reunion last night—their caterer had canceled—in hopes of seeing Jillian.

There was a moment last night where his blood seemed to spark with awareness and he'd thought he caught a glimpse of her, but he didn't. It wasn't surprising not to have run into anyone. He'd only been back a few days. He'd gone straight to his parents', listened to his dad complain about him being "home for no reason," and crashed in the spare bedroom of their houseboat before agreeing to step in for the cook who'd bailed on the reunion.

Setting the chalk down on the ledge, he went down the next aisle, grabbing some brown rice and whole-grain pasta. His dad would bitch but Levi knew how to make even dull ingredients dance with flavor. They might not see eye to eye, but his dad was getting older and Levi didn't want tension between them anymore.

Maybe the surgery wasn't a big deal, but it reminded Levi that no one stuck around forever. He'd gone away, chased his dreams, and learned that joy—and sadness, if he was honest—felt better when shared with people who loved him. His mom's call and the hint of fear in her voice, regardless of her words saying everything would be okay, were all he needed to get back to the place he'd missed.

With his head down, he double-checked his basket, and rammed straight into something that turned out to be a person with a dozen or so packages of mini cupcakes piled high in their arms.

"I'm so sorry," he mumbled, even as he hurriedly set his basket down, reaching out to steady the person or, at the very least, maybe the baked goods. His hands covered dainty ones, and little flickers of heat danced over his skin, through his fingertips, and up his arms. The muscles around his heart tightened uncomfortably and he knew, even before the top two packs fell to the floor, who was behind the cupcake tower.

The plastic containers made a loud *splat* noise on the linoleum—*cupcakes down*—but all he could see was Jillian Keller. An unexpected fluttery feeling slapped his rib cage and wiggled its way up to his heart as he stared at her, waited for her gaze to move from the mess on the floor to his face.

When it did, the sparks on his skin paled in comparison to the bolt of lightning that hit his gut. *Goddamn* she'd grown up to be stunning. That wasn't a surprise, but the way looking at her stole his breath absolutely was.

Because she had very little, if any, makeup on, it was easy to take in her natural beauty: the soft pink of her round cheeks, the shape of her eyes and their striking color, the slope of her cute nose. A gentle blush settled over her face. They'd grown up together, they were friends in the "little-sister-of-my-friends" sort of way. Until she'd turned thirteen to his fifteen. Some sort of switch had flipped that summer, and when he saw her, his palms got sweaty, his words got tangled in his mouth, and his heart acted like it was on speed if she got too close.

Levi had fought the crush hard because of his friendship with Beckett and Gray. But by the time he'd left Smile at seventeen, he'd known if he spent another summer around her, he'd kiss her for sure. Or she would have kissed him. The one time she'd gathered the nerve to try hadn't ended so well, but the memory still made him smile.

Without thinking about it, one of his hands moved to his chin, where his fingers rubbed over the small scar from that night. They were older and wiser now but she was still off-limits. There were strict "guy rules" about these things: female relatives of buddies were off-limits. Even if, after fifteen years apart, his tongue felt thick, his mouth frozen, just from looking at her. From the way his blood hummed beneath his skin, he didn't think it was going to be any easier to remember the rules at thirty-one.

Last night, when he thought he saw her, he'd searched a little longer than he should have, but he told himself it was just to catch up and say hi.

His heart thumped in his chest like it was chanting, *li-ar, li-ar* with its beats.

"Levi," she said, her voice a husky whisper.

"Hi, Jilly." He smiled at her, wishing he could hug her, but with the cupcakes in her arms and the mini time lapse as they stared at each other, it would be awkward. Hell, *he* was awkward, gawking at her like he'd never been around a gorgeous woman before.

"You're really home," she said, almost more to herself than him.

He laughed, ran a hand through his hair. "I am. Were there rumors I wouldn't be?"

Her eyes widened a bit, like she realized she'd said it aloud. "No. No. I just thought I saw you but didn't think it could be you." She glanced down at the mess, pulling his gaze to the same spot.

He crouched down to grab them. "Shit. I'm so sorry."

The packages crinkled as he turned them right side up. He winced as he stood straight, looking at the mushed pink icing smearing the inside of the lid.

"They aren't so pretty now," he said, giving her a sheepish smile. "I'll go see if there's a couple more packs?" He looked around, realizing the baked goods aisle was exactly where it'd been when he moved away.

"It's okay. Really. Eight packs should be enough. Those two were just extra. I grabbed all there was. I should take them up front, though, if you don't mind putting them back on my pile?"

Levi grinned. "It's bad enough I almost took you out with miniature cupcakes. The least I can do is walk you to the front."

"Good thing they weren't full size," she said as he scooped up his basket with his free hand.

Her lips twitched and he had the urge to make her laugh. She had a deep, full laugh that he could almost hear when he thought of it. "It could have been catastrophic."

A small, barely there giggle left her lips. "It wasn't entirely your fault. I was hurrying and couldn't see. My daughter, Ollie, forgot to tell me she signed me up to bring treats for the activity day at school this afternoon."

Right. She'd been married and had a kid. He couldn't remember all the details, but he knew she'd moved back a while ago with only the kid. "Ahh. Not just a cupcake emergency but a last-minute one."

Jillian laughed, and the sound delighted him. Just like he remembered: rich and carefree and so absolutely sweet. "Adulting with a kid is never dull. But never mind that; are you visiting your parents?"

As they walked side by side to the front of the store, he leaned a bit closer. He hadn't forgotten that Smile's official pastime was gossiping. "I'm home for good. I was already packed and headed this way when my dad had to have emergency gallbladder surgery."

Jillian stopped, turned toward him, her compassion radiating in waves that pulled him closer. "What? Is he okay? How did I not know this?"

He laughed, resisting the urge to smooth her brow with his fingertips. "Despite a lot of evidence, you actually can keep a secret in this town. Not well, but he told his crew not to say anything. You know him—stubborn as a mule and can't stand being helped."

"Aw. I'm glad he's okay. I should cook something and bring it over."

He wasn't going to say no to seeing her again, but before he could say anything, her face scrunched adorably.

"Right. As if he needs my lazy lasagna when he's got a chef on hand."

Levi cringed. "Lazy lasagna? Jilly." He shook his head in mock disappointment. "Good thing I'm home. That sounds like a crime."

She rolled her eyes, amusement shining, and started walking toward the front of the store. He'd forgotten how easy she was to talk to. His work kept him so busy and so focused, he'd forgotten a lot of things. But they were coming back to him.

"Let's never talk about that again," he teased.

When he looked down at her, his arm brushed against hers, and sensation traveled through him like a current. Jillian stared up at him for a minute and the muscles in Levi's chest tightened, making it harder to breathe. Her bottom lip slipped between her teeth and Levi fought the urge to press his thumb against it, tug it out, and replace it with his lips. *Shit. Redirect. Redirect.*

"I can't believe you're home," she said, her voice breathy.

He couldn't read her expression, which shouldn't have been a surprise. He wanted to; he wanted to know what she was thinking. Did she remember the crush they'd had on each other? It wasn't one-sided, and if he was right about her intentions the night he left, she'd wanted to kiss him every bit as much as he'd wanted to kiss her.

"I'm right here, so it must be true," he said in a whisper.

Shaking her head and the somewhat dreamy look out of her eyes, she walked to the checkout.

Maureen, the store owner and Smile's part-time psychologist, was scrolling on her phone when they approached the counter. Her dark brown eyes widened as they closed the distance, a little smile tipping her lips upward. She wore a purple silk scarf around the base of a thick bun that didn't hide all the gray. Another reminder that time passed. He didn't want to miss any more of it with these people. Maureen's happy, all-seeing eyes and wide welcoming smile hadn't changed a bit.

"Well, look at this," Maureen said, setting her phone down. "It's like turning the TV to a retro channel. Last time I saw the two of you here together, I don't know if either of you were old enough to drive."

"Ouch. Way to age us all," Levi said, setting the mangled cupcakes on the counter.

Maureen's laugh was deep and smoky. "Oldest one in the
room is allowed to do that. Levi, you're not supposed to rough
them up first." She picked up a pack, stared at the smooshed
baked goods.

Levi set his basket down on the counter, then helped Jilly unload her arms. "There was a bit of a collision. I'll pay for them."

"You don't have to buy them, Levi. I couldn't even see where
I was going." Jill opened her wallet, which was handily hooked
around her wrist.

Maureen shushed them both. "Don't be silly. I'm not charging
for them. Miles will eat them."

Miles was her husband. Levi hadn't seen him yet, but usually
he worked in the back of the store, which acted as a post office and
shipping depot. Maureen took the cloth bag Jilly produced out of
her pocket, started ringing the cupcakes up. "Levi, heard your
dad's surgery went well. Hopefully he won't go back to eating all
that greasy food. Your mom says you're home for good?"

It felt great to reply with "I am." It felt even better to see Jilly's
gaze drift to his with the same spark in them he felt in his chest.

"Wonderful. Welcome back. Now, did you get a craving, Jilly,
or are you and your brothers meeting up?"

"Ollie forgot to mention she needed cupcakes for sports day
today," Jill said.

"I could have gotten Miles or Anderson to deliver them,
honey. No need for you to be running around more than you already do." Maureen shook her head, loaded the cupcakes into the
bag. Then she glanced at Levi. "Though, I suppose things work
out as they're meant to sometimes, don't they?"

The silence stretched too many beats, which made Levi laugh

awkwardly, which in turn made Maureen hoot with unrestrained laughter. Jilly got them back on track by telling them about the sports day at the school.

He liked listening to her talk, and when she spoke about her daughter, her entire body seemed to shift into high gear, like just the thought of her kid energized her. It made him want to move closer and ask more questions to keep her chatting.

Jilly paid, but waited at the end of the counter for Levi's order to be rung through.

"What will you do now that you're back? Your mom is always telling us about the fancy restaurant you worked in," Maureen said, scanning the items.

His end goal was always food. Right now, though, he needed to build some bridges. Literally and metaphorically. "I'm hoping to pitch in for my dad so he doesn't get behind on his jobs. He's coming home from the hospital today."

No need to tell anyone that he was thinking about a food truck that served elevated comfort foods. He gestured to the chalkboard with his thumb. "Maybe I should put that on the board so everyone doesn't have to ask?" He paid, then scooped up his bags as he joined Jillian at the end of the counter.

"People do love our chalkboard. Even with the new Smile Facebook page, people list everything on there." Maureen leaned on the counter.

"That's really nice that you're going to help your dad out. It's not always easy to put your own dreams on hold for others," Jillian said.

Something tweaked in Levi's chest. The way she said it suggested she knew, personally, how that felt. He hadn't done that at seventeen, but he could do it now while he got settled and started building his life here. "Let's hope he thinks so."

The phone on the wall—which Levi couldn't believe still existed; the thing was a relic—rang.

"Better get that. You two be good. Glad you're home, Levi. Tell your mom Miles can deliver if she needs anything."

His chest warmed. His own tally was proving more people were glad about his return than not. In fact, so far his dad was the only one in the "not" column. He pushed that thought away for later.

They waved to Mo as she picked up the receiver. When they stepped off the little porch and onto the sidewalk, the sun was lifting in the sky, casting a warmth over them that Levi wanted to soak up. He'd enjoyed the city, but damn it was good to be home where he felt like he could actually feel the sun on his skin.

When Levi looked over to tell Jillian how glad he was to be home, his words caught in his throat. Something about her, even before he'd had the ill-fated crush and even after all these years, pulled at his heartstrings.

No one could blame him for the bit of nostalgia and longing that hovered around his heart muscles. She brushed a strand of her long, wavy auburn hair behind her ear. Her dark brown eyes found his, making his heart bounce like a rubber ball. Shit. He realized right then that at the top of his list of things he'd missed, but hadn't let himself think about for all these years, was spending time with Jillian Keller.

Four

Jillian reminded herself that she needed to get the cupcakes to the school before they melted. *Or before you do, under the heat of Levi's gorgeous green-eyed gaze. Home for good, like thinking of him conjured him up.* She glanced his way, smiled. It was like the hue of his eyes had matured and aged as well as the rest of him. And yes, he still had the goddamned sanity-melting dimple.

Focus on something safe. Work. Kids. Not the way his biceps stretch the fabric of his T-shirt or the way he fills out those worn jeans. Definitely not the way the hint of stubble makes you want to rub up against him like a cat. Or the way his hair still falls in his eyes when he lowers his chin. The way his laugh still makes you smile without warning. She'd worn a sweater to fight off the brisk morning air, but now she was practically sweating. Jillian wasn't opposed to working up a good sweat in a scheduled and preplanned way. Like a hike. A bike ride. Jillian preferred things she could be in charge of; things that allowed her to orchestrate, or at least guide, the outcome.

Levi fell into step beside her like he had nowhere better to be. The natural move filled her with nostalgia and a bit of déjà vu for the times when they'd all stroll together down this very street. The shops on Middle Street were open but, lucky for her, none of the shop owners were on their stoops chatting or hanging out. That could change at any moment.

When Smile was founded, Ernest Simel had focused on creating a town center near the water. For years, the town was a total of five streets, this one right in the middle. The island town had grown exponentially, but one of the things Jillian loved was there were no cars allowed on Middle Street. This allowed it to keep the old-timey, slow-paced feel even with the updated shops and amenities.

"It feels weird. So much is the same but it's also completely different," Levi said as they crossed at the rainbow crosswalk toward the water. There was a walking and bike-riding path that would lead them to the school.

She felt like Ollie must when adults told her to hang on to her questions. They were bubbling up inside of her like water in a teakettle. What about the food industry? That was why he left. What happened to his job? What would he do here now that he was home? Had he fallen in love while he was away? Oh, gosh, had he brought someone home with him? *Breathe. Or at least, try to chill.*

"I get that. It's an accurate description. On one hand, we still have the community chalkboard, but on the other, there's been over a dozen new shops that have opened up in the last three years."

She'd felt similar when she'd come home. There were enough similarities to feel comfortable but enough progress and changes to not feel claustrophobic after living in a big city. Coming back, being surrounded by her family, back where she belonged, where Ollie belonged, smoothed many of the jagged edges married life had left her with.

Levi glanced at her. "You look good, Jilly. You went into accounting, right?"

Catching up just like regular friends would. No one had to know that being near him unearthed a longing she thought she'd buried years ago with her old diaries. She didn't even have to admit to herself that hearing him say she looked good made her want to stand up straighter. Or maybe hug him. *Because that wouldn't be awkward.*

"I did. I worked at a firm here in town but took a break to help Grayson with his lodge and ended up loving it. I mean, I do his accounting, but there's more to it than that. I gave up my old job but kept a few freelance clients. I also work a few days a month as the office business manager for the school." *Babble much?*

"My mom told me about the lodge. I need to see your brothers. I can't believe all three of the Keller siblings are back here and working together."

He stopped on the cobblestone walk, the breeze coming up off the water making his hair dance and her fingers itch to tame it.

He was different but so much the same, she didn't know what to do with the feelings wrestling each other in her chest. "Trust me, none of us could have predicted it."

Levi's eyebrows rose, a mischievous smile on his kissable lips. *Lips, Jilly. Just lips.*

"How's Beckett, besides on the fence about being engaged? I cast a 'yes' vote on the whole proposing-in-public debate," he said.

Jillian laughed, shifting the bag in her hand. "Beckett hates that their names are up there. Honestly, I think Presley put up the poll just to tease him. He's not really on the fence. He's so in love with Presley, he'd marry her tomorrow if he thought she'd say yes. They're just taking their time. He opened a bike shop, so they're busy with that."

"Right. I got an email last summer about a grand opening," he said, watching her closely enough that she worried she'd blush under his gaze. "It's perfect for him. Everyone is doing what they love. You can't ask for more than that."

Jillian bit her lower lip. There was something beneath the

happiness in his gaze; something she recognized. Longing? Her stomach tightened with unfamiliar feelings. It'd been a long time since she'd worried about anyone's happiness, other than Ollie's or her family's.

"No. You really can't."

He started walking again so she did as well, wondering if he was going to accompany her all the way to Ollie's school.

The quiet between them wasn't awkward or stilted the way it could be in certain situations. Like during her last date, or a conversation with Graham.

"Your mom must be glad you're home." She said it softly.

Not only had she caught the comment about hoping his dad felt the same, but the discord between him and Steven Bright wasn't a secret. Levi's dad had planned for him to join his construction business. Obviously, it was still a sore spot.

"She is. I think all parents are probably the same; they want their kids close. How about your parents?"

"They love that we're all here; especially Ollie. But the weird thing is, now they're the ones leaving." Jilly lifted one arm to wave at Anderson, who was down by the docks talking with Gramps, Smile's mayor and, as far as they knew, no one's actual grandpa.

"They're moving?"

The words put a kink in her breathing. She hoped not. "Traveling. They want to follow a band they love in their RV like a couple of groupies."

Levi's laugh chased away the melancholy the thought of them leaving brought.

"I can't imagine my parents doing that. I don't know how my dad is going to manage the summer of taking it easy."

He shifted his grocery bags to his right hand then put his left one on her lower back as they stepped off the curb and crossed over to the next street. Little licks of heat traveled up over her back from each of the spots where his fingertips rested. Jillian shivered.

Tilting his chin, he looked down at her with a sweet smile, so much of the old him mixed with the mature, too-hot-for-her-own-good him. "Cold?"

She swallowed, shook her head. It wasn't good to feel this much. She'd done that once before and ended up a divorced single mom with a low-key distrust of men.

"No."

Levi turned so they were facing each other, looked at her like he was waiting for her to say more. Nope. She wasn't putting her foot in her mouth. Not this time. Though, the last time she'd seen him, before he left, it was her mouth she'd tried to put on *his* that left her swimming in a pool of mortification.

"I'm glad I ran into you, Jilly."

She could be honest. She was a grown woman. He was a friend of her brothers'. A *family* friend. "Me, too. I'm glad you're home."

He shuffled closer, reached out, and tucked a strand of her hair behind her ear. She had to stop herself from leaning into his touch. *You're just remembering the boy you once loved.* Yet, the man looking back at her was every bit as intriguing.

"I feel like it's where I'm meant to be."

Because her chest felt too tight, she stepped back. "I should get these to Ollie."

"I won't be helping my dad out forever. My end game is to cook." He started to say more but stopped, pressed his lips together, and then started again, making her wonder what he *didn't* say. "Maybe I could make you dinner?" His words came out quick and loud. "I mean, you could also help me with some ideas for what kind of cuisine is missing in Smile and ways to reintegrate myself into the community."

"You know who you should talk to? Presley."

He smiled, the lines by his eyes crinkling adorably. Could something be sexy and adorable at once? Yes. *Levi Bright.*

Focus. "She's a marketing and media expert. She's running Smile's tourism and recently founded a Smile Vacation Concierge service. She puts together packages, gets shop owners to offer coupons and deals, and helps people make the most of their time here."

Levi took another step closer, and even though there were cupcakes and bags between them, it was like he'd sucked a little of the air right out of her lungs.

"I can't wait to meet her. So? Dinner? Maybe next week?" His gaze was strong and intense, like he could read her mind if he stared long enough.

Her heart vibrated like a nest of bees, creating a slow, subtle, but powerful hum along her skin.

Jilly's mouth went dry. Was he asking her on a date? Were her teenage dreams coming true? Did she want them to? She knew people had talked behind their hands, in whispered voices and low murmurs, when she'd returned to Smile. *Poor Jillian. Did you hear about her ex-husband? It's good she's home with her family.* It made her want to hide away.

Dating anyone—but definitely dating Levi—would be something different, but people would still talk. Gossip was fine as long as it wasn't about her. She couldn't shield Ollie from stories the way she had when they'd returned home. Levi continued to stare. Why couldn't she force words out of her mouth? *Because you've wanted Levi to ask you out since you were fifteen years old.*

He grinned, making her stomach jump in a way she felt all the way through her body. "You can't say no. We have a lot of catching up to do."

Jillian laughed, a needy, usually silent little voice in her head telling her to say yes.

Before she could, he put a hand in his pocket and said, "I'll ask Gray, Becks and his girl, my parents and yours. It'll be like old times."

Everything lurched to a stop. Just like old times. *When you were his friends' little sister.* Of course he wasn't asking her out on a date. *Go home, fifteen-year-old Jilly. You're all grown up now.*

"I have Ollie."

"Bring her."

What was the opposite of a date? *This. This is so not a date.* "Sure. Yeah. That sounds great."

"Good." Without warning, he leaned over the bundles in both of their arms and pressed a quick kiss to her cheek. She heard and felt his sharp inhale as his lips left her skin. Her heart bounded against her ribs like an overeager puppy who couldn't control its feelings. *Down, girl.*

"I'll see you." *Obviously.*

"Yes you will. Have a good day, Jilly."

She nodded, probably looked like a fool staring after him when he waved and turned back the way they'd come.

She released a pent-up sigh. Ten minutes back in Levi's presence and she was living out fairy tales in her head, seeing things that weren't there when she knew better. Even if he was attracted to her, he was close to her brothers. Guys had rules about these things. "No little sisters" was somewhere near the top, even if they'd all grown up.

Seeing things that weren't there was sort of her specialty. She'd let herself believe Andrew loved her enough to last a lifetime, when in truth, they hadn't even made it through the first year together without her wondering what she'd gotten herself into. She'd doubted his affection early on, but what scared her, and unfortunately stayed with her long after he left, was that she doubted herself. Her judgment and her ability to make someone stay. In turn, that made her question whether she ever wanted to take that risk again. Even with someone as special as Levi Bright.

Five

Levi's gut rolled with the gentle sway of his parents' houseboat and he realized, as he lay in bed staring at the off-white ceiling, thinking about Jillian's smile and the way her eyes crinkled, it was like being a teenager again. Back then, he hadn't known what to do with his feelings, but as an adult, he knew what he *wanted* to do about them. Seeing her the other day had brought an onslaught of emotions, but it wasn't just nostalgia or sweet memories.

His skin felt like it vibrated in her presence. It made him want to get closer, hold her hand, see if her hair was as soft as it looked. He'd dated here and there over the last several years, but being the head chef at a high-end restaurant was a life-consuming job. He wanted more out of life, and even though he knew the past was part of his feelings, he wanted to know who she was now. What made her smile besides Ollie? What did she do when she wasn't working one of her ten jobs? She'd looked so adorably flustered when he'd asked to make her dinner, he switched gears, saying he'd include the others. Seeing her with everyone was better than not seeing her at all.

Rolling off the twin bed, he shivered when he set his feet on the chilly, bare-wood floor under him. As a kid, he'd thought the short bank of colorful homes on the water in Tourist Lane, on the northern tip of Smile, was the coolest thing ever. Now, he was more than a little inclined to find a place on solid ground.

Glancing out the window, despite the unsteadiness of his stomach, he couldn't help but grin. A few guys were fishing off the end of the dock. A couple of boats were leaving, probably heading out to Mackinaw City for deliveries or pickups. A little girl and her mom walked out of the purple house at the end of the row, the girl's pigtails bouncing with her jumping steps.

He might not like houseboats anymore—other than looking at them—but he loved being in this part of Smile. It was tucked away down a long, narrow bike and walking path. He'd felt like a tourist himself a few nights ago when he'd first shown up, coming down here with a memory as solid as a photograph about what it looked like. What had once been—the few houseboats and a couple of shops, along with several fishing boats—still existed. But there was so much more. Now, there were over twenty houseboats and a row of shops longer than the walk in. There were picnic tables set up in the green space, clusters of purposefully planted trees, and strategically paved walking paths.

Jonesing for his first cup of caffeine, he hurried into track shorts and a running T-shirt. The metal stairs from the loft his parents rarely used wound down to the first floor and made him a little dizzy. His mom and dad were sitting at the small table for two, chatting over coffee.

His mom rose immediately, pulling her oversized cardigan closed even as she opened her arms for a hug. "I can't get used to you being here. It makes me so happy."

He laughed, squeezing her tight. He pressed a kiss to her soft, dark hair that she refused to let go gray. "It's okay to get used to it, though I think I'll start looking for somewhere to live more permanently."

She pulled back, her eyes, just like his, shining, and patted his chest. "There's no rush."

His dad shifted in his chair, covering a wince. His mom went back to the table, murmured something quietly to him before his dad shook his head. Levi clenched his jaw, knowing his dad was too stubborn to ask for help. He pulled the cookies he'd made out of the fridge, set about warming a few up as he ignored the tension for a few minutes.

"What are your more long-term plans, honey?"

Levi grabbed a plate, set one of the cookies down in front of his dad. "I've got some ideas, Mom. Morning, Dad. How you feeling?"

"I'm fine. No reason for everyone to be worrying so much. What's that? I can't eat cookies for breakfast. Is that what you learned at your fancy restaurants?"

"Steven," his mom hissed.

Levi grabbed another cookie and set it down in front of his mom. "Actually, it's one of the recipes I created. I made them last night. It's a cross between oatmeal and a cookie. It's made with whole grains, cane sugar, cranberries, and no dairy. I researched foods for recovery and came up with it. You were never a straight-up oatmeal guy."

His dad stared at the cookie and took a bite, and his mom followed. Levi went back to the counter, certainly not expecting praise. Steven Bright believed working with your hands meant building something a person could live in; like a house. Not making cookies or fancy meals. Levi grabbed his coffee, added a generous pour of milk and a spoonful of sugar.

"Levi, this is delicious. Isn't it, Steven?" There was a tired edge to his mom's voice. Levi didn't want to add discord between them. His mom struggled with Steven's dismissal of his profession and the way they'd left things all those years ago when he'd gone off to culinary school against his dad's request that he stay and be part of Bright Builds.

"Not bad." Steven pressed the pad of his finger against the crumbs and licked them off.

Not bad. *High praise.* Levi held back his smile as he joined them at the table with his own cookie. "So, back to the question, my short-term plans are, I'd like to step in for you while you're off work, so you can recover without worrying about jobs."

With deliberate slowness, his dad turned his body toward Levi, his lips in a firm line. His dad's dark hair, once so similar to Levi's, was thinning on the top and liberally sprinkled with gray. His always-calloused hands were lined with age. But he was still strong and solid and a damn good man. If they could get past what his father saw as a betrayal on Levi's part, maybe they could get back to the way things had been before he'd chased his own dream.

"You know I have a crew, right? You think I'm going to bench Eddie and let you just boss my guys around because you're home on a fool's errand?"

His mom groaned and moved away from the table, taking the empty plates.

Levi tamped down on his irritation, kept his voice calm. "It's okay, Mom. I knew this was coming. I'm sorry I didn't want to follow you into construction or become a partner in your company. I loved working with you growing up, but it wasn't my dream. It still isn't. But I want to help out if I can. However I can. I still know how to use a hammer. I'm not looking to step on toes, but I know you always pull your weight at every job, which means no matter who is in charge you'll be down a man, and I want to pitch in until you're on your feet again."

His mom put her hands on his dad's shoulders, like maybe her touch could put him in a better mood. To be fair, from what he remembered of his parents' relationship, it usually could. "That's very sweet of you, honey."

A derisive noise left his dad's lips. "Then what?"

Using his need for caffeine as an excuse not to snap at his dad or lose his patience, Levi took a long sip. It wasn't a good time to tell them about the food truck. Not with his dad's surly mood.

"Then I'll figure out what I'm doing and start building my life here."

Getting up a little slower than Levi liked to see, his dad took his coffee cup to the sink. "You need money? That why you're asking for a job?"

Jesus. Levi huffed out a breath. "I don't need your money, Dad. I was head chef at one of the best fine-dining restaurants in Vermont." He'd cooked for senators and dignitaries and under chefs who'd received James Beard Awards. His career had been, quite literally, a dream come true. But it hadn't filled his soul the way he thought it would. "I have money. I'm offering to help. You can think about it, but I don't know why you'd have to." Other than stubborn pride, which Levi knew a thing or two about.

Before his dad could answer, Levi pushed back from the table and took his own cup to the sink. He'd grab a coffee in town. This houseboat was too fucking small, especially with his dad's shitty mood.

"Let me know." With that, he scooped up his phone and his keys, gave his mom a kiss on the cheek, and took off.

He hadn't finished tying his shoes on the front step before his phone buzzed.

Beckett

Happy you're back, man. Come meet my girl, see my bike shop.

Levi

Will do. Need to get settled then I want to make a big meal for all of you. Not at my parents' though. Too small in too many ways.

Beckett

Let's do it at the lodge. Lots of room and we're not booked until June 1.

Levi

Perfect. Next week. You and Gray are running your own businesses. Maybe I can talk to you about my plans. Look at us, growing up. And you're getting married. If you ever get up the nerve to ask her.

Beckett

You saw the poll.

Levi

And voted.

Beckett

Jackass.

Levi

Can't wait to meet her. I'll try to talk some sense into her; warn her off.

Beckett

I repeat: jackass.

Levi

Admit it. You missed me.

Beckett

About as much as a sliver in my ass.

Levi

I won't ask how it got there. See you soon.

Beckett

Levi's fingers hovered over the screen. *Oh, by the way, is your sister dating anyone? Mind if I ask her out?* He shook his head. "That would go over well." *Are sisters still off-limits?* A laugh burst out of him as he pocketed his phone. "You know the answer to that."

Two things never failed to clear his head—making an excellent meal, and running. Since his dad had bitched and complained about the grilled chicken and rice he'd made the other night, Levi was in no hurry to cook him another healthy meal. Running it was. If he ran into Jillian, so be it. He grinned as he stretched, remembering that this was Smile and there was always a good chance of running into someone, whether you wanted to or not.

With his muscles loose, he started with a slow jog off of the docks, letting his mind wander. No surprise, it zipped back to Jillian. Waving to people he passed, he cut down a back alley between two of the shops along Tourist Lane, hoping it still led to a trail he remembered. Thankfully, it did.

AirPods in, his pulse matching the beat of some old-school AC/DC, sweat pooling at his spine, Levi slipped into the zone. Would have stayed there, too, if he hadn't looked to the left and kept looking, because what he saw made his pulse race faster than the exercise. In the middle of the green space, several women—though there was only one who captured his attention—were bent into some very awkward-looking positions he wouldn't even attempt on a dare. Jillian's hair was twisted into a pretty braid down the back of her pale blue tank top that showed off toned arms, soft curves, and tantalizing skin that . . .

He heard a muted "Dude" seconds before his shin came into direct contact with something cold and hard. He caught air before he felt the rough slide of crushed gravel abrading the skin of his knee, thigh, and hands when he landed. He would have gladly concentrated on the stinging, burning pain but Anderson—freaking do-it-all Anderson—was in his face, checking him out, telling him not to move, even as the women hurried over. Reaching him first, because it wasn't bad enough that he'd tripped over a cooler—in front of people—or that he'd have cuts all over him, was Jillian, the woman he couldn't stop thinking about.

"He's okay. Just some cuts and scrapes," Anderson said, pushing their shoulder-length hair back from their face. "I'm so sorry. I tried to get your attention, Levi. You were in the zone."

"Oh, honey. You fell ass over cooler," an older woman who looked familiar said.

Levi's gaze was locked on Jillian. Her expression of concern morphed into one of mild amusement at the woman's comment right before she crouched down next to him. God, she smelled good. How could she be out in the sun, bending into pretzel shapes, and smell so good?

He was quite certain the same couldn't be said of him.

"Sue likes to state the obvious," she said under her breath, touching his knee, her brows furrowing.

Her fingers on his skin sent an electric charge through his whole body, making him flinch. She pulled her hand back, looked at him.

"Did that hurt? You might need to go see one of the Doc Williamses and make sure you didn't break anything."

Levi gave a rough laugh, remembering that there were two general practitioners in Smile and they were married to each other. The Williamses. It was the female Doc Williams who'd put four stitches in his chin the night he left. Levi pushed to his feet. "Pretty sure you can't break pride."

Jillian rose with him, her top lip pulled between her teeth, and it took all of his effort not to stare. Not to wonder what it would be like to . . .

"She's right, sweetie. We should get you checked out." Sue, whom he still couldn't place, took his arm.

Anderson held out a bottle of water, dripping with condensation. "On the house."

"Thanks." Extricating himself from the older woman's grasp, wishing he could walk away and pretend the last three minutes had never happened, he opened it, swallowed down half the bottle.

When he lowered his chin, he caught a look in Jillian's gaze—he was *not* the only interested party here—that made his skin sizzle all over again.

"You're sure you're okay?" Anderson asked.

He didn't usually lie, but looking at Jillian and knowing he wasn't going to be able to sidestep his feelings so easily, he had no choice. "Completely. I'm absolutely fine."

"You could join us for yoga," said one of the older ladies, with her gray ponytail tucked through the back of a ball cap. "That'll stretch those muscles." Her gaze wandered down his length and back up before she whistled, shook her head. "You're going to be sore tomorrow."

Jillian pressed her lips together but they quirked anyway.

Sue, whose gray hair was cropped into a stylish bob, clapped her hands. "Yes. That's an excellent idea."

"A good Downward Dog never hurt anyone," Anderson added.

Levi closed his eyes, took a deep breath, and opened them again. This time Jillian wasn't hiding her laughter. Neither were the other ladies.

"If you do it right, it feels really good," another woman said, nodding along.

"Kill me now," he whispered under his breath.

Jillian ducked her head, avoided his gaze. The women slowly dispersed back to their mats while Anderson went back to their lawn chair next to the cooler.

"What are you doing, Anderson?" he asked, tucking his Air-Pods in their case before shoving them in his pocket.

"I like to make sure the ladies stay hydrated."

Of course. That made perfect sense. In Smile.

"Are you going to clean that all up?" Jillian asked softly from beside him.

Levi looked down at her, resisted the urge to touch her in any way even though he really wanted to reach out, maybe take her hand. "Yeah. I guess I'd better."

She hooked a thumb over her shoulder. "I have a first aid kit in my car." She gestured with a tilt of her head and started walking toward the far parking lot.

So much for avoiding her; Levi fell into step beside her.

"You realize you have to embarrass yourself in front of me now, right? To even the score?"

Jillian sucked in a breath, stopped in her tracks, and turned to face him. His heart beat faster as she stared up at him, hands on her hips.

Sounds rumbled out of her mouth but nothing coherent as her eyes widened. She shook her head, mumbled something he didn't catch.

His fingers went to his chin without meaning to and he rubbed the scar there, that long-ago night flashing through his head with startling clarity. He hadn't thought about her being embarrassed. Really, all he'd thought about other than the fact that his chin was gushing blood was that Jillian Keller almost kissed him. And he'd been really disappointed that she hadn't.

The way she'd acted the other day, he wondered not only if she'd forgotten about it but if he'd imagined her feelings. Clearly, she remembered, but obviously it wasn't the smile-provoking memory for her that, to this day, it was for him.

Six

At well over six feet with wide, muscular shoulders, Levi barely fit in the passenger-side opening of her yellow Beetle. If he was uncomfortable with the lack of space, he didn't show it. If he thought she was staring too hard or her breathing was oddly erratic, he gave no signs. Other than the slightest of flinches when she cleaned his cuts and scrapes, it almost felt like he was holding his breath. Jillian was doing her very best to not think about his legs or his calves or what it would be like to crawl right onto his lap and—

"Is this the same car you had when you were younger?"

She startled. "It is."

He pursed his lips, nodded like he didn't know what to say about that. But it was better than talking about who had embarrassed themselves more. She won that battle hands down.

"When I came home after . . ." She stopped, glanced up to see him watching her intently. "When my marriage ended, I moved back in with my parents. Right after I got home, my dad asked me to come out to the garage one night." She smiled, returned to the spot on his calf that she was bandaging up, as she thought about how a little piece of her resurfaced when her dad gave her the car. "I'd sold it before moving away but he got a chance to buy it back, so he did, as a surprise."

She swallowed past the thickness in her throat. She hadn't wanted to be a failure at marriage, but God, she'd wanted to come home. She was so happy to be back in Smile, and getting her teen-age car back made her feel lighter. Hopeful. It was step one in a pretty long healing journey.

Levi was still looking at her as she crumpled the Band-Aid packages. She tried to breathe through her nose as she reminded herself he was just a man and she was no longer an innocent young girl who plucked petals off flowers as she chanted "he loves me, he loves me not." She hadn't been that girl in a very long time.

The memory of getting her car back, along with his proximity, was doing strange things to her nervous system. She let out a sharp breath, exhaling the rough pieces of the past, then stood up. Before she could move back, he unfolded his long body, rose slowly, like he was allowing her time to adjust to his nearness. Smart would have been stepping away; *staying* away. Jillian was smart. Just not in this particular instance. Not when it came to Levi.

"Thanks for taking care of me," he said.

Her pulse wobbled. "You should watch out for coolers."

When he laughed, she felt it along her skin, and for one split second, she ached to close the distance and take the kiss she'd craved all those years ago.

She frowned up at him, remembering that night and what he'd just said about evening the score. She *wasn't* a kid anymore. They could address the long-buried mortification head-on. He might not even remember.

"Back to the whole embarrassment tally. Pretty sure I have you beat for the rest of our lives."

He didn't follow her when she walked over to a garbage can, got rid of the wrappers, then wandered back.

Instead, Levi leaned against the side of her car, seemingly perfectly at ease. "I think you're wrong, Jilly."

The playful way he said her name made her want to smile and shove him at the same time. She rounded the hood of her car, firming her shoulders so she didn't melt into a puddle of lust.

The past was the past. "Then we aren't remembering things the same way."

Levi turned and, because of his height, leaned casually with his arms folded on the roof of her vehicle, tapping his fingers while watching her from across it.

"Maybe not. I'm glad your dad got your car back. You deserve good things. Plus, this car is like happiness on wheels, so it suits you."

She didn't know what to do with his kindness, his sweet smile, and the way he held her gaze.

"Do you want a ride somewhere?"

His smile widened, reminding her of the boy he'd once been. The line between then and now would be tricky to stay on the right side of. He was just starting his life over. She was just getting hers on the right track. *Stay in your lane, Jilly.*

He looked down at his legs then back up. "I guess my run is over for today. I need to talk to Pete. You headed near there?"

It was Smile. Nowhere was truly far from anywhere.

She nodded, fidgeting with her keys. "Passing it. Indirectly, at least." Since it was on Middle Street.

They both seat-belted, him after he moved the seat back to stretch out his legs. It was silly to feel nervous with him in her car. They were adults. But she'd dreamed of driving around Smile in her yellow bug with Levi riding shotgun, his hand on her thigh while music blasted and they stole kisses at stoplights.

"You've got a sweet smile on your face," he said softly.

Heat spread over her body like it was being tattooed into her skin one cell at a time.

Keeping her eyes on the road, she took a small leap. Not like both of them hadn't been fully aware of her feelings. Maybe acknowledging them as a thing of the past, she'd settle herself on firm ground right now. "I was thinking about how my sixteen-year-old self used to imagine driving in my car with you."

She felt him angle his body, giving her his attention. Jilly kept hers on the road. Safer for everyone.

"I'd be curious to know what else sixteen-year-old Jilly imagined."

Oh, good lord. So much for that theory. Fortunately, Smile was small, and she turned into the school parking lot.

"Easier to park here than behind Pete's. You good to get there from here?" It was less than a ten-minute walk. Her brain and body weren't communicating so she was out of the car before he answered. With his long legs, he easily met her at the front of the bug.

Levi put a hand on her arm, stilling everything about her except her pulse, which did a little tap dance. "I wasn't trying to embarrass you again, or scare you off."

Lifting her gaze, she saw the gentleness in his and it settled her heart rate. "I know . . . I'm . . . Okay, let's just lay the cards face-up. I liked you back then, I obviously thought of kissing you, I tried, I broke your face, you moved away. The mortification score is Jilly a thousand, Levi one." She closed her eyes, took a deep breath, realizing she'd just added plus one to her score.

His whole body shook with his laughter, and she felt it because his hand lingered on her arm. She opened her eyes, stared at him.

"I don't even know which part of that to address first," he said in between laughs.

"I'm glad you find this so amusing," she said, not angry but wishing again that she had the magic potion for chilling the hell out when he was within touching distance. If she wasn't careful, she'd forget her own hard-learned, self-imposed rules about keeping an emotional distance from any man. Even the one she'd wanted forever. Truthfully, no one she'd met in the years since her divorce had made that difficult.

Levi leaned his butt against the rounded hood of her car in a move so effortless and casual a gust of longing struck her right between the ribs. Whether it was for him or the way he felt so at ease in every situation, she wasn't sure.

His hand slipped from her arm down to her fingers in a barely there grasp she felt everywhere. How could something feel exhilarating and new while also feeling familiar and sweet? With very little nudging, she moved closer to him, his legs almost on either side of her hips. She'd imagined this as well, long ago. The logical part of her brain—the *mom,* sister, professional, and *adult*—knew this was not the time or place. But she'd like to meet the woman who could resist Levi Bright looking at her like she was all he could see.

"I don't think it's funny that you're struggling with any of this. But I do think our memories are slightly different. First of all, you didn't break my face." He pointed to his chin.

Jilly leaned forward, right into the scent of his skin. Her lips pursed as his head tipped back. "You have a scar." It wasn't prominent; just a pale faded line. But still. She'd put it there. Her fingers itched to trace over it. To touch him.

He dropped his chin, meeting her gaze. "It makes me smile every time I think of it."

"You're a strange man," she said.

His index finger brushed under her chin, lifted it. "True. But when I think about that night, I think about how badly seventeen-year-old me wanted you to kiss me. How much, even though I was excited about school, I didn't want to leave in that moment."

It was like fifteen-year-old Jilly and almost-thirty-year-old Jilly shared a dramatic chest bump inside of her rib cage. He'd wanted it too. *Okay. Let that be enough.*

Jill stepped back, did her best to school her expression and calm the fizz of energy inside of herself. "Teenaged Jilly would be happy to know it wasn't one-sided."

Mature. She mentally patted herself on the back.

Levi pushed off her car. His expression was a strange mix of longing and determination. He gave a barely visible nod, like he'd decided something for himself. "Yeah? How about *this* Jilly? How does she feel knowing it's still not one-sided?"

Her gaze widened, and because she simply couldn't maintain her chill around him and the universe clearly hated her, she moved back, tripped over a raised piece of the path that led to the school. Levi might not have seen the cooler in his path earlier but his reflexes were *not* lacking. His arms darted around her, yanking her against him and stopping her fall. Of course, this meant she was tucked up against his chest, all too aware of how good he smelled, despite having run and rolled around a bit on the ground, and how solid his abs felt under her fingers.

"Careful," Levi said, his voice gruff, his breath warm against her face.

Careful. A good word to focus on. "I am." *For very good reason.*

The recess bell rang and, like they'd been waiting at the door, dozens of children sprinted out into the sunshine.

An electric energy filled the air with the pounding of feet on the ground as students aged five to thirteen fought for every single second of freedom in these final days before summer.

Jillian stepped away, grateful for the timing. She'd never actually been *saved by the bell*.

"Mom!"

Before she could turn fully, Ollie body-slammed her thighs, her small arms snaking around all she could grasp of Jilly. A unique kind of happiness that could only be inspired by her daughter rose through Jill, reminding her of the here and now.

Jilly's world righted and focused on her little girl. With the ease of a well-practiced mom, she bent her knees, boosted her daughter up for a hard squeeze before letting her go.

"Hey, sweet pea. How's it going?"

"I'm good. I gotta go. I'm it for Man Tracker. I like to give them a head start 'cause I'm so fast. Who's this? I'm Ollie." She stuck her hand out, staring up at Levi.

His lips twitched as he crouched down so they were eye level. "I'm Levi Bright. A friend of your mom and your uncles."

Ollie nodded. Her reddish hair had grown out and the curls were more pronounced so they bobbed along with every movement. "Hi. You should come to our lodge. It's the coolest."

Jillian couldn't help but laugh at the unfiltered mini-marketer she was raising.

Someone shouted her name. "I gotta go. Bye, Mom. Bye, Levi."

Ollie raced off as fast as she'd shown up, a little blur of movement and energy that fueled Jilly's soul.

Levi rose, his gaze meeting hers, and she noted the softness in his eyes.

"She's adorable. Feisty."

"You have no idea." And she was the reason Jillian didn't do impulsive things like dating just because her hormones were in overdrive. Her ex had let her down in more ways than she could count, but she never wanted Ollie to feel the emotional impact of that. The men in her life were steady. Secure. Not that Levi wasn't, but he was a threat to Jilly's heart and carefully curated life. He stared after her daughter a minute, then looked into Jilly's eyes. "She looks like you. I'd love to get to know her."

Damn it. Her heart surged. While other men might see a child as an obstacle to get to the mother, Levi wouldn't. But that didn't make him any less dangerous. If anything, that might make her more vulnerable.

"I'm sure you'll get a chance. We're all friends," she said, reminding herself as much as him.

She might have sucked at marriage, fumbled her way into divorce, and been subpar at dating, but friendship she could do.

Seven

Despite the rough start to the day, timing was on his side when Levi sat down at the long, diner-style countertop of Pete's. Who better to talk to about a food truck, or any culinary venture, than a man who'd run a restaurant successfully for Levi's entire life?

A big, burly man who looked like Santa and often acted like Scrooge, Pete ran the go-to place for breakfast, brunch, and lunch in Smile. Pete's was a favorite of tourists and locals alike, not just for the great food but the vibrant and utterly unique art that adorned the tables.

Levi was waiting for the big guy himself to come out and chat with him, but according to his line cook, Pete was on the phone with a supplier. The man liked to cook his way. He didn't like any other parts of the business. But he knew them, and hopefully he'd share some trade secrets.

Sipping his coffee, his stomach eager for the waffles he'd ordered, Levi turned when the door jingled and saw Beckett strolling through with a gorgeous woman at his side, her head tipped back in laughter. He wanted that.

Some might think tripping over a cooler and making a fool of himself wasn't great luck, but not Levi, since it gave him some time with Jillian. He could picture her laughing at his jokes like Beckett's girlfriend was. He wanted that more than he'd considered. That familiarity, the right to touch and laugh and kiss. Inside jokes and all the rest of it.

"Levi Bright," Beckett said, spotting him as the pair started toward a booth. They detoured toward him as he rose from the stool.

They met in the middle of the floor and a lightness invaded his chest. He'd really missed his friends. Texts, emails, FaceTimes, and a random visit here and there hadn't been enough. They hugged, both of them laughing, before he pulled back and held a hand out to Beckett's girlfriend.

"You must be Presley. I'm Levi. I voted in favor of this guy asking you to marry him, but if it's not what you want, just blink twice and I'll rescue you," he said, moving quickly when Beckett went to give him a shove.

"No horsing around in my diner," Pete said, coming through the swinging door.

"Or smiling or laughing," Levi whispered, making the other two laugh.

Pete stopped beside them, looked down his bulbous nose at Levi. "You want to eat these waffles or wear them, Bright?"

Presley laughed, tucked herself under Pete's arm, and gave him a squeeze. Clearly, the woman didn't value her life.

To Levi's surprise, everything about Pete softened. He handed Levi the plate of waffles, gave Presley a half hug, and told them to find a booth.

"Are you magic?" Levi looked at her then Beckett. "Is she magic?"

The two of them slipped into one side and Levi sat on the other. They held hands and grinned like loons in love.

"She's magic, all right. Pete's sour moods are no match for Presley's sunshine."

Presley rolled her eyes. "Please. He's a teddy bear."

Levi unrolled his fork and knife, cut into the thick, vanilla-scented waffle, his mouth watering. "Maybe you ought to come meet my dad."

"Actually, I did a little bit of website work for your dad," Presley said.

Holy shit. The fork paused halfway to Levi's mouth. "And he let you?"

She laughed again. "He *hired* me."

So, it was just Levi he didn't want in his space or business.

Groaning around his bite of waffle, he closed his eyes.

"Jesus, dude. Want us to leave you alone?" Beckett said.

Opening his eyes, Levi swallowed and laughed. "I missed these."

"You're a chef, aren't you?" Presley asked as Pete approached.

"I am," he said, cutting another bite but tipping his head in Pete's direction. "But this guy has a secret recipe that he won't share for anything."

"Family only." Pete squeezed in beside Levi without an invitation.

Levi slid his plate over onto Mona Lisa's face—each table was a re-creation of a painted masterpiece, all done by Pete's wife and his daughter. Every one of them was gorgeous. Van Gogh's night sky was Levi's favorite, but it had a family of four around it right now.

An older woman hurried out of the back, tying an apron as she rushed over to their table. It was the older woman from the park. Her bushy brows lifted when she saw him, a smile twitching on her lips.

"Hey, Beckett. Hi, Presley. Sorry I'm late, Pete. Some runner went ass over cooler, not looking where he was going, and we had to help him out." She kept her gaze on Levi, who did his very best not to turn the color of ketchup. *Pete's sister!* That's who she was.

"What an idiot," Pete mumbled.

She laughed. "What'll you two have, since I see this one's already eating," she said, gesturing to Levi.

The two of them ordered, Pete's sister went to ring it in, and the four of them caught up a bit. Presley was delightful, and seeing his old friend so happy—another person who'd gone away only to realize his life was right here in Smile—gave Levi some courage.

"I know you have to get back to the kitchen, so I wondered if I could meet up with you sometime soon to pick your brain on starting a food truck." Dragging a bite of waffle through syrup, which he also thought was Pete's special recipe, Levi did his best to appear calm. Casual. Like getting advice on the next phase of his life was no big deal.

"A food truck? That's a great idea. What kind of food?" Presley asked, turning her cup over for the waitress to pour in coffee.

"Comfort food with a bump," Levi said.

"A lump? You want lumps in your food? Didn't you go to some fancy-ass school?" Pete asked.

"Give him a chance to talk, Petey."

Pete practically snarled, but Sue ignored him and filled the rest of the coffee cups before walking away.

"A *bump*. Elevated. Elevated comfort food. Twists on old favorites," Levi said, clutching the fork tighter.

"Smile is going to keep growing, and you're not far from Northern Michigan. A food truck lets you wander if you need to, but I honestly think you'll have more than enough business right here," Presley said, then bit her lip. "Sorry. I get excited about this stuff."

Beckett put his arm around her shoulder, kissed her temple. "Don't apologize for being amazing." His gaze settled on Levi. "She's excellent, man. She's doubled the bike shop's bookings through social media and cross advertising."

Pete sighed. "It's a good idea. I'll give you that. Not sure about the cuisine, but I've never wanted to move beyond breakfast foods. What's your schedule like?"

"Other than finding a place to live as soon as possible, pretty clear."

Beckett's brows scrunched. "Everything okay with your parents?"

Levi set his knife and fork on the plate. He was full, but sorry it was finished. "Dad's surgery went well so now it's just recovery, but he's not real thrilled about me being home. Plus, the houseboat makes me queasy."

Pete and Beckett laughed but it was Pete who said, "Wimp. Few years off the island and you can't handle a boat?"

Levi chose to ignore him as Sue set down Beckett's and Presley's food. Pete shifted, rose out of the booth.

"You could stay at the lodge, but we're fully booked starting a month from now, and Jilly's working on getting some different groups in and out before then. Could probably work around it, though."

"Be here tomorrow morning at eight thirty," Pete said. "I might have a solution for your living situation." Without another word, he went back to the kitchen.

"Full of details and words, that one," Levi said, picking up his coffee.

"Oh my gosh, it just gets better and better," Presley said around a happy sigh as she ate a bite of waffle smothered in blueberries.

Beckett sat up a little straighter as he cut into his egg, bacon, and tomato sandwich. "She's talking about me."

Presley shook her head. She had a sweet softness about her that made her approachable, but when she'd talked business, her tone and demeanor had shifted, showing Levi she could probably lead the charge on just about anything. She was confident, even in her quieter moments. Unlike Jilly, whom he seemed to have to coax smiles out of, Presley seemed to wear a permanent one. *Makes getting one from Jilly more special.*

"A food truck, huh?" Beckett said around a mouthful of sandwich.

"That's the hope. I wanted to be available to help my dad, but I'm not sure he wants me stepping on toes at any of his construction sites."

"Sorry things are still rough with him. Give it some time," Beckett said.

"What happened?" Presley asked, picking up her coffee.

Levi sighed and leaned back in the booth, thinking about the day he'd told his dad he won an early-entry scholarship to a distinguished culinary school in New Hampshire.

"I followed my dream instead of his."

Like she sensed he didn't want to get into it, they spent the next little while chatting and catching up.

"Why don't we do a get-together at the lodge this weekend. You wanted to cook for everyone. Your dad should be okay to travel by then. It's a short ride. You could see the place, feed us, and maybe your dad could give us some advice on a few outbuildings Jillian was thinking of." Beckett polished off the last of his sandwich as a larger party filed through the door and took up the booths on the other side of the diner.

Levi could take care of anything the lodge needed. If the job wasn't started yet, he could help his dad without messing up any existing projects. "Yeah. That's great. I'll talk to my parents. I told Jilly about it," he said, hoping his tone didn't give off any "I'm still crushing on your sister after all these years" vibes.

"Great. She'll be in, and my parents, too. And Ollie."

"I met her," Levi said, pulling his wallet out of his back pocket.

"Ollie? When?"

"Uh, today." After being the idiot who fell over the cooler. He glanced at his phone and stood up. "I should go. Presley, it was great to meet you. Becks, I'm glad to be home, man. I'll figure out a menu and text you. You'll clear it with Gray?"

"For sure. You sure you're okay cooking for all those people?"

Levi smiled. "More than okay. I'm going to try out my food truck ideas on you guys."

"Better not be waffles," Pete hollered.

Levi paid, lifted his hand, and said he'd see the chef tomorrow.

As he walked out of Pete's into the sunshine and fresh air, his heart felt a hell of a lot lighter than it had earlier today.

Eight

Levi stood with his hands on his hips, staring at the two-story building behind Pete's, in the alleyway that separated the businesses from another street. Technically, it was a garage, though not even a Mini Cooper or Jilly's Volkswagen would fit inside. It was narrow like the other few garages with apartments over the top. Not every shop had one. Pete had been in the middle of plating orders when Levi showed, on time, and said he'd meet him out back.

The breeze lifted some random debris along the concrete. Dressed in a hoodie and sweatpants, he wasn't cold, but he was tired and wouldn't have minded a few extra hours of sleep.

Pete came out the back door of the restaurant. "Sorry. It got busy at the time it usually dies down. Jilly should be here any minute."

Like his heart recognized her name, it surged in Levi's chest. "Jilly? What's going on?"

Pete gestured to the garage. "She was going to go through some of this stuff when she had time. Her and Gwennie insist it shouldn't just be tossed in a dumpster, but when do I have time to clear this place out?"

He grumbled the words, and Levi was trying to follow along.

What did Pete's wife and Jill have to do with this? Why was he here?

Pete pulled a set of keys from his apron pocket and pointed to the side of the building. "You wanna clean it out, it'll help Jill, get Gwen off my ass to get it done, and you can rent the space. It's a bachelor pad and you'll need to clean it up, but there's enough room for you. I won't gouge you on rent and I'll give you a deal on the first few months for cleaning it out."

Levi's head was already spinning, trying to process everything the chef, who usually strung six words together max, was saying when Jillian hurried down the alley dressed in leggings and a dark green sweater that read: GET LOST. As usual, the sight of her made him smile. His gaze swept over her from her high, thick ponytail to her pretty pink running shoes.

"Here I am. Hi, Levi." She leaned into Pete for a side hug like the man wasn't a burly bear of a human.

Pete kissed the top of her head and, though it meant absolutely nothing, Levi felt the prickle of jealousy. Even if nothing happened romantically, he wanted a familiarity with her that allowed him to be in her space. He couldn't get over how much he enjoyed being in her orbit. Even when he hadn't had nearly enough coffee.

Pete stepped back. "Jilly helps out some with the Smile museum and historical society with Gwen. If you guys can sort what needs to go to the museum and take it over there, I'll take care of the rest. Just get it all piled up out here. If there's anything even worth keeping. Who knows? Maybe it's all junk." He tugged at his beard. "I should have tossed it all but I couldn't make myself do it."

Jillian lifted her brows, looking at Levi, and gave a small shrug. He'd gone years without seeing her or thinking about her, and now she infiltrated his thoughts and brightened his day. Seeing her might actually be better than a shot of caffeine.

Pete led the way up a narrow set of stairs along the side of the building. Jilly followed but glanced back at Levi. Fortunately, he wasn't staring at her ass in those pants, so he could smile without embarrassment.

"You want off of the houseboat this bad?"

"How bad can it be?" His heart twitched when she smirked at him. She knew something he didn't.

Pete had the door unlocked and opened when they reached the landing. Hopefully the ceiling only looked so low because the space inside was beyond full. Boxes, old PETE'S signs, vintage-looking posters—framed and unframed—vinyl benches and stools, a jukebox, a couple of street signs, and random chairs were visible from the door. When he stepped in, his arm bumped an antique popcorn maker. Levi could almost smell the butter.

His jaw dropped to his chin. Holy. Shit. He continued to look around. If he tried hard, he could visualize the space without decades' worth of random items being piled on top of each other. Somewhere beyond some weathered paneling was the top of a fridge, so that was likely the kitchenette.

"There's a bathroom off the back there. You can't see it because I turned that couch upright to save space."

Levi bit his lip hard to stifle the comment that his effort hadn't worked. There was barely any visible floor to walk on.

Jillian stepped up beside him, her shoulder brushing his arm, her fingers dangling close enough to touch.

"You've added more. I'm glad you didn't get rid of it all, Pete. There's a lot here, and most of it might go, but I definitely see some things worth salvaging." She ran her hand along the handle of the popcorn maker. It came away with dust that she wiped on her pants.

Levi realized he was smiling. This was going to be a hell of a job but, in the end, it would be a cool little space for him to live in while he started building his future.

"They say you can't go back, but I'm pretty sure the entire history of Smile is tucked away in there." If his tone leaned toward reverent, it was because Levi actually felt like he was stepping into long-ago summer days, remembering, viscerally, stopping by Pete's for an ice-cream cone or, even better, a root beer float.

When he glanced at Jillian, her smile was brighter than the goddamn sun. His fingers grazed hers again. This time, it wasn't an accident.

How could looking at her steal the breath from his lungs and make him feel like he could breathe in the same second?

"Pete," Jillian said, running a hand over a stack of boxes that came to her waist, awe in her tone. "How long have you been storing things?"

Levi took a tentative step forward. "Since the dawn of time, from the looks of it."

Pete growled. "I'm not a hoarder. I got busy."

Jillian sent Levi a chastising look, which he figured was a very practiced mom move.

"That's okay, Pete. This stuff has a history. Your history here in Smile."

Levi glanced at the older man and saw the way Jilly softened him just with the kindness in her tone, expression, and body language. A completely underrated skill he admired.

"It does. Thirty years of my restaurant in there. Thirty years of Smile. I'm not even sure I'm attached to all of it, but it's just too much to dive into. Gives me hives thinking about digging through it all. But I said I'd do it. So, now I found a way." He grinned, pinning Levi with his gaze as his teeth peeked through his beard. "I'll let you stay through the summer for free."

Levi nodded rather than saying he sure as hell hoped so. It might take them that long to clean this place out.

Pete turned and walked away, leaving Jillian and Levi staring at the past. He smiled, thinking that there was no one he'd rather sort through the past with to get to the future. Looking over, he was struck again by the way she stole his breath by doing nothing more than being herself.

"Why are you smiling?" She stepped into a small square of space between a couple of boxes.

"Because I like looking at you. And being with you. And I was just thinking, there's no one I'd rather do this with."

Jillian turned and he saw the hesitancy, the nerves, dancing in her gaze. Levi stepped closer to her, took her hand. She had little freckles across the bridge of her nose and he couldn't take his eyes off of them. Like Pete, he was scared to dive into this, but holding back had never been his strong suit.

Jillian's breath faltered. "What? Why are you looking at me so intently?"

His gaze darted up, then back to her freckles, counting them. Seven. "One day soon, I want to kiss each one of your freckles."

This time she sucked in a sharp breath that worked to erase the space between them.

She stared at his mouth as a gentle hue of pink splashed over her cheeks. "Levi." He recognized the desire that surged in her eyes, because it echoed his own.

He reached out, slowly so she could stop him, and brushed the strands of hair that had escaped her elastic behind her shoulder, letting his fingers linger. Her lips parted and Levi was pretty sure he'd never wanted to kiss a woman this badly except for one other time in his life. And it was the same woman.

Jillian's breath hitched in and out, her gaze wide as his hand moved down her neck, along her shoulder, in a gentle caress.

A loud, growly noise startled him away from Jillian but he kept her close to his front, turning to see Pete glaring at them. Him. Pete was glaring at Levi. Not Jillian.

Jillian bit her lip and ducked her head with a shy smile. Her forehead landed on his chest.

"Thought you two might want some lemonade," Pete said, setting both large glasses down on one of the boxes.

"Thank you, Pete," Jillian said without looking up.

"You're welcome, Jilly," Pete said, his tone amused despite the way he narrowed his gaze at Levi.

Levi rubbed his hand soothingly over Jillian's back.

"You make sure you don't break anything special," Pete said to Levi.

Jesus. There was a warning he'd hear in his sleep. "I know how to take care of things that matter, Pete."

The chef's lips twitched, moving his mustache. "Good."

"Is he gone?" Jillian whispered, still looking at their feet.

"He is."

She stepped back, not looking at him as she went to the lemonade and took a long drink. Like she needed to center herself, Jillian inhaled deeply, set her drink down, and turned to face him. Uncertainty trickled back into her eyes, making his muscles tense. "We're not kids anymore. I *have* a kid, and both of us live here on the island."

He smiled teasingly. "Sure will make it easier to hang out with you."

She sighed, a soft smile on her lips but worry present in her gaze. "It's complicated."

Levi nodded. He didn't need to push. She'd been right there with him, wanting that kiss every bit as much as he did. She might need time to process and sort through whatever she felt, but this thing between them was too big for either of them to ignore. This wasn't just a teenage crush or fond memories pulling at his heartstrings. It was his future bursting wide open. Of course, he could tell just by looking at her that if he said that, she'd run. Jillian

Keller had always been cautious and careful. Being divorced and having a kid probably made her more so.

"I'm in no rush. Some things are worth the wait."

She pulled in another one of those shuddery breaths and he had to stop himself from crossing over to her and pulling her into his arms.

"I don't want to screw up our friendship. You've always mattered to me."

He had that fear in the back of his head too. He trusted his own instincts, though, and everything inside him told him this was worth the risk. They weren't teens anymore. They were adults capable of compromise and flexibility. He'd never shied away from working for what he wanted. And he'd never wanted anyone like Jilly.

"Didn't I just promise Pete I wouldn't wreck anything special? He might bury me in some other storage space if I don't make good on my word."

Jill looked up at him, her brows furrowing adorably, her arms going out wide to gesture to the room. "He was talking about this stuff."

Levi loved that she really thought that. "No, sweetheart. He was talking about you." He let that sink in. Watched her features as it did, loving the way her eyes lit up from his words. "You're the something special, Jillian Keller. You always have been."

Nine

Jillian felt like two different people: one who wanted to lead with her heart and one who knew to lead with her brain. Her heart was still swooning like the heroine of an old-timey black-and-white movie over an almost kiss. What would it be like if they had an *actual* kiss? Her head was telling her to smarten up and protect herself.

Wanting and taking were two different things. She couldn't take for herself without directly impacting her daughter. And no matter how she felt, Ollie would always come first.

She bit her lip, still staring at Levi like he was a complex riddle she could solve.

"You keep looking at me like that, we'll never figure out what to do here," he said, smiling at her from as far across the room as he could get given the mass amount of . . . stuff packed into the room.

Jilly's heart did an unsteady jig in her chest. At nineteen, she'd met Andrew, had a whirlwind romance, gotten pregnant, and moved away. Getting caught up in "feelings" was how she'd ended up a thirty-year-old single mother who didn't date.

Who didn't want to date. Until Levi.

Giving herself a little pep talk about acting like an adult, she went to see what he was looking at. Levi lifted a framed photo out of a box he'd opened.

Jilly took it, ran her fingers over the dusty glass. "This is amazing." It was a picture of Pete and Gwen standing in front of Pete's, a sign over their heads saying: GRAND OPENING. They looked so young and full of life, happiness, and hope. She loved knowing that in some cases, happily ever after really did work out.

When she looked up to say as much to Levi, he was so close, her mind went right back to what it would feel like to kiss him. She set the frame down, stepping back, because she couldn't breathe if they were sharing air, and nearly tumbled over a box. He caught her, both of his hands reaching out to steady her.

"You need to stop falling for me," he said.

Jillian laughed, and she *knew* he'd made the cheesy joke to settle her nerves. Which just made her want him more. He dropped his hands and gestured to the room.

"There's so much history in here," she said, looking anywhere but directly at him.

"What should we do? I feel weird letting you help with this. I'm getting an apartment out of it. What do you get?"

Time with you. She took another step away, looking around the room, trying to picture what it could be like when it was cleaned up. She marveled at how much fit inside what had to be less than five hundred square feet.

There were boxes stacked higher than she was tall. Some had MENUS scrawled along the side, others had COOKBOOKS. Standing in the center of the room, because the ceiling was pitched, was a ten-foot lamppost clock that looked vaguely familiar. The metal was battered by time and weather. It was amazing. There were tin signs, old barrels, wooden boxes, and pallets.

Levi picked up their lemonades, and passed her hers. She took another long sip, enjoying the taste puckering her tongue.

"Just as good as I remember," Levi said. "This might be too much for just the two of us."

He was right. "On it."

Jilly pulled her phone from her pocket and texted Grayson, Beckett, and Presley in their group thread. "Gray was heading over to the mainland to grab some things but he should be back soon. I'll see if he or Beckett can help."

"I can't ask everyone to drop what they're doing and help with this." He set his lemonade down and put his hands on his hips. They were narrow, but his chest was wide, and she wondered what he did, besides running, to stay in shape. *Way to stay on topic, Jilly.*

"Isn't that part of why you're home? To help your dad?" She put her lemonade on one of the boxes.

Levi turned to face her, his gaze cloudy. "That was part of the plan, but he's too stubborn to take help from me."

Jillian pursed her lips, fighting the urge to point out the irony.

Levi pointed a finger at her. "I see what you did there."

"Beckett said you're making dinner for all of us at the lodge. Consider this our way of working for our supper."

Levi laughed and Jillian felt a little thrill rush through her. It was nice to be funny to someone other than a nine-year-old.

"Okay. If we can sort through some of it here," he said, picking up a box and testing its weight before bringing it closer to the door, "we can decide what needs a more thorough look. Pete didn't seem very discerning about what to keep."

Jillian turned her body so she could slink between some of the boxes and see what else was hiding.

"What kinds of things do you want for the museum?"

Jillian smiled, an idea formulating. "Originally, I'd thought it would be great to take vintage pieces that represent Smile, but looking around," she said as she did, "I think we can do more. Pete's been feeding people in this community for thirty years. What if we put together a retrospective of sorts? A way to show him what he means to everyone."

Her phone buzzed in her pocket. Checking it, she smiled and held it up before setting it down. "Help is on the way. Gray will be here in an hour. Beckett's doing a tour so he'll come by this afternoon, and Presley is headed over now for a little bit before her town council meeting."

Levi walked closer, his gaze locked on hers. "You're a problem solver."

She huffed out a short laugh. "I guess so." It wasn't like there was someone else around to solve problems for her. She was used to seeing what was needed and putting a plan into action.

He stopped directly in front of her, and this time, reached out and stroked his thumb over her cheek.

"I have a problem," he whispered.

Jilly swallowed past the dryness of her throat. "What's that?"

"I really like this woman but she's scared. How do I spend time with her without spooking her?"

Despite the fact that her heart was racing like a speedboat, she managed a laugh, and finally, her head and her heart merged into one being again. "Just be patient."

His gaze flashed with understanding. His fingers curled around the nape of her neck.

"I can do that," he whispered.

He didn't move to kiss her or close the distance between them. She realized, as her breath caught in her throat, that she wanted him to. In this moment, right now. Not because of the past or because she'd always wondered. Simply because she still had a very real crush on the man in front of her.

Maybe it was reckless not to think this through. Or maybe it was time to stop overthinking every little thing. The space between them dwindled.

"Knock, knock," Presley said from the open doorway.

"We need to shut that door," Levi muttered, stepping back.

Presley's gaze locked on Jilly's and the excitement in her eyes nearly made her groan. There was no way Presley wouldn't corner her about this at the first opportunity. More than that, she knew Presley would push her toward Levi, because despite her own rocky past with love, Beckett's girlfriend was a hard-core believer in happily ever after.

Especially if it meant she got to play the role of Cupid.

Ten

Somehow, Pete offering him a place to live turned into a lively get-together that Levi couldn't have anticipated. And hadn't realized he'd been missing out on for years now. His life in Vermont was full and busy. He spent anywhere from fifty to seventy hours a week at work. He ran, planned meals, and every now and again, had a few beers with the kitchen staff. Whatever friendships he'd forged, however, had nothing on these ones. This. This was what he'd been missing; the kind of friendships where it didn't matter if an hour or a year had passed, you easily fell back into the groove of what you'd always been. It's what he'd come home for. His gaze lingered on the doorway where Jillian had disappeared to take a phone call a few minutes ago.

By dinnertime that night, Pete's little above-the-garage apartment was nearly emptied out. The downstairs storage space was fairly open, so they'd put all of the possible museum items there for him and Jilly or Jilly and Gwen to go through. Gray had shown up at noon with sandwiches and a truck. Now, it was full of items to take to the dump in Mackinaw City.

Presley had shown up right when he was almost certain that Jillian was going to kiss him. Of course, Presley was too happy and eager to help to dwell on it. Beckett's girlfriend was some sort of Tetris wizard when it came to seeing and sorting things into stacks, piles, and more efficient spots. She immediately started going through boxes that weren't really museum worthy but might have sentimental value to Pete and Gwen.

Beckett joined them later in the afternoon with his "favorite sidekick, Ollie."

"Bet Pete won't mind you using this couch. Might as well," Beckett said, a hand on the still-upright piece of furniture.

"Where will you sleep?" Ollie asked.

Levi looked over at the kid. She was pretty freaking cute. She was lying on the floor reading, but her legs were up against the wall, straight in the air, and she was using her backpack as a pillow.

"I'll get a bed. Put it in the corner where you are now. Maybe a smaller couch so there's more room."

"You should live at the lodge," Ollie said. "It's the coolest."

Levi smiled and continued scrubbing out the fridge. It had nothing in it but a funky smell he didn't want to think too much about. Grayson walked over to his niece, bending at the waist to look at her upside down.

"It is the coolest, isn't it?"

Ollie grinned up at him. "Yup. And I'm going to work there all summer."

"If your mom says so," Beckett added. He and Gray worked together to set the couch down, now that there was room.

"Uncle Gray already said I could," Ollie said, lowering her legs to the side with a thump before rolling into a seated position.

Grayson came back, tapped her on the nose. "Mom's the boss, kid."

Levi tossed the cloth he was using into the sink as Jilly and Presley walked back into the apartment. Presley had three pizzas in her arms and Jilly had a smile so wide, it immediately brought out Levi's.

Ollie scrambled to her feet. "Pizza!"

"Wash your hands," Jilly said, glancing at Levi, causing a little glitch in his chest, before walking over to Grayson.

Helping Ollie reach the sink, Levi washed his own hands when she was done, listening to Jilly's excitement.

"It's a small fitness company based in Northern Michigan. They're looking at two team-building retreats a year. Their other booking fell through, so if this works out, we could scoop them and have a steady client during the offseason. What do you think? We could offer the end of next week. It would be a perfect trial run."

Grayson Keller was exactly as Levi remembered him. Steadfast, serious, thoughtful, and he loved his family. The guy was loyal, smart, and made him laugh. Levi was always closer with Becks because Gray was older, but he'd missed them both.

"What?" Jilly said, looking up at Gray as Beckett, Presley, and Ollie set the pizza on a few boxes and began to open the lids. "What aren't you saying? I can go over tomorrow and do a virtual walk-through with them."

"I have my field trip to the mainland tomorrow!" Ollie added. She'd been talking about it off and on for the entire afternoon. They were going to the Mackinaw Bridge Museum. Levi had chuckled along with the others because they'd gone on a similar trip back in their elementary school days. It was weird to him, how so much could change yet so much stayed the same.

Jilly was fidgeting with her hands, wringing one with the other, and he wondered why this phone call had her so nervous.

"Shane asked for the week off. He's taking Louis on a surprise trip before the summer season kicks into gear," Grayson said.

"Oh, I highly recommend that. Mine worked out perfectly,"

Presley said, leaning over the box to kiss Beckett. They shared a sweet smile; Levi needed to ask about that story later.

For now, he was confused as to why Shane being away impacted Jilly's plans, and who the hell Shane was.

Jilly frowned, tapping her chin with her finger. "If they come midweek to the weekend next week, maybe we could do premade foods? It's only a trial run."

"Could work with Mrs. Angelo. She'd be able to do breakfast and lunch easily. Maybe some Costco lasagnas or something for dinners? It's what? Less than ten people for two days?" Beckett pulled at the cheese on his slice to detach it from the rest, then handed Ollie a napkin.

"Sorry, can I jump in and ask who Shane is?" It couldn't be someone Jilly was interested in. Someone who was interested in her?

Everyone looked his way, intensifying his out-of-the-loop feelings.

"Shane's the lodge chef. He made plans because he knows the summer is packed. He's cut back his hours because his husband retired last year—you know Louis, Mo's brother. He taught us PE. We've worked around it for the new schedule with some help from Mrs. Angelo. You remember her? Actually, you probably remember her niece, Katara. Didn't you date for a couple weeks one summer?" Grayson's smile broadened as he shared all that information.

Okay. No reason for his face to heat. He'd been sixteen, but he didn't miss the way Jillian's brows arched or her lips twitched. *Redirect.*

"Barely. Okay, so, you need a chef." He pursed his lips, put his hands on his hips. "If only there was someone you guys knew who not only is a kick-as—butt chef—"

"Uncle Becks says 'ass' all the time. It's okay," Ollie said.

Beckett threw a napkin at his niece, making her giggle, while Jillian reminded her, quietly, to watch her words.

"As I was saying, too bad you don't know a chef who has time on his hands who could help out."

Jillian turned her body toward him. She felt too far away. When she was in the same room, he wanted some part of his body, any part, to be touching hers. A pinkie finger, his hand, his thigh. His mouth.

Grayson moved around his sister and grabbed a slice of pizza. Levi did the same, pretending that nerves weren't percolating in his stomach. He could do this. He could help out, spend some time with Jilly, and maybe feel useful while he got things figured out and settled. It was the time-with-Jillian thing that was making bubbles of excitement pop inside of him.

Grayson passed Jilly a piece of pizza. Being with all of them reminded Levi how close they were. He wanted Jillian. More than he'd anticipated. But he needed to move slow. Now that he was home, there was no way he'd risk his friendships with any of them. These people made him feel *home*.

"He's cooking for us at the lodge this weekend. We can make sure he knows what he's doing," Beckett teased, starting in on his second piece.

"Can I help?" Ollie said around a bite of food. "Chef Shane lets me help. I'm a really good sous-chef."

Levi laughed, locking eyes with the kid and nodding even though he didn't have Jillian's "yes" yet.

"You're in the middle of all of this, Levi," Jilly said, gesturing with her arms and losing a piece of pepperoni from her slice.

Gray reached down and grabbed it, then walked it over to the garbage. "What's wrong with that, Jill? That would be awesome,

Levi. If you're sure you have time. Aren't you helping out your dad?"

Levi shrugged, still irked at his dad's refusal to let him pitch in. "Maybe. But not much even if he lets me. I can cook for you guys. It sounds cool. I'll come with you tomorrow and check out the kitchen setup."

Grayson and Jilly shared a look and Levi wondered if her brother picked up on the subtle hum of nerves shimmering around her. She wanted this but was thinking about being alone with Levi. Grayson was looking at it like an answer to a problem.

"Problem solved," Levi said, catching Jilly's gaze with a smile.

Gray squeezed her shoulder and looked at Levi. "Make a list of what items you need once you talk to Jilly about the menu, and I'll grab everything."

A smile hovered on his lips as Jillian stared at him, silent messages passing between them. He liked the restlessness inside of him; the anticipation of what could come. Both with cooking and with the lodge.

He'd been home almost a week and finally felt useful to people who mattered to him. Not the ones he planned, but he was okay with that. It'd been a hell of a day. A new apartment, reuniting with friends, pizza, and beer. He'd hoped to end it knowing exactly how it felt to kiss Jillian Keller, but he could wait on that. For the first time in a long time, neither of them were going anywhere.

He was up early the next morning in hopes that the idea he had would put Jillian at ease. There was the old adage that the way to a man's heart was through his stomach. Levi was flipping that narrative and hoping if he wowed her with a delicious lunch—maybe they could even picnic by the water—Jillian's guard would drop a bit further. He kept telling himself that it wasn't a race. But when Levi was sure about something, he dove in, headfirst and determined.

Levi stirred the barbecue sauce once more before bringing a taste to his lips.

"Mmm. Perfect," he said, tossing the spoon in the sink of his parents' kitchen.

His dad walked into the room as he was coating the chicken he'd baked with the sauce. He slipped it into the oven to caramelize it. His old man was moving slow and, surprisingly, hadn't been pushing himself too hard. Levi had a feeling his mother was behind that.

"Smells good in here," he said, grabbing a mug from the cupboard to pour himself a coffee.

He hated the way his shoulders tensed just from being in the same room with his dad. He loved his dad. Respected the hell out of him. He just didn't understand why he was so mad at Levi.

"Thanks. I'm heading over to the Keller lodge with Jilly today. Have you been there since Gray took over?"

His dad grabbed the milk from the fridge while Levi dug through his mom's Tupperware drawer for containers.

"I haven't. I haven't been over there since you were a kid. I'm not even sure who owned it way back then." His dad took a seat on one of the stools they kept tucked into the island, leaving the milk out.

Putting the milk away, Levi started transferring the potato salad from the bowl he'd chilled it in to a container. He'd been up early baking blueberry muffins with streusel topping. He'd also put together some homemade granola that he liked to have on hand for quick snacks. For lunch, they'd have barbecue-glazed baked chicken, potato salad, and biscuits, along with veggies and a lemon-dill dip.

He'd used his mom's short mason jars as serving containers for the strawberry custard dessert he'd made the night before.

"That look on your face worries me," his dad said, setting his coffee down.

Levi bit back a sigh. "Happiness?" He huffed out a laugh and started cleaning up. Jilly was picking him up in a half hour, which should be just enough time to pack everything up. "My happiness worries you?"

"We've known the Kellers a long time. Not sure that's a road you should travel down."

Irritation pricked his skin. He closed the lid on the salad, put it in the fridge. His parents had a couple of coolers in the garage. "Jillian's not a road, Dad. She's a smart, beautiful, funny woman I've been intrigued by since I was a teenager."

His dad grabbed one of the blueberry muffins that sat cooling on a rack, broke off a piece, and shoved it in his mouth. If nothing else, at least he was eating healthier with Levi home.

Levi went about cleaning, hoping the chore would keep him from telling his dad to mind his own business.

"You've been gone a long time. You say you're back for good, but right now you have no plans other than pitching in with my crew. Jilly's not the kind of woman you date and drop."

Levi's hands tightened around the sponge he was holding. Lifting his head, he stared at his dad across the counter.

"I'm not sure what's bothering me more," he said, deciding that bed or no bed, this was his last morning waking up in his parents' home. "Your low opinion of me in regards to Jillian or your attitude about me being home."

Setting the muffin down, his father brushed his hands together, sprinkling crumbs. "I don't have a low opinion of you. Stop being dramatic. You might be older, but you obviously still jump into whatever you want with your eyes closed. I'm just saying, the Kellers are our friends. Upstanding members of the community. And Jillian came home five years ago a shell of her former self. Acting on whatever—" His dad paused, then gestured toward Levi with his hand. "—spur-of-the-moment urges you've got, can only end poorly for everyone."

The muscles in his neck tightened. Holy fuck. His dad wasn't just mad at him. He didn't think Levi was good enough for Jilly.

Levi tossed the sponge in the sink. "I do jump in. I'll give you that. But I'm not an idiot and I'm not careless with other people's feelings."

His dad let out an exaggerated breath that was clearly a disagreement.

"I've been cooking since I was a kid. It used to make you proud. I'm truly sorry if I let you down by not joining Bright Builds. But going to school wasn't a whim. It was my dream."

How could his dad, who'd built his own dream right here in Smile, not get that?

"And yet, here you are, walking away from that dream as fast as you ran toward it. What happens when you get tired of being home? It'll be hard enough on your mother to have you move away again. What about Jillian? She doesn't need another man she can't count on."

His dad's words felt like an uppercut to the ribs. He'd drastically underestimated the amount of resentment his dad held toward him and his decision to leave.

Levi shook his head, like maybe that would clear up the myriad of thoughts ricocheting inside of his brain. The timer on the stove went, so Levi turned, took the chicken out, and set it on top. His movements were deliberate and slow because he felt like tossing the dish into the sink and asking his dad what the hell he was talking about. Instead, he removed the oven mitt he'd donned and turned to face the man who'd raised him. The man he'd looked up to and admired.

"I'm almost thirty-two years old. Running a kitchen was my dream. I went for it, and I appreciate that you sacrificed things to make that happen. I truly do. It's a lonely life, the one I was living. And I'm getting older and so are you and Mom. So sue the hell out of me for wanting to come home and start a new phase. I didn't run away from my dream. I lived it for almost fifteen years, and it changed, morphed into something else. I'm sorry you don't think I'm good enough for Jillian Keller, but fortunately, the only person whose opinion matters on that is hers. I need to get ready to go. I'll have my stuff out tonight. Thanks for your hospitality, Dad. And for opening my eyes so I could understand how you really feel about me."

"Levi? Steven? What's going on?" His mother came into the kitchen as he and his dad stared at each other across the island countertop.

Pulling on every Zen meditation technique he'd learned at a team-building event he'd attended a few years ago, he forced a smile when he looked at his mom.

"Nothing. I'm headed out with Jillian today. I'm helping the Kellers out with something." He glanced at his dad, hoped the message *because they actually trust me* got through. "If you're not busy Saturday, I'm making everyone a big meal at the lodge. I'd love if you came—I'm sure you could boat over with Jilly's parents. I'm taking my stuff. I've got my own place behind Pete's now."

His mom gripped his hand. She might have missed the conversation, but the tension was a presence in the room as real and tangible as the three of them.

"You don't have to go. You're welcome to stay as long as you like."

Levi leaned down, kissed her cheek. "I won't be far. I love you."

She squeezed his hand. "I love you."

It was like ripping a Band-Aid off an open wound to hear the sorrow in her voice.

He heard her whispered voice behind him. "What the heck did you do?"

Nothing. His dad hadn't done anything other than lay his cards on the table and show his hand. He was disappointed in Levi for leaving, for choosing something other than the family business, and for coming back.

Upstairs, he tossed the few things he had in his duffel bag. He'd had his few belongings—mostly kitchen items, some framed posters, photographs, and odds and ends—shipped to a storage facility in Mackinaw City. He wouldn't need anything other than what he had here for a while yet.

Making the bed, Levi thought about the day he'd left. He knew his dad wasn't happy with his choice, but maybe he'd been too caught up in his own desires to really absorb how upset his dad had been.

No, he hadn't come home for Christmas or holidays, because once he started his life, he'd been sucked all the way in. The couple of years he'd tried, his parents had gone on a cruise. They talked on the phone, but now that he thought about it, Levi mostly talked to his mom. He'd known his dad was hurt by his choice, but figured time and success would smooth things over. It hadn't. He'd been able to ignore that for a long damn time. Now he was home and he knew, even if his dad wasn't right about everything, he wouldn't feel entirely settled, like he was once again part of Smile, until things were okay with his dad. He just had no idea where to start.

Eleven

Jillian eased up on the throttle as the dock for Get Lost Lodge came into view. A glance at Levi caused a spectrum of feelings to spin in her chest like a Tilt-A-Whirl. Leading the way, currently, was amusement.

"You can let go of the seat now," she said, parking next to the dock with the ease of someone who had done it dozens of times. "I don't remember you being scared of boats."

His face had gone a soft shade of green, amplified by the dark sweater he wore with his jeans. His hair was windblown, his back rigid, his fingers likely leaving permanent imprints on the leather of the boat seat.

"Boats? No. Love boats. You driving one? I might be scarred for life. Is there a boat equivalent for the Indy 500? Because that's clearly your calling. Maybe stunt driving?"

She cut the engine with a laugh. "I'm an excellent driver. You sound like Presley." She pursed her lips. And Beckett, Gray, and Anderson, now that she thought of it.

Jilly stood, stretched, and noticed the way his gaze followed the movement, lingered on the little sliver of skin that revealed itself with her arms up in the air. Goose bumps prickled her skin. She lowered her arms, awareness humming in her blood.

"Fine. When Ollie's not with me, I drive a little faster. But I'm safe."

Levi stood, tested his own steadiness with his hands out on either side. "I'm alive, so I guess I can't argue."

The good thing about his judgment over her excellent driving was it distracted her from obsessing over the idea of being alone with him, spending the day with him, being near him with no one to stop them from getting too close.

She'd spent most of the night thinking about him and the tension that hovered between them like another person. Somewhere around 3 A.M. and an elbow from Ollie, she'd decided he was worth the risk. Because she talked a good game about being over Andrew, and she *was*, but she was still letting her relationship with him dictate her future by being scared to try again. That pissed her off enough that she'd fallen asleep with the determination to move forward and stop looking back. She was in control. She wasn't about to let any man upend her life the way Andrew had. The way she'd let him.

Levi wasn't like any other man. Definitely not Andrew. She'd told herself that any relationship, temporary or long term, in a small town came with the risk of scrutiny. Any connection that ended would inevitably mean she'd run into that person. Right? So, why shouldn't it be Levi? Why shouldn't she take a chance on herself? And him? She'd even convinced herself that she could date without thinking about the future. Or too deeply about it. Okay, she could try to not worry about the future.

What she *was* actually worried about—other than losing what was left of her heart—was Levi's mood when she'd picked him up.

He'd smiled when he greeted her at the door of his parents' home. The delicious scents coming from the kitchen had distracted her from the way the smile didn't reach his eyes, from the tension thickening the air when she'd said hello to his parents. The day before, Levi's determination and confidence about the two of them, the couple of near kisses, his head-on acknowledgment of their mutual feelings, had opened some of the locks around her heart without much effort. But this morning, she realized, he could easily have changed his mind. And likely not because of her driving.

The water was currently calmer than her stomach as she stepped out onto the dock before Levi could offer to help her.

"I think you're supposed to let me be a gentleman," he teased, setting the cooler beside her before getting himself out.

Jilly tied the boat up, doing her best to breathe and count the way she'd taught Ollie to do when she was worked up.

"I'm pretty independent," she said, pulling on the rope to secure it. She'd had to be when her marriage fell apart, and even before when she was basically raising Ollie alone while her husband disassembled their lives and friendships brick by brick.

She stood, brushed her hands off on her pants, and when she turned, Levi was right there, the early-morning sun casting a glow around his head. He was more than hot or just good-looking. He was classically handsome in a way she hadn't let herself appreciate nearly enough. The chiseled jaw, the scar on his chin barely visible even though she knew it was there. Those dark green eyes that made her think her feelings were see-through. His straight nose and soft hair. All of it together was a lot to take. A lot to want. Especially if he didn't want her back.

He wasn't touching her but his gaze was so intent, it felt like he was. "I don't think I told you how good you look today. You were always pretty, but you're a beautiful woman, Jilly."

She sucked in a breath, doing her best not to swoon at the intensity in his gaze, the surety in his voice. She'd pulled her hair into a tight ponytail because she didn't want it flying in her face while she drove. Her oversized cable-knit sweater hung off her right shoulder, revealing a hint of color with the pink tank top she'd worn beneath. Like him, she wore jeans, but she'd added good boots. He continued staring. He didn't seem distracted now.

"Thank you." What else could she say? *No one else has ever looked at me the way you do? Can this kind of heat and desire last beyond the initial burst of attraction and become something real and long term?* Did she want it to?

She could see, though, because Levi's eyes were like a story-book, that there was more. There was something on his mind that he wasn't offering, so she pushed down the part of her that wanted to kiss him, pull him close like she had the right.

Learning what was within her control and what wasn't had been a hard lesson. She couldn't control Levi's feelings—or her own, apparently—but she could keep them on the right path. Slow and steady, and if anything came from it, that was fine. *Yeah. You're so cool and breezy, Jill. And good at lying to yourself.*

He let his fingers brush hers, like they were dancing, weaving in and out and around each other. "You're welcome. You know I wouldn't say it if I didn't mean it, right?"

Whatever else she was unsure of, she knew Levi was true to his word. Letting her index finger loop his, she nodded.

"I do. And you look good, too. You always have."

"Are you nervous, Jilly?"

She let out a high-pitched, short laugh. "Why would I be nervous?"

He inched closer. "Because you feel what's between us?"

Her lips twitched but she shoved his chest gently. "A minute ago, I wasn't even sure you still wanted to . . . explore things. You seemed off this morning when I picked you up. I thought maybe you'd changed your mind. Which is fine. I'm a big girl. Trust me, I can handle not being wanted, but I meant it when I said I didn't want to impact our friendship. Because before anything else, that's what we are."

Maybe if she'd voiced her concerns earlier in her marriage when red flags started popping up, she could have saved it. Probably not, but she knew she couldn't just sit on her worries anymore. It would take away from everything else.

Surprise and shock flashed in Levi's eyes, then his hands cupped the sides of her face, holding her steady like his gaze. "There's no world where I've changed my mind or *don't* want you, Jilly. I know you've been hurt. Your ex is a fucking idiot, but I'm grateful for that even if it caused you pain, because if he or any other man had shown you what you're truly worth, what you deserve, I wouldn't be standing here with you right this minute."

He let out a long breath, seemingly letting go of the tension in his shoulders even though his gaze hadn't softened. It was earnest and dark and really freaking sexy.

"I'm sorry about this morning. My dad and I argued. I've always known he wasn't thrilled with my choice to leave Smile and pursue cooking, but I didn't think it was this enormous chasm between us getting wider and deeper the longer I was away. You showed up shortly after he suggested I'm not good enough for you."

Ouch. "That's a horrible thing for him to say. That must have made you feel terrible." She liked Mr. Bright because of what she knew of him, but the thought of someone saying that to Levi brought out a protective streak in her she'd thought was reserved for only Ollie and family.

Levi shrugged, his gaze moving beyond her. When it came back to her, she could see there was no hesitation now. He was confident and sure. Maybe enough for both of them. "There's time to make things right. I'm not sure how yet, but I don't want to focus on that. I want to focus on this. You. Us. This day. Right now. I don't mind making you nervous in the right way, Jilly. But I don't want to push for more than you're ready for. We've known each other for years. It's been a minute since we spent any real time together, but I'm not reading you wrong, am I? Do you want me to kiss you?"

She swallowed, audibly. He'd laid it all out there, opened up to her honestly. He deserved the same from her. He made her want to be brave.

"I feel like I've wanted you to kiss me for as long as I can remember," she said, her voice low but her words steady.

He sucked in a breath, one hand moving to her waist as his other cradled her face. Other than that, he stayed still, letting her lead, and *that* made her feel powerful. Anticipation hummed over her skin and she realized how much she wanted this. Years of want that must have been buried as deep as the boxes in Pete's place seemed to fill her entire body. Sometimes, people tucked things away for so long, they forgot they existed, and when they stumbled upon them again, it felt brand-new. And yet, somehow, familiar.

Jilly slid both of her hands up the hard planes of his chest, watching him, feeling his heart beat beneath her hand. Before she could press her mouth to his, he smiled and leaned in, brushed the tip of his nose over each of those freckles, the little rainbow spattering across the bridge. He grazed his lips over her nose, touching each little mark, moved up to press a feather-light kiss to her forehead and then to each of her closed eyelids. A tremor worked its way between them and she didn't know if it was him, her, or both of them.

"Levi," she whispered, surprised by the desire evident in her voice. *No hiding now.*

He rubbed the pad of his thumb over her full bottom lip. The first touch of his lips made Jilly certain the fire between them was always meant to burn. It was gentle at first while he learned the shape of her mouth, angled her head to take the kiss deeper. Then she pushed herself closer to him, changing the kiss from sweet and innocent to one full of promises and demands. While one of his hands pulled her closer, his fingers pressing into her skin in a deliciously exciting way, his other trailed lightly down the side of her body, then back up, from her hip, over her waist and up, along the outer swell of her breast and up more until it was buried in her hair.

Going up on tiptoes, Jillian closed both of her arms around his neck, murmuring and sighing in the same breath, letting her tongue tease his, spurred on by the growl that left the back of his throat. Her own hands wouldn't stay still. They curled into his hair, and it was every bit as soft as she'd imagined. Her thoughts scattered to dust until she was consumed by everything about him: the shape of his body, hard edges against her curved ones, the differences complementing each other, the taste of his lips on her tongue, the scent of his earthy shampoo.

It shocked her to hear the little hitches in her own breath, followed by her barely there whisper asking for "more." His hand at her hip roamed up her back, his fingers dancing over her spine, sending little sparks in every direction, before moving down to her lower back to fit her against him like a lost piece of a puzzle he'd meant to finish long ago.

When he finally pulled back, both of them were breathing like they'd run to the top of the mountain behind the lodge. If she'd been on the fence, unsure of what she wanted, Levi's lips had given her all the certainty she needed. She wanted *him*. She'd been kissed plenty in her life and no one else's kisses had ever made her whole body feel like it had been warmed by the sun. Like just the act of kissing was enough to make her head spin and push the world away. She'd had good kisses; seductive, sweet, sexy kisses.

But kissing Levi was unlike anything she'd ever experienced, and she wanted to make it her new hobby. Or better yet, her full-time job. She touched her lips with her fingertips, like she could still feel him there.

She was glad he looked as shaky as she felt. Still, his voice was strong as he brought his hand to her neck, stroking her cheek with his thumb. "I'd say that was worth the wait. I know you're unsure of what's next, but it's up to you. You're in charge. When you're ready to kiss me again, I'm here."

Their chests were plastered against each other so she could feel their heartbeats and thought it was kind of cool that they played off of each other. Him. Her. Him. Her.

"Just like that? I'm in charge? No pressure, just kiss you anytime I want?"

His smile brightened his entire face. "Yes, please."

Her fingertips curled into the black sweater he wore. She didn't know how to respond to his words or the feelings swirling inside of her.

Though energy coursed between them like the waves beneath the dock, she didn't want to rush. Or maybe she just knew that if she kissed him, she wouldn't get anything else done all day.

Stepping back, she took his hand while he scooped up the cooler, and tugged him toward the grounds.

"Welcome to Get Lost," she teased, swinging their joined hands.

Levi squeezed hers before bringing it to his lips and kissing the back of it. "I think I'm going to like it here."

Twelve

Levi wasn't out of shape. He did cardio and weights a few days a week, played sports when he could, and ate reasonably healthy meals. When Jillian asked if he was up for the challenge of a harder hike, he'd scoffed like the answer was obvious. He should have read into her sexy, subtle smile but he'd been seduced instead and would have, quite literally, followed her anywhere.

They stayed side by side for most of it, her chatting about Ollie and the lodge, how they'd worked their asses off the summer before to get the place up and running. He loved the sound of her voice, the way the pitch and tone changed depending on who she was talking about. About forty minutes in, he wondered how the hell she was still carrying on a conversation when he was completely winded. She took videos at different points so she could send them to the company she was giving a tour of the lodge to before lunch.

"Uh-oh," she said, stopping in the middle of the trail. She put her hands on her hips. "Maybe this one is too much for you."

His lungs burned even as he took the opportunity to sip water. "No one likes a smartass," he said, unable to hide the unevenness of his breaths.

"That can't be true. If it is then it doesn't apply to me, because I know many, many smartasses and I like all of them," she said, her gaze twinkling and her breathing, thank freaking God, a little heavy.

"I don't remember you being so funny," Levi said. He set his pack down, stretched his arms up over his head. He'd ditched his sweater a while ago and had considered hiking in his boxers just to get out of his jeans but figured he should hang on to a bit of his dignity.

Jillian's gaze tracked his T-shirt, making his skin heat up with the blatant perusal. He lowered his arms, stepping into her despite the fact that he was sweating. So was she. That had to cancel things out, right?

She didn't seem to mind as he stepped close enough to touch. It was hell not reaching for her, but he'd put the ball in her court. He wanted her. There was no way he could look at her and not want her. Likewise, there was no way she couldn't know that he did. But, as his dad had pointed out, she was the one with more to lose.

Though she kept a sliver of space between them, he felt her everywhere. "I was usually too shy to talk to you."

"Or reading a book," he remembered, catching the scent of her shampoo and pure Jillian. His muscles tightened, ached to pull her against his body.

"I think I came into my funniness later in life." She gave him a wide, goofy grin that made him laugh.

Fuck it. He reached out, ran his thumb along her cheek, reveled in her sharp breath. "Hmm. It looks good on you. Like everything else."

Her smile made his heart turn over. "I don't remember you being so smooth with the lines."

He took her hand instead of kissing her, which is what he wanted to do. Scooping up his backpack—they'd left the cooler at the lodge—he pulled her forward at a much more leisurely pace.

"It's not a line. Nothing I say to you is. I just tell you the truth. I try to do that in most areas in my life," he told her.

She tugged on his hand so he turned to face her. He'd slung the pack over one shoulder, so it whirled with him when he turned.

"In which areas of your life *don't* you tell the truth?"

He hated the way her eyes filled with trepidation. He hated that she'd been hurt and those scars still showed; those fears still hovered. In that moment, he understood his dad watching out for Jilly. Their parents were friends. He cared about the Keller kids. But shouldn't he give Levi the benefit of the doubt?

Levi bent his knees a bit to bring their faces closer like he was going to tell her a secret. He trailed a hand up her arm, lowered his lips beside her ear, felt her tremor, and smiled. The ball was in her court, but he could make sure she had a reason to play.

"When my mom asked if her chicken pot pie was delicious, I lied and said yes because I didn't know how to tell her it wasn't supposed to have lumps in it that *weren't* chicken and veggies. At the dentist, when the hygienist asks if I floss regularly, I say yes even though I don't. In high school, I told Beckett and Gray that Jenna Meyers had a boyfriend even though I knew she didn't because I didn't want them to ask her out."

He pulled back far enough to see the amusement dance over her features.

"Hmm. Did *you* ever ask her out?"

"Jenna?"

She gave him a deadpan look. "No. The hygienist."

He snaked his arm around her waist, pulled her closer. "The hygienist was old enough to be my grandmother, so definite no there, and I waited too long with Jenna. She and Kyle Greggory got together about a month after I lied to your brothers."

Jilly ran her fingers over his chest, and he liked the feeling more than he should. At least if he wanted to concentrate on her words and not how she made him feel.

"They're still together. They moved to Chicago about three years ago," she said quietly, tracking the movement of her fingers.

Levi lowered the pack and used both hands to frame Jillian's face, tilting her head so she looked at him. "I heard that. I'm happy for them. Maybe people end up where they're meant to be."

"You think so?"

"I do. I wasn't so sure for a while, but now? Nowhere I'd rather be."

She stared at him so long, he wondered what she saw. Did she think she could tell the truth of his words by looking at him? Levi had learned that the best way to prove something was continuous follow-through. It was okay that she was unsure. He'd show up day after day and give her reason not to be. Same as he'd eventually do with his dad.

He thought she'd step away, impose that control that seemed to shield her like a titanium cloak, but like a switch flipping, Jillian took control and pulled him down so she could kiss him. He needed absolutely no encouragement to jump on board. He felt her sigh into the kiss and all but melt against him. One of her arms went around his waist as he tilted his head, his fingers tangling in her hair. She tasted like his homemade granola and Jillian, a sweetness he knew he could get addicted to if she gave him the chance.

"Lightning," she whispered, pulling back.

She literally left him dazed. He stared at her through lowered lids. "What?"

"It's not supposed to strike the same spot twice, but every kiss with you is good."

Well damn. It was hard not to puff his chest out at that.

"I defy all of those theories."

Jillian laughed. "Why don't we get to the summit. The walk down will be easier. We can have lunch, I'll show you around, and maybe later we can sit in the hot tub for a bit."

Levi smiled. "You didn't mention a hot tub. You know, I've seen a summit before. You see one, you've seen them all, right?"

Jillian stepped back, picked up his pack and handed it to him. "We have to reacclimate you to the great outdoors. You've been citified."

He laughed at the term. "They have parks and hiking in Vermont. And skiing."

Walking side by side, they veered to the right, Jillian pointing the way. "I lived in the city for a while, too, you know. Somehow, even when it's right there, you forget to take advantage of it." She glanced at him. "Or were you out in the wilderness every chance you got?"

He sent her a mock glare. "I'll have you know, I walked to work each day and it took me right through the local park."

Jillian bit her lip. "Right. My bad. That's exactly the same. It's strange that you were a bit winded earlier what with your vigorous outdoor routine in the city."

Levi laughed and the sound carried along the breeze, the birdsong accompanying it.

When they finally reached the peak, she was right; the view was breathtaking. He could see Smile in the distance. It felt so close and so far away at the same time. Life was like that, he supposed. He'd lived in a busy city, worked in a crowded restaurant, knew dozens of people between colleagues and customers, but felt entirely alone. Now, standing on a mountaintop with only Jilly by his side, he felt surrounded. Fulfilled. Connected.

He took Jillian's hand in his, stared out at the water and the sky, and the feeling intensified. He felt . . . home.

Thirteen

Levi Bright was making it incredibly difficult to remain cautious. If Jillian were making a spreadsheet the way she did for work, he'd check every box. And then some.

Makes me laugh? Check.

Gorgeous, sweet, and funny? Triple check.

Kisses make me feel like fireworks are going off inside of me? Oh yeah. Definite check.

As if all of that wasn't enough, he could cook. Like, really, probably-wouldn't-get-thrown-out-of-Gordon-Ramsay's-kitchen cook.

Glazed barbecue chicken, fresh potato salad with herbs, homemade biscuits that melted in her mouth, and a dessert of strawberry custard were too much for her to resist. She should just propose marriage and be done with it.

She licked sauce from her finger, ready to sing his praises, when she caught the way he was staring at her, his gaze hooded, his eyes watching the way her tongue moved over her finger. Her breath caught and she couldn't help her smile.

"This is absolutely delicious. I'm talking best barbecue sauce I've ever had," she said. She'd worried that she'd forgotten how to seduce a man, but apparently it didn't take much, because if he stared any harder, they might both go up in flames.

Levi made a sound that was somewhere between an agreement and a groan. It made her laugh, which made him scowl.

"What's funny?"

"I've been worried all morning that maybe I'm not cut out for this; flirting, starting something with you. I didn't exactly win any awards growing up for being sexy or seductive. I sure as hell didn't feel like either of those things by the end of my marriage. But if I'm reading your expression correctly, I don't need to worry so much about it. Not with you."

The farm-style dining table at the lodge sat twelve to fifteen people comfortably, but they'd sat side by side and right now, she was grateful for the lack of space between them.

He reached out, cupped her cheek with one hand, looking at her like he couldn't believe she was real. She was pretty sure no one had ever looked at her quite the way he was right now. It made her head spin like a Ferris wheel; slow, almost dreamlike.

"I think you read me better than anyone has, which is strange given that we haven't been around each other in a very long time. There's this sense of familiarity because we knew each other as kids," he said, his voice soft and serious as his thumb brushed back and forth over her cheek. "But a newness that comes from who we are right this minute, who we've become in the time we've been apart. You're reading me exactly right, Jilly. You are the sexiest woman I've ever known, and you don't have to do much more than breathe to intrigue me and make me want to get closer. Maybe it's too soon or too much . . ."

She didn't think before she responded, her hand reaching out to cover his mouth while the words fell from her own. "I've craved someone wanting me *too much* for most of my life and twisted myself into tiny, painful knots trying to make myself *enough*. Maybe it is too much, too soon, but that doesn't make it any less real. Or true." She hadn't expected that buried truth to spring out of her.

When her phone buzzed, she nearly jumped, dropping her hand. Glancing to where it sat on the table, she frowned at the large script reading UNKNOWN NUMBER.

The client's numbers were in her phone. She let the call go to voicemail, not wanting to get caught up before the meeting. Levi was watching her, that appreciative gaze making her skin warm. She leaned closer as he did the same. In tandem, their mouths met, his lips skimming, brushing, making her reach out for him, ready to dive all the way in. Her phone buzzed again.

Levi laughed and leaned back. She recognized the caller this time.

"That's your meeting. I'm going to go check out the lodge. Come find me when you're done." He pressed his lips to her forehead, rose from the table, sliding her phone closer so she could answer.

Right. Life. Back to her regularly scheduled life and the things she wanted outside of Levi.

Taking a deep breath, she wiped her hands on a napkin, grabbed her phone, and stood up.

Swiping her thumb across the screen, she smiled at Eva Hale, the CEO of a fitness company.

"Hi," she said happily, her pulse slowing.

"Hi, Jillian. Thanks for taking us on a tour today. We've got you on our big screen. I'm here with a few of my employees and a couple of my partners."

Jillian smoothed her hair back with one stroke, hoping that going for a hike before this wasn't a bad idea, that she looked presentable. Levi seemed to think she was, but he might be biased.

"I'm so happy to do it. I really think your team would have a great time at our lodge. Let's get started. This is the dining room. It seats up to fifteen comfortably."

Pride suffused her as she led the team through the cabins—all but number four, which belonged to Bernard Dayton, a guest who'd become family. She showed them the grounds, the dock that they planned to widen this season, the hot tub nestled in tall trees with twinkle lights strung around it.

"It's really gorgeous at night with the stars and the lights," Jillian said, trying to keep her words well paced and timed. She didn't want to babble out all of the information in her excitement.

"What kinds of activities do you think you could organize?" Eva asked.

Jillian had spent time chatting with Presley about this very thing. They didn't want to go more in debt, but there was a lot they could offer with what they had available, and more they could do for relatively cheap.

"There's all of the obvious ones—boat tours, fishing, swimming, trail walks, multi-level hikes, and overnight camps at the summit. But I think we can also create some activities suited to your company. We've got some faux survival scenarios that I think would work perfectly for your team. As I mentioned before, we're just dipping our toes into this area, and first and foremost, this is a family-run fishing lodge that caters to that demographic. But we'd really like the opportunity to show your team a great time in a place that will give you plenty of room for creating and strengthening connections."

Damn . . . did she sound like an infomercial?

"Are all meals and snacks included in the price you quoted us?"

Jillian smiled, heading toward the back porch, which led to

a door off the kitchen. "Actually, I can introduce you to the chef who would be taking care of all of your meals."

She found Levi at the long countertop, scrolling on his iPad. When she walked closer, she saw food trucks and made a mental note to ask him more about that.

"Eva Hale, let me introduce you to Levi Bright. He's recently returned home to Smile but for the last ten years, he's been working in Vermont at a high-scale restaurant in the heart of Burlington."

Levi straightened his shoulders and sent her a quick questioning glance before turning on his natural charm, greeting the team and answering all of their questions about meals and dietary restrictions.

When they finished the call, Jillian was practically vibrating. She set the phone down, stared at it, and felt Levi's presence like a cloak of warmth and support.

"You okay?"

Turning, she nodded. "I think that went really well. I wasn't sure if I could sell it but I think we did."

"*You* did, Jill. You did that. It's a kickass idea and they were very impressed."

She spent so much time working to support others, she didn't often stop to take credit for her contributions. Which was fine. She didn't need applause. But she'd almost forgotten what it was like to take an idea, nurture it into fruition, and see it all the way through to implementation. It was heady. Empowering.

Levi grinned at her like he wasn't just impressed but proud. And that unlocked more of those chains around her heart.

"Everything you said about the menu, it was perfect. They're going to email and say yes."

He stepped closer, keeping just enough space between them to make her want. "Yes they are. We're a pretty good team."

She nodded, afraid to admit that out loud. Even with Andrew, whom she'd committed to fully and completely, she'd never felt like the other half of a partnership.

Because her emotions in this moment were not only inexplicable but threatening to overwhelm her, she pointed to Levi's iPad.

"Show me your dreams."

He held her gaze and she realized at least one of her own dreams had a very good chance of coming true. If she wasn't too scared to let go of all her safety nets.

Fourteen

They moved their family date, as Ollie called it, to Sunday, as it seemed easier for everyone. Other than Levi's dad, who said he couldn't join them. Jilly hated seeing Levi look so defeated over his father's reactions to his being home, to them starting something, and toward Levi's dreams in general.

"I'm going to be a chef, a wilderness survival guide, and a game show host," Ollie said as Levi cleared the counter for them to get to work.

Jill knew he didn't need their help but it was nice that he followed through on his word to Ollie, telling her she was his sous-chef.

The sun shone through the wide kitchen windows. It was a perfect, breezy May Sunday. Ollie, Levi, and Jill had headed over to the lodge early today to get things set up and give Levi time to cook.

"That's a lot of jobs," Jill said, meeting Levi's amused gaze.

"I like to be busy," Ollie said, washing her hands at the kitchen sink.

Levi laughed as he set out items he'd need. She and Gray had offered to pay for the food since he was feeding them, but he insisted that he wanted to host even if it wasn't his kitchen.

"That you do." She passed Ollie a tea towel, noting that their supply was low.

She pulled out her phone to add it to the list of things she needed to pick up. Her gaze wandered to Levi double-checking his ingredients. She liked watching him like this. Usually, he had a carefree aura about him, an easy laugh, a quick smile. But in the kitchen, when he was getting ready to cook, he was focused. Serious. Kind of like when he looked at her when they were alone.

Levi passed a small cloth bag to Ollie. "I got you something."

"You did?" Ollie took the bag, her grin so wide it was easy to see the spot where two of her teeth were missing.

"Sure. Every chef needs one of these," Levi said, folding his arms across his chest.

Jill couldn't deny that her attraction to him increased with the way he watched her little girl open the gift.

She unwrapped a white chef's jacket. "This is so cool! Gordon Ramsay wears one of these. Do you have one?"

Levi nodded, grabbed his from one of the bins on the other counter, and put it on while Jilly helped Ollie.

"What do you say?" Jilly asked, meeting Ollie's excited gaze.

"Thanks, Levi. This is the coolest."

He held out a fist to her, which Ollie quickly bumped. "No problem. Now, we match."

Jilly stared at him a moment. There was nothing but genuine interest when he spoke to Ollie. He didn't look at Jill and gauge her response or see if she was impressed.

"Sorry I didn't get you one," he said, then one side of his mouth curved up in a sexy smirk. "I haven't forgiven you for the lazy lasagna yet."

Jilly laughed. He couldn't know that this was better than a gift. So much better.

"Okay," Levi said. He clapped his hands together. "Let's get started. Have you ever made biscuits?" He didn't speak to Ollie like she was a little kid, something grown-ups tended to do.

She could see Ollie noticed it as well. "Mom and I make the Pillsbury ones. Does that count?"

Jilly bit her lip, fighting her smile when Levi's gaze met hers again and he groaned.

"It doesn't. Though I'm not too much of a food snob to admit they're yummy."

Ollie nodded. "They're delicious. And I've made pancakes. And once, Pete let me help him make waffles."

Levi stood straighter. "He did not," he said, his tone full of shock.

Ollie nodded quickly. "He did. He said I was the best helper."

"He won't let me anywhere near his waffles," Levi said, his tone low and awestruck for her daughter's benefit, which had the effect of turning Jilly's heart to mush. "You must be a pretty great helper."

"I am. I work here at the lodge, too. If you visit this summer, I can take you for a hike."

Levi glanced over Ollie's head toward Jillian. She saw affection mixed with amusement. "As long as it's easier than the one your mom took me on."

Jilly's phone buzzed in her hand. Unknown number again.

"If you have things to do, we can handle this," Levi said.

"Yeah. We got this, Mom." Ollie grinned at her.

"Why don't you go grab the stool so it's easier for you to reach everything," Jill suggested.

When Ollie ran out of the room, Levi stepped closer, leaned in, and kissed her cheek.

"I like your kid," he whispered.

Mush. "I think she likes you back," Jilly said, putting one hand on his chest, mostly because she liked touching him but also because it steadied her.

"How about her mom?"

Jilly shook her head, looking up at him. "She likes you a little too much, I think."

He made a low sound in his throat before sealing his mouth over hers in a quick, electric kiss. Like he heard Ollie coming, Levi stepped back and turned toward the counter, leaving Jillian somewhat dazed as her daughter set up the stepping stool.

"I'll just . . ." Her words didn't work properly. "I'm going to make some phone calls."

"Sounds good," Levi said.

She watched for a moment as Levi showed Ollie how to set up her ingredients to make better use of her time. As she backed away through the swinging door, she realized that Ollie had her uncles and grandfather but this felt different. Ollie got along with everyone. She had an easy way about her and a genuine interest in so many things. She wondered how she'd feel about Jillian including Levi in more of their activities, or if that was even wise at this point.

Her phone buzzed again and this time she answered it as she walked through the dining room toward the front lobby.

"Hello," she said, thinking about the things she wanted to get done while they were here.

"Jillian."

Andrew's voice stopped her in her tracks. She looked around the high-ceilinged room that both welcomed the guests and offered them a place to relax, like he might materialize out of thin air.

"Why are you calling me?" Leaning against the front desk, she slowed her breathing.

"That's not a very nice way to say hello."

Her shoulders stiffened. "I don't want to say hello or anything else to you. Why are you calling?"

"I'd like to see you."

Why? Why now? After all of this time, after letting her go and letting them down, why would he reach out now?

"No."

"I'd like to see Olivia."

Nothing strengthened her resolve like protecting her daughter. "That's unfortunate because the answer to that is no as well."

"I have business in Michigan. I'd like to see you and my daughter. It would be easier if you wouldn't fight me on this."

That was the story of their marriage. How could she make it easier on him? But she wasn't in love with Andrew anymore, she wasn't blinded by the vows they'd taken. She was five years wiser and stronger than she'd been when her marriage ended.

"Funny thing," she said, hoping her voice sounded steadier than she felt. "I'm not interested in making anything easier on you. I don't want to see you. And neither does Ollie."

She hung up, her hands shaky. Taking a minute, she forced herself to take a deep breath in through her nose, hold it, and let it out.

Then she did what any grown adult woman would; she texted her best friend. Then she texted Presley. They'd be here this afternoon and Jill could talk to them about Andrew. About Levi. About what the hell she was doing and how, even at thirty, she still felt like a mixed-up teenager.

Fifteen

Levi looked around the lodge dining room, and even though his dad didn't show, his heart was full. Cooking for anyone soothed his soul. Cooking for people he loved was a next-level high. His gaze landed on Jilly, standing over by her parents near the end of the long table. They were chatting with Gramps, who was good friends with Mr. Keller and had ended up tagging along. Jill's brothers and Presley chatted animatedly with Jill's best friend, Lainey, whom he remembered from when they were younger. He'd definitely seen her early last week at the reunion.

Jill seemed a little off when he and Ollie had found her weeding the garden in front of the house. Ollie really was an impressive helper and a hard worker. Levi had told her mom as much but there was a stormy look in her gaze, and before he could get her alone to ask if she was okay, everyone had shown up.

It'd been nonstop since. The most charming of all, Ollie bounced on her knees on a chair beside his mom, telling her a story that had her laughing. His heart actually flipped over in his chest like a pancake. He decided to ignore the fact that his dad didn't show. His mother said he wasn't feeling up to the boat ride, but Levi knew it was more than that.

It didn't matter. Levi was right where he belonged. This was the start of it. Something big. Something he'd wanted for longer than he'd let himself acknowledge. Picking up a fork, he tapped it on a glass, getting everyone's attention.

"Thanks for letting me cook for you guys tonight. And for the use of the kitchen," Levi said, a hint of nerves sliding over his skin, making their presence known. Several of the items he'd prepared were things he was considering for his food truck. Their opinion mattered.

He looked at his mom, nodded, hoping she understood how much it meant that she'd come tonight. Of course, the Kellers were hard to say no to, and Jilly's mom had taken care of corralling at least one of his parents into a yes.

"I'm excited to be home. I've been away for a long time but I think, in the back of my mind, I always knew I'd return."

Everyone clapped, making his neck hot. His gaze naturally found Jillian, who watched him, a little smile ghosting her perfectly shaped lips.

Time to share the news. "Tonight is a chance for me to try out a few menu items for the food truck I'm planning to run. I wanted to cook for all of you and have a happy-to-be-back celebration, but I also wanted your opinions on some menu items that I'm considering."

His mom put a hand on her chest. "A food truck?"

Levi found it difficult to swallow around the sudden dryness in his throat. He held her gaze, bracing himself.

"That's a very fun idea. Everyone is going to love your food, honey. Even if it comes out of a truck," his mom said.

People chuckled, and Levi bit back his groan. He was pretty sure he could make Kraft macaroni and cheese with little hot dogs and his mom would praise him like a gourmet chef.

Presley caught Levi's gaze. "It's an excellent idea and a sound business. You can literally drive to more populated areas if it's a slow day. Or you could rent a space on Tourist Lane, put some picnic tables out front."

Beckett nodded, putting his arm around Presley's shoulder.

He could do this. He would do this. Just like going away to school—he could succeed without his dad's full approval. Or presence.

"I love food trucks," Ollie said, settling on her seat. "We went to Mackinaw City and there was a dessert food truck. That was the best thing I've ever seen in my life."

Everyone laughed and the tension in his chest loosened. Became bearable.

"Yes. And someone let you try one of everything," Jillian said, shooting her dad a pretty good side-eye.

Mr. Keller winked at his granddaughter. "No regrets, right, peanut?"

"Nope." Ollie looked at Levi. "Will you have desserts?"

He smiled at Jilly's daughter, seeing enough similarities that his heartstrings tugged, tying a new knot.

"Some. Let's get started. I'm going to drop off sample platters with an assortment of items. Don't be shy. I want to know what you think. I'm looking to fill a void in Smile's offerings. Not that there are many," he said, knowing his audience and the locals' love of supporting their own. "Think about what's easy to grab on a lunch break, at a festival, or at the Sunday market. I want my food to be different but fit the vibe of a town we all love."

"Let us try it, son," Gramps said. He ran a hand over his bushy gray beard, smoothing it down.

Grayson and Beckett got up to help him grab the pre-plated platters he'd already set up in the kitchen. He'd made two different chicken sliders, one breaded, one baked; a smaller version of his secret-recipe cheeseburger (barbecue sauce and cheese mixed right into the meat); homemade hash browns; three kinds of fries (sweet potato wedges, sea-salted wedges, and thick-cut regular ones). He had some lemon ricotta pancakes with a blackberry coulis he'd been playing around with, but he wasn't ready to share that yet. The breakfast foods might be a touchy spot since locals often liked their favorite standbys and he wasn't sure he wanted to operate breakfast hours.

Using four cheeses, he'd made a grilled cheese on thick-sliced bread. Of course, there were two different kinds of biscuits that his sous-chef had assisted with. She'd been a kick in the kitchen. He'd had to slow his timing and take a couple of breaths, reminding himself he wasn't looking for perfection. He was happy that Ollie only seemed to grow more comfortable with him as they worked. She'd helped him with a couple of vegetarian options including zucchini sticks and loaded baked potatoes. Telling his friends he had the rest, Levi returned to the kitchen, giving himself a minute. His gaze landed on the dessert.

He wasn't sure he'd offer it on a truck but he'd wanted to serve it tonight as a nod to the past, with the Keller siblings, and to the future he hoped to have with Jillian. Her brothers loved her and thought he was great. So, his friends wouldn't be opposed to him asking her out on an actual date. Would they?

He figured Ollie, if she was anything like her mom, would love it, too. Levi was more concerned with getting her kid to like him than he was worried about her brothers having an issue.

Either way, he had some hurdles to jump and looked forward to it, because the more he thought about it, the more he and Jilly made sense. And the more he thought about her, the more he wanted to act on the undeniable chemistry between them. Kissing her was like nothing else he'd ever known. Other than cooking, it was the only thing that ever made him feel like the rest of the world disappeared.

When he was a kid, his mom had read romance novels with half-naked guys on the front. He and Beckett had snuck one and found some of the spicier bits. At the time—they were maybe eleven or twelve—they'd laughed their asses off at the proclamations of love the guy professed. Now, he understood why people wrote love stories. How the hell was anyone supposed to feel so much and not share it? And he hadn't taken her on an actual date yet. *Shit. You should take her on an actual date, you idiot.*

Murmurs of delight and exclamations traveled to him in the kitchen, and Levi pushed down on the emotion coursing through him. This mattered. Their thoughts, his success. He wanted this badly. Tonight was a big step toward making it happen. He and Jilly had looked at food trucks on his iPad the other day and he'd learned that she was incredibly smart and savvy when it came to business decisions.

"Stop procrastinating, Bright. Get out there."

He sat next to his mom, adding a couple of small things to his plate. His stomach wouldn't settle; he hoped his mom wouldn't mention his lack of appetite. The platters were all but empty. Laughter and chatter filled the room along with the delicious aroma of sauces and spices.

"Oh, Levi. This is delicious," Mrs. Keller said from across the table as she grabbed another hash brown.

"I don't remember you loving to cook when we were growing up," Gray said, grabbing a grilled cheese square and setting it on Ollie's plate.

"Sure he did," Beckett said. "We couldn't go anywhere without him and his backpack of homemade snacks. What was that sandwich you made when we were thirteen?"

Levi grinned, breaking a biscuit in half and spreading some

honey-lime butter on it. He'd forgotten about that sandwich. They'd been hanging out at the Keller house and Beckett complained there was nothing to eat so Levi had rooted through the fridge and cupboards and made something up.

"That was gross, man," Levi said.

Beckett picked up a slider. "It was awesome. He used leftover chicken Mom made, added mayo, lettuce, onions, and crushed-up Doritos."

Levi's mother laughed. "Him and his sandwiches with chips on them." She shook her head and sent him a warm smile.

"I don't know about his sandwiches," Jilly said as she added a couple of each type of fry to her daughter's plate while the others chose their favorites. "But he made the best s'mores of any of us."

Levi's chest constricted almost painfully. She remembered.

"Hey," Beckett said. He and Presley were sharing a plate, which he'd give his buddy a hard time about if it wasn't absolutely fucking adorable. His friend was deeply in love. "My s'mores are fantastic."

"Agreed," Presley said, leaning her head against his shoulder.

Beckett kissed the crown of her head and Levi's gut clenched. Somewhere in the middle of achieving all of his dreams, he'd realized what he was missing. Levi wanted what he saw right in front of him: a partner. Someone to lean on, love, fight and make up with. Someone to grow old with. How would he define the kernel of energy and desire that lit him up from inside when he looked at Jillian Keller? Whatever it was, whatever he called it, she was the only one, then and now, that made it ignite into an all-out inferno.

Jillian's arm brushed his as she shifted in her chair. He turned to her, surprised at the duality of his feelings. It was weird to feel so excited near someone who also made him feel so comfortable.

You okay? She mouthed the words.

He nodded, cleared his throat, and looked around the table. "What do you guys think?"

"I think the fries are awesome sauce," Ollie proclaimed loudly.

"Me too," Gramps said.

"This is the best grilled cheese sandwich I've ever eaten," Grayson said.

Lainey nodded even as she took the other half off of his plate. "Agreed."

"Hey!" Gray said, shooting her a look that straddled the line of amused and irritated. "Get your own."

"You took the last one." Lainey took a large, exaggerated bite before making loud *mmm* sounds.

Mr. Keller met Levi's gaze as he picked up a lemon-pepper-and-dill wing. "I'd say when adults fight over your food, you're doing something right."

"Definitely high praise."

His mom used her fork and knife for her zucchini stick.

"You can just pick that up, Mom. Try it with the red chili jelly." He picked up the small bowl and passed it to her. She beamed at him.

"I'm so proud of you, honey. The food is delicious."

"Thanks, Mom. I'm sorry Dad couldn't make it."

"He acts tough but he knows he needs to rest. The surgery went well, but it's still surgery."

The conversation went from there, the Kellers and Gramps asking about his dad, the Kellers talking about their summer trip.

Jilly smiled at him, nudged his shoulder. She picked up a quarter of a grilled cheese. "Lainey's right. This is my favorite of what I've tried."

He wanted to cover her hand with his or slide his onto her

thigh. He wanted the right to do that, the familiarity that Beckett had with Presley. *Slow your roll. A date, remember?*

"A food truck, huh? Was that your plan all along?" Gramps asked.

Levi nodded. "Other than getting home, yeah." Gramps, being the mayor, would spread the word better than the chalkboard. And that was saying something.

Grayson grabbed a loaded baked potato. "I was wondering about extending the dock. Making it wider so more people could fish off it or sunbathe. Would that be something I need to talk to your dad about?"

Levi glanced over at his mom. She shrugged.

"Jilly mentioned that as well. On my way home tonight, I'll drop my mom off and ask him about it."

Because he wanted people to feel free to taste and share their thoughts, and because he needed another minute to catch his breath and just settle the thoughts in his head, he drifted back to the kitchen. Music from an old-school, probably vintage radio, with an actual antenna, came in bursts through the static as he cleaned up. He smiled, thinking the Kellers ought to invest in a Bluetooth speaker.

When the door to the dining area swung open, he turned, expecting, maybe hoping, to see Jill. Instead, it was his two oldest friends instead. Something about the way they walked in together, the set of their similar jaws, and the way they watched him, set him on alert. This wasn't his friends coming back to congratulate him on the food. This was Jilly's protective older brothers coming to give him the talk. He should have expected it. Hell, he should have talked to them first. But he'd been blindsided by the intensity of what he felt seeing her again. It shouldn't have surprised him that they picked up on it. He didn't mind them taking care of their sister. As long as they didn't cross a line that wasn't theirs to tiptoe over.

Grayson, just a touch shorter than his younger brother, had a year and a bit on Beckett and Levi. Both brothers had dark hair, wide shoulders, and the kind of facial structure that made them universally good-looking. God, they'd had some good times over the years.

"Coming to give your compliments to the chef?" Levi leaned his body against one of the back counters that housed all the baking dishes, crossed one foot over the other and his arms across his chest. Home field advantage. *Except it's technically their home field. Shit.*

"For sure. Your food is delicious, man. Jilly said you guys nailed the meeting the other day, too. We'll get a contract written up for that and of course, pay you a more than fair wage," Grayson said.

They split up at the island in the center of the kitchen, each coming down one side of it. Levi would have laughed at the picture they made, like they'd choreographed the move, but he knew their sister had been hurt before.

"What's going on with you and Jilly?" Apparently Beckett was taking the lead on their real reason for coming in.

Levi held up his hands. "Nothing. At all."

Both of them relaxed their shoulders, like he'd popped a pin in their worries.

"But I'm going to ask her out."

"Dude. There's a code," Beckett said.

Levi chuckled, wrapped his hands around the edge of the counter behind him. "Come on, guys. It's me. You know I won't hurt Jilly. If I'm being honest, I've liked Jilly for a long time."

"Correct me if I'm wrong," Gray said, his tone quiet, his gaze . . . *not.* "You've been gone a *long time* and only just recently decided to move home, right?"

Levi nodded. "Sure. But I've been wanting to for a while. This wasn't a whim." He did know how to make informed and thoughtful decisions. "I care about your sister. I know she's been hurt. I'm not looking to add to that. If she didn't want my attention, she'd shut me down."

"She was married. Her divorce wasn't pretty." Grayson's voice was solemn and Levi realized that it had hurt them to watch what Jilly went through.

"I know." Maybe not all of the particulars yet, but he knew she had scars. "But it didn't break her. She's one of the strongest women I know. I'm not going into this lightly, not that it's technically any of your business."

He and Jilly didn't even know what they were yet, so he didn't want to hash this part out with her brothers. Though, it was like needles under his skin to know that maybe his good friends didn't think he was good enough for Jilly either.

"You've been back a week and what? Now you're all in?" Beckett stepped closer.

Levi shook his head, pushed off the counter. "No. Not yet. I don't know. But there's something between us. We're both unattached adults and you know I wouldn't hurt your sister. I love your family and both of you like brothers. Give me some fucking credit."

"And if you can't," Jilly said from behind them, making Levi curse under his breath because none of them had heard her come in, "then give me some."

Both Keller brothers seemed to shrink a little. Beckett ran a hand through his hair. "Aw, Jilly."

"We're just looking out for you, Jill," Grayson said, walking toward his sister.

Jill let the door swing closed behind her. "That's almost as sweet as it is unnecessary. I'm a big girl and fully capable of making my own choices."

Beckett scoffed. "And you choose this guy? He cried when he fell off a roof and he never even broke anything."

Grayson snorted, covered his mouth. Levi shoved Beckett from behind. "We were eight and you shoved me, you ass."

Jillian laughed. "And y'all got in so much trouble for being on top of that shed, none of you did it again. I get that there's history here, but I don't need you two poking your noses into my business."

"Sorry, Jilly." Beckett turned, clapped Levi on the shoulder, and started for the door, stopping to pull his sister into a side hug.

Grayson's lips pursed as he met Levi's gaze. He gave one sharp nod then followed Beckett's lead.

That left Levi alone with Jilly. And a dining room filled with their friends and family. But right this minute, with her looking at him across the gleaming countertops, the scents of his favorite foods in the air, all he saw was her.

He grinned. Levi was a big believer in going after what he wanted. "I think you really like me, Jillian Keller. Will you go out on a date with me?"

Sixteen

The night had been going so smoothly. She'd set aside her growing worries about Andrew—Lainey had texted that he was probably going to bail on seeing Ollie anyway so why get in a panic over it? She hadn't gone into detail with Presley, instead saying she'd talk to her tonight. With her ex pushed to the back of her mind, she'd been able to enjoy Levi's creations and presence. Mostly. Being around him tended to make her pulse and brain scramble like crossed circuit wires. *Not* thinking about him was impossible. The way he'd kissed her, how much she wanted him to kiss her again. Jilly had been listening to Ollie tell her grandparents about making the biscuits, and her chef jacket, when Jill realized her brothers had been gone too long to simply be paying their compliments to Levi for his amazing cooking. She knew exactly what they were doing.

Hadn't she *just* thought how nice it was to have her big brothers close by? Ha.

Levi continued to stare at her, bringing her all the way back to the moment. With startling clarity, his question settled like static electricity in the air between them. It was *charged*. There needed to be a word in between "like" and "love" on the whole falling-for-a-guy scale. *Will you go out on a date with me?*

Why did his words evoke a response similar to kissing him? *Because it means it's real to him, too.*

He didn't come closer but it felt like she had no space. No room to move. Or breathe. Fifteen-year-old Jilly had invaded her senses and was on the verge of passing out.

Fortunately, she was a mature woman who had been asked out plenty of times. *Not by your childhood crush.*

"Levi." His name came out like a strangled croak. She closed her eyes, inhaled deeply, and let it out before opening her eyes again.

When he did step forward, after what felt like several tense breaths, he didn't come to her. He detoured and picked up something decadent-looking, bringing it over to the counter where she now stood.

Her heart gave one tight squeeze before melting into a puddle of emotions all over her rib cage. The dessert didn't look traditional but she definitely recognized it.

"You made me a s'more?"

When she was ten to Levi's twelve, she'd burned her finger badly on a marshmallow at the start of the summer. For the rest of the season, she'd insisted she didn't want s'mores because the rule was, you want one, you make your own. But Levi made her one every time they built a fire on the beach that summer.

"You can say you don't want it but I know you do." He nudged the plate closer to her, saying the words he'd said all those years ago.

The dessert was stunning. He picked up a fork, carefully slid it through what he'd made.

"Instead of a graham cracker base, it's a milk-chocolate sponge cake on the top and bottom. Between the layers is a vanilla cream mixed with fire-roasted marshmallow fluff." He lifted the fork with a sample of each part. "Then I topped it with dark chocolate drizzle and crushed graham crackers." Levi held it up for her to taste.

With her gaze on his, her hands shaking enough to keep a grip on the counter, her mouth opened. He slid the fork between her lips slowly, watching her the entire time.

Her mouth closed around the bite and Levi pulled his hand away slowly. Jilly hummed appreciation for the delectable bite of ooey-gooey goodness on her tongue. Desire flared in Levi's searching gaze even as he moved closer, setting the fork down with a soft clang on the countertop.

"Jilly," he whispered.

Between the chocolate, the look in his eyes, and his proximity, Jillian felt like she was caught in a dream she'd had a thousand times.

I think you really like me, Jillian Keller. Will you go out on a date with me? YES. But fear blocked the word. A date was a real start. *Which you're more than ready for.* Hearing Andrew's voice earlier had reminded her that she deserved better. When she came home, it was to build a life for Ollie *and* herself. She wanted Levi in it.

"Hey, Chef Hottie. We need more—Oh. My bad." Lainey froze but the smile on her face said she wasn't sorry at all.

Jill's heart hammered so hard she could feel it throughout her entire body; hear it echoing inside of her head.

"I should go. That dessert is delicious." The words tripped out of her mouth like she wasn't sure how to use them.

He reached out, put a hand on her arm.

"I can come back," Lainey said, making no effort to move.

Panic flared to life inside of her. She couldn't explain it but she didn't want to agree to anything today. She'd say yes, but not now, not with all of these people here. "No. I should go. I need to go."

Jill turned and left the kitchen, pushing past Lainey, whom she knew well enough to know would give Levi the third degree and then follow after her. Ollie and her dad were debating which fries were the best. Beckett and Gray looked at her but she looked away, sitting down next to Presley.

Presley turned her head to face Jilly. "You okay?"

Mostly. She was fine. She could stay absolutely fine and mostly okay. But part of her didn't want to, and that was the part that needed to talk to Presley.

"I need to go for a walk. Or just get some fresh air."

Presley leaned closer. "A wine walk?"

All the breath left Jilly's lungs. "God, yes."

Presley nodded. "We're going for a walk. I say guys are on cleanup. Except for Levi. He cooked."

Lainey came back through the swinging door, and Jilly could have kissed her. She had a bottle of wine and three glasses in her hand. "Walk?"

Presley nodded.

"Can I come, Mom?" Ollie asked.

Jilly glanced at her mother, who, somehow, read her like a book. "If I'm not mistaken, you owe me a rematch for Uno," her mom said, smiling at Jill.

Ollie tipped her head back and laughed. "You always say that when I win, Grams." Ollie hurried out of the chair. "I'll get it," she called and ran down the hall toward the family suite they'd stayed in last summer. Levi came through the door, glancing at her and then her brothers.

Grayson nodded in Jilly's direction then rose from his seat. "We're on cleanup, Bright. Why don't you grab a coffee and sit down while we take care of it?"

Levi watched her closely and she could feel the energy humming between them. This was real. And if she didn't want to mess it up, or land flat on her face, she needed to pull herself together.

"We're going for a walk."

His lips tipped up on one side. "I'll save your dessert."

"I like dessert," Ollie said, coming back into the room with her card game.

Everyone laughed. Levi shrugged. "I'll try to save you some, but if she's anything like you, she's going to love that s'more."

He winked at her. She had wine, good girlfriends, brothers who cared enough to show it, and Levi Bright winking at her before going to feed her daughter a homemade, gourmet s'more. As teenaged Jilly would have said: What even was her life right now?

Seventeen

The walk was short-lived and easily traded in for some back-porch-under-the-stars time. There were technically two back porches; one with the hot tub, built farther out from the house, sort of off to the side. This one, attached to the house, was a place Jilly had grown fond of last summer when she and Ollie had been living in the lodge's family suite.

Jilly curled into one of the cushions on the outdoor sectional couch, careful not to jostle her wine. Presley was wrapped in a plaid blanket, curled up at the far end, her own wine in hand. Lainey lit the propane fire table before sitting down between them, right in the corner, then picked her wine up from the table and lifted it in cheers.

After filling them in on the things making her heart and her mind wrestle with each other, Jilly stared up at the night sky, trying to count the stars until her breathing calmed.

"Andrew is a monkey butt," Lainey said, breaking the silence.

Presley sipped her wine. "That sounds like something Ollie would say."

Jill laughed. "That doesn't make it less true."

"Levi's a good man, from what I've seen for myself so far and definitely from what I've heard," Presley said, pulling the blanket tighter around her shoulders.

Noises creaked and croaked through the trees. Looking toward the lodge, Jillian could see shadows of people moving in the dining area. Her family. Gramps. Levi.

She'd miss her parents when they left. This lodge had become a second home to them. It didn't have the backyard where she and Beckett and Gray had played and argued, made up games, and chased each other around, but they were making new memories here. When Ollie was seven, her brothers and dad had built a cute little playhouse that mimicked her parents'. It now sat nestled in some trees near the start of the kids' hiking trail. Her mom had created a little garden around the cobblestone walkway her dad built last summer. It made her smile every time she looked at it. Even though now, Ollie said she wished she had a zipline instead of a playhouse.

"Spill," Presley said, nudging Jilly in the shoulder.

Jill looked at her would-be sister-in-law. "I've known him since we were kids. I can separate the past from the present. I'm not a kid anymore. I *have* a kid. There's already too many feelings for it to be a fling or one-night stand. And that's not really my thing anyway. Though, relationships aren't my strong suit, and who knows what he's actually looking for."

"He looks at you like you're a hell of a lot more than a fling, Jilly," Lainey said, leaning back in her seat. "You might be jaded toward relationships because of your dipshit ex, but you're not blind and Levi Bright is not subtle."

She wanted to believe that it meant as much to him as it did to her, but Andrew calling today had messed with her belief in her ability to separate fact and fiction. Maybe she was just looking at it all through a fifteen-year-old's rose-colored glasses.

"She's right. He looks at you the way I hope Beckett looks at me," Presley said.

Both Lainey and Jilly quickly confirmed that Beckett looked at her with hearts in his eyes.

"And if he still wanted to kiss you after your first attempt, you know he's into you," Lainey said with a quiet giggle.

"Shut up," Jill warned.

"When was your first attempt? Why haven't I heard this?" Presley sat up straighter.

"You have to tell her," Lainey said.

"You have to tell me," Presley said, scooting closer.

Jilly sighed. "I wanted to kiss him so badly. I was only fifteen. He was leaving because he'd gotten a scholarship to an elite culinary school."

"So, I set up a meet cute," Lainey said.

"She staged an intervention so I could get my kiss," Jilly said.

She could still feel the mortification rising up inside of her as she recounted the tale to Presley. She told her how she'd met him on the side of his house, back when his parents didn't live on a houseboat. She'd wanted to say that she would miss him, but she'd stood there, her heart beating so hard it felt like it was outside of her chest. It felt like he'd moved closer, maybe so he could hear her or maybe because he'd wanted to kiss her, too. He'd smiled, that stupid dimple breaking her brain so it could only focus on one thing. Kissing Levi Bright. When she'd gone for it, she'd tripped over a root coming out of a bush. He went to catch her, he *did* catch her. She'd tried to right herself, to turn and run, anything but face him. Instead, she'd made it worse and accidentally slammed the back of her head into his chin. He'd been lowering his head to ask if she was all right. He swore, dropped her arms, and she'd stumbled, looked up to see him holding his bleeding chin. Later that night, her brothers told her he'd had to get stitches but they didn't know what really happened. Levi said he'd tripped.

Jilly felt like she was really back there in the moment and didn't realize she was crying until the tear trickled down her cheek.

"Oh, sweetie. It was so long ago," Presley said. "That must have been awful. Plus, it sounds like you guys made out—ha, see what I did there—just fine this time. He might have fond memories of before, like you do, but I don't think what he felt then is tied to how he feels now. He sees you for who you are, all grown up."

"She's right. He's into you *now*, Jilly. He baked all afternoon with your kid," Lainey said, setting her wine down and reaching out to squeeze Jilly's hand.

He had done that, and Ollie had such a great time. Why was she so scared of moving forward? Standing still wouldn't get her anywhere, but it was a more surefire way to prevent getting hurt again. *There's that maturity you pride yourself on.*

"He's a good man. Maybe he's just trying to mend a teenage girl's heart."

"Did he break it?" Presley asked, lowering her wineglass to rest it on her leg.

Jilly smiled. "Not really. It broke when he moved away and I never got a chance to see if we could be anything. But you know, it broke in the way a teenager's heart breaks."

Presley tilted her head. "Is that somehow different than an adult heart breaking?"

Shifting to get more comfortable, Jilly tried to find the right words to explain it. "It is. As a teen, I didn't know what a broken heart meant. I pined for him, dreamed about him, imagined us together. But as an adult, when my marriage failed and my heart broke, it was different. It had implications on the rest of my life, not just whether or not my crush would make me roasted marshmallows and sit by me at bonfires."

The moon created a soft glow in the sky, shining down on

them even as different creatures added a strange, chirpy kind of music to the night.

"I think a teenage heartbreak can have some pretty big implications. Over time, how we define love might change, but that doesn't lessen your feelings from back then. It's part of who you are. If anything, when you're young, you don't know to put your guard up or watch your step. You love uninhibitedly before you learn to try and protect your heart, or only share small pieces of yourself."

Jilly swirled the wine in her glass, staring into it like it had all the answers. "But I'm not fifteen anymore. I have responsibilities."

"Everyone has responsibilities. Even at fifteen. They just change. The question is, do you want him to kiss you again?" Lainey didn't shy away from the hard questions.

A surprised laugh left her lips as she looked over at Presley. "Well, yes, I do. Why is *that* the question?"

Lainey shrugged. "Because regardless of what happened in the past, him leaving, you embarrassing yourself, your marriage, his stuff with his dad . . . if you still want to take that step, if his kiss made you feel the way you said it did, then it's worth taking the step, seeing if there's anything there to build on. You can protect yourself all you want, but living in a way that doesn't allow you to get hurt isn't really the kind of life you want to live, is it?"

Jilly sighed. "I like who he seems to be now more than I liked who he was back then. And that was already a lot."

Reaching out, Presley put a hand on her arm. "Figuring out who he is now isn't a legally binding contract, Jilly. Beckett and I are proof positive that you can plan it all out or wing it on a prayer and life will do what it wants regardless. We like to think we're in control of the whole journey but really, we just get to choose our responses to what happens along the way. Don't let what you know now, as an adult who has been through what you've been through, stop you from believing in the things you did when you were fifteen. When we stop overthinking things, the answer usually turns up."

Jill took a long swallow of her wine, then looked at Presley. "It's like you had a dozen fortune cookies memorized for this moment."

Her friend looked out at the darkening sky. "I thought I had it all planned out. Falling in love with your brother showed me that there's no amount of planning or preparation you can do for where life leads you. I'm just grateful my ex didn't want to come to the lodge with me, because honestly," she said, looking at Jilly now, a sweet smile on her face, "I would have fallen for Beckett anyway, and that would have made for a hell of an awkward trip."

"There's a lot at stake," Jill said quietly.

Presley poked her shoulder. "Yeah? You think you'll upend your life for him and make a gigantic move just to be closer to him and his family?"

Lainey laughed. Jilly bit her lip, nodding at the point Presley made. She'd done exactly that for love. "We're all glad you did, but obviously, no. I think I'll make a fool of myself while we live in the same town and everyone will be here to witness it."

Lainey got up and moved closer. Presley did the same, only sitting on the other side. She could have used these two around when her marriage fell apart. Lainey had been in contact with her, but the more Jilly found out about Andrew stealing money from his company, from some of their *friends,* the more she'd hidden and the lonelier she'd felt. This was better.

"That's what I'm learning about small towns. They're all up in your business, they have way too much input, but they celebrate your wins, and lift you up when you fall. You're not alone, Jilly, whether you go down this path with Levi or not. And either way, people will speculate. You have to make the decision for you. You deserve that."

Huh. It'd been a long time since she'd thought about what *she* deserved. Her thoughts were generally consumed with what she had to do, had to get done, what Ollie needed, the lodge needed, who would take care of what.

What did she want? Maybe it was time to figure that out. Or acknowledge that she already had.

Eighteen

The night had gone really well. Better than he hoped. When Jill, Lainey, and Presley had come back in after sharing wine on the back patio, there'd been a lightness to Jilly he hadn't experienced so far. Like she'd come to some conclusion and was content. The way she looked at him from across the room as they'd pulled out board games and set up teams was enough to make his mind wander about what decisions she might have made.

He wanted to be one of them. His mom held his arm as he walked her to the houseboat. Twinkle lights hung over the entrance to the docks that surrounded the homes.

"You're really talented, Levi." His mom stopped walking and looked up at him. There was a soft breeze coming off the water that made them sway in a barely noticeable way. If a person were used to it. He noticed and was happy, once again, that he'd taken the apartment over Pete's.

"Thanks, Mom. That means a lot to me. I'm really happy to be home. Even though . . ." he said, his voice trailing off as he looked down the lane his parents' home was on.

His mom patted his arm. "Do you remember being seventeen and full of dreams, sweetie?"

Levi looked down at his mom, aware of music in the distance. Sunday night in Tourist Lane brought a lot of locals who shopped and ate or just strolled in the park.

"I do."

His mom nodded. She was aging well. There were subtle lines and creases on her face and her hands were weathered but she took care of herself. He'd missed her when he was gone and liked that he could check in on her, on them, frequently now.

"Your dad had dreams, too, honey. When you were born, he really put his all into the business. And when we couldn't have more babies, he was okay with it because we had you."

A stitch lodged in Levi's side. He hadn't thought about his parents having or wanting more children. Being an only child had been okay with him. He'd had Gray and Beckett and a lot of other friends. He'd never felt lonely or left out. He wondered how Ollie felt about being an only child. Or if Jillian wanted more children.

His mom squeezed his arm, getting his attention again. "I wanted more and was sad for a long time, but as you grew, you had so many friends, I didn't have to worry about you being alone. It's hard when you put your whole heart into something and then it goes a different way. Even if he shouldn't have, your dad did that with you, thinking you'd be his partner. It wasn't just that he lost that, but you went away and he felt like he lost *you*."

Levi's mouth went dry. He nudged them forward because the emotions swirling inside of him were too strong to stand still. "I didn't move across the world, Mom. I tried to come home to visit, asked you guys to visit."

"I know, honey. And you did what you were meant to do. I'm not saying any of this to make you feel guilty. Just trying to help you understand. And I did visit! Two summers in a row. I was and still am very proud of the man you've become, Levi. Your father will come around. Just give him some time. He might be scared to get his hopes up about you staying."

Nodding, Levi bent and kissed his mom's head. "I'm staying, Mom." For more reasons than he'd originally expected.

When they got to the houseboat, the door opened before his mom could take the first step up onto the little platform entryway. Anderson stepped out of the doorway, tucking a strand of brown hair behind their ear, smiling when they saw Levi and his mom.

"Hey, guys. How was dinner?" They held a dented old-school red toolbox.

"It was lovely. What are you doing here, Anderson?" His mom stepped back so Anderson could exit as Levi's dad shuffled to the doorway.

"You're home earlier than I thought," his dad said, a soft smile for his mom.

"What are you doing here, Anderson?" Levi asked, looking back and forth between Smile's go-to for any problem big or small and his own dad.

"Your dad just needed some help with a leaky faucet. Couldn't get down there to check it out." Anderson stepped onto the dock, their expression neutral.

"You knew I was dropping Mom off. You could have asked me," Levi said, stepping away from his mom.

"It's not a big deal," his dad said, moving so his mom could enter the house.

"Levi," his mom said.

Levi shook his head. "No. I just . . ." He cut himself off, not wanting to say things in anger. He scrubbed both hands through his hair and let out a deep sigh.

"You'd ask anyone before me. I'm sorry if I hurt you, Dad. But

I was a kid, focused on making his dreams come true. You're an adult who has ignored my apologies, shown absolutely no remorse over not supporting my move home, and shut me out purposefully. You win. I'll leave you alone. You made a life that didn't include me even though that was *never* my intention. I won't try to force my way in anymore."

"Levi, please. Don't say that," his mom said.

"I didn't mean to step on any toes, Levi," Anderson said, shuffling in the awkward aftermath of Levi's words.

Levi shoved his hands in his pockets. "Not your fault, Anderson. You didn't. I did."

He heard his mom's whispered anger toward his dad but didn't hear his dad's gruff response. Levi hurried off the dock and went back to his apartment, ignoring his mom's phone call. He'd smooth things out with her later, but it was time for him to admit that the tear between him and his dad might be too jagged to patch back up.

When he let himself into his apartment, he stood by the doorway, staring at the space. It was bigger than he'd expected, but that could be the lack of furniture. Pete had lent him a television and said it was fine to use the couch.

Throwing his house keys on the counter, he opened the fridge, grabbed a beer, and popped the top, taking a long drink.

"You can't control everything. You wanted a life here, start building it," he told himself.

He'd had a few of his boxes brought over from the storage unit he rented. He needed to order a bed, some linens, unpack the stuff for his kitchen. He needed to focus on something other than the past.

Telling himself that, he nearly laughed at the irony when the first box he opened had his high school yearbooks.

Taking two of them and his beer, he went over to the surprisingly comfortable couch that was too long for the space and sat down. He set his beer on the floor and flipped through, seeing old signatures, photographs of him, classmates he remembered and couldn't recall for the life of him.

His fingers traced over a picture of him and Beckett smiling like idiots for the camera. Despite how small Smile was, there were two schools. One went from kindergarten to eighth grade, and the other, on the far end of the island, went from ninth to twelfth. Which meant running across pictures of Jilly, too. He found one of her sitting with her back to a tree, a book in hand, smiling up at something Beckett was saying. Beckett was doing something—probably showing off for some girl he'd had a crush on—and Jillian was waving him away with a grin on her pretty face.

She'd been part of his life for so long, he'd taken it for granted. Or just hadn't thought about it. She'd been at every one of their basketball and volleyball games, making signs when they'd made the finals. She baked cookies and left them for Beckett and his friends so when they all rolled into the Kellers' kitchen after practices, they had something to eat.

Levi continued to flip through the pages, nostalgia and a bit of regret twisting his stomach into knots. There was nothing wrong with going away. But he shouldn't have stayed away. He shouldn't have avoided coming home—which he had to admit, he'd done a fair bit—just to sidestep conflict. Conflict was part of life. He shouldn't have let so much time go in between, because the people he cared for, all of them, had carried on with their lives. It was his own fault he had to find a way to fit into who they were now. He was the outsider.

But he didn't want to be.

Setting the yearbooks on a cushion, he pulled his phone from his pocket and dialed the number before he could change his mind.

"Hello?" Jillian's voice was hushed and, whether she meant it to be or not, sexy.

"Hi. Were you asleep?" Guilt cramped his gut.

She laughed. "No. But I came into my room to grab my book, and Ollie is."

Right. She had a kid. He hadn't thought about wanting a family. In truth, he compartmentalized his life, focused on work most of the time. Now that he was home, he realized how many of those compartments were empty. Ollie was a cool kid and Levi could see little pieces of Jillian in her actions and the way she spoke. Instead of making him wary that he wanted a woman with a kid, it only made him more certain.

"You didn't answer me tonight," Levi said quietly.

"I guess I thought the answer was obvious," she said, her voice still low.

He wished she were right beside him. "I don't want to take anything for granted." No more assumptions. They hurt.

"Yes, Levi. I'll go on a date with you."

Levi smiled, the rest of his stress and uncertainty slipping away. He'd focus on what he could control and that would include showing Jillian how very good they could be together. If he were still a naïve teenager or a hopeful romantic, he'd even say they were meant to be.

Nineteen

Jilly's nerves popped like champagne bubbles.

She forced a deep inhale, held it, and let it out. Glancing in the mirror to check her outfit, she told herself she was ready. It was just a date. *With a man you've known and cared for forever. In a town that knows you both.* Her phone buzzed and this time she recognized the "unknown caller" and pressed Dismiss immediately.

She deserved tonight. This chance with Levi. They'd be seen as a couple. This was the Smile version of a relationship hard launch, as Presley would say. Nobody would wonder after tonight.

She'd had a fairly busy day getting everything organized for Eva Hale's team to visit the lodge this week, emailing a few other potential clients, setting up emails for returning lodge guests, and getting in touch with a student needing graduation volunteer credits to arrange having her work the front desk so Jillian could deal with paperwork and have a break from it when needed.

Tonight, she'd forget about work and everything else and just enjoy going out with Levi.

She hadn't been on a date that she was truly excited about since Andrew at the very start of their relationship. And that was way too many years ago.

Her mom knocked on her bedroom door. Her parents had gone for a two-day trip to the mainland to look at a couple of newer RVs. Before leaving, they'd said they needed to have a family meeting, something they hadn't done in years. It hadn't happened yet. Jillian had a strong feeling they were going to talk about selling the house, so she didn't mind putting the conversation off.

"You look beautiful, honey." Her mom leaned on the doorframe.

Her own whitish-blond hair was loose around her shoulders. Between yoga and walking, her mom was fairly fit and looked younger than almost sixty. According to Edie Keller, laughter was the secret to staying young.

"Thanks, Mom."

Jillian wore a cute black sleeveless dress. A layer of sheer overlay with soft pleats fanned out over a looser satiny slip underneath. It was, she hoped, sexy and sweet, highlighting her toned arms over her rounded belly.

She didn't work out at the gym, but she kept herself busy enough that most of the time it wasn't a complete chore to stay in reasonably good shape. She didn't want to be nervous. Not about her looks. Levi obviously found her attractive or he wouldn't kiss her like his life depended on it.

"It's hard to believe I'm going on a date with Levi Bright."

Her mom smiled. "He's just a man, honey. Don't idealize him or find a way to convince yourself you don't deserve someone like him."

Jillian met her mom's gaze. "Does this mean I'll still be giving Ollie advice at thirty?"

Her mom pushed off the doorjamb. "Probably. And unlike how it'll be for the next several years, once she's older, she might actually think you know a thing or two."

Jillian laughed. "I can't imagine that."

Ollie was getting restless. Summer was coming, she was eager for the break, she was excited to be at the lodge, but a little worried about missing friends. She'd had a lot of freedom at the lodge the summer before but this summer was much busier and she couldn't do all the things she wanted. Part of Jilly felt guilty about focusing on herself—taking time to explore with Levi when she could be hanging with her kid. But truthfully, her kid had a more active social life than she did.

Her phone buzzed again. When she looked at it, she frowned. Andrew kept calling. Kept leaving messages. It was like he could sense, for the first time in almost five years, she was truly ready to move on.

Her mom came over to stand in front of her so Jilly lowered her phone. Focused on what was right in front of her. "I'm proud of you. I don't think I tell you that enough."

An unexpected lump formed in her throat. "Thanks, Mom. What brought that on?"

Edie brushed a lock of Jilly's hair back over her shoulder. "You've always been careful. Measured. I feel like your marriage and divorce made that part of you more . . . intense. It was like you decided if you weren't his wife, you'd just be Ollie's mom. And you'd be the very best one in the world. Then, Gray got the lodge and you let that into your life. But I worried that you wouldn't let yourself have something just for you again. That you'd be too careful or cautious to take a chance on something for yourself."

Tears burned under her eyelids. "It's scary."

"But you're doing it. Which is why I'm proud of you. You can't have what you don't go after, sweetie. There are no guarantees, but being willing to put yourself out there, especially with someone you've cared about for so long, shows how strong you are. How brave."

Jilly wrapped her arms around her mom, hugged her tight. She wanted to ask if they were selling the house but didn't want to cry before Levi arrived, so she didn't.

The doorbell rang. Jillian pulled back, her heart rate spiking. "I don't feel brave."

Her mom cupped her cheeks, kind of like Ollie used to do. "You look beautiful. You're going out with a wonderful man. Enjoy yourself."

"Your gentleman caller is here," her dad said, coming down the hallway.

Jilly shook her head, gave her dad a side hug. "Are you that old?"

Her dad kissed the top of her head. "Old enough to know how to scare Levi if he hurts you."

"Dad."

"I won't hurt her, sir," Levi called from the front room.

Awesome. The date hadn't started yet and she was blushing. "Ollie's at her friend Christopher's. His mom should be dropping her off around eight." Because Ollie had argued when Jilly said seven. "You two can have a date night as well."

Her dad laughed. "We just had a two-day date in Michigan. There's baseball on and your mom is going to book club."

Levi stood by the door, looking at family pictures hanging on the wall. He turned, and his expression—the light in his eyes and his smile—brightened when he looked her way.

"Hi," she said, feeling that familiar and unavoidable warmth on her skin.

"Hi." He held out a small bouquet of pink carnations. "These are for you."

"You didn't have to do that." She took the flowers.

"What she means is thank you, Levi," her mom said, coming up behind her. She took the flowers from Jillian. "I'll put these in water for you. Have a good time. We'll be fine and I'll tell Ollie to text you goodnight, so don't rush."

She kissed her mom's cheek. "Thank you."

When they were outside, she stopped on the porch steps and looked at Levi, who stood one stair below her, bringing them close to eye level.

"Thank you. For the flowers. They're so simple and pretty."

He smiled, his hand cupping her cheek. "So are you." He squeezed his eyes closed for a second then opened them. "Pretty. Not simple."

She laughed, some of her own nerves lessening. "Thank you. You look really nice."

He grinned at her, took her hand. "It's been a while since I dressed for a date." She could probably beat him on the length of that while, but he cleaned up more than nice. He wore a dark gray polo shirt, dark jeans, and his hair had been styled but still looked like it wanted to do its own thing, little strands here and there. She loved it.

When they reached his car, he opened the passenger door for her, helped her in. He was so easy to be around. "This is already fun."

He leaned in, gave her a soft kiss. "I hope you didn't doubt that it would be."

She didn't, but she hadn't expected to feel at ease so quickly. Like she was doing exactly as she should; with the right person.

When Levi got into the vehicle, which she was pretty sure he'd borrowed from his mom, he reached over and squeezed her hand. She hadn't thought about how much she missed the little things

in a relationship. A look, a gentle kiss, holding hands. That reminder that someone wanted to be near you every bit as much as
you wanted to be near them.

She was grateful he looked away before he caught the sappy gaze
she knew would be in her eyes. Because even though she knew it was
too much too fast, she was falling hard and didn't know how to stop.
The very least she could do was not advertise it in every look she
gave him. They chatted about the lodge, their days, and he gave her
the rundown on the three food trucks he was considering as they
drove the short distance to the pub.

When he helped her out of the car at Brothers' Pub her body
brushed against his as she stood. With his hand on her hip, he
stared down at her in a way that made her breath hitch, her stomach tighten, and her pulse scramble.

"You look gorgeous, Jilly. I like this dress."

Her breath whooshed out of her lungs. "I like you." She didn't
mean for it to come out all breathy, but Levi was good at stealing
her breath. Then and now.

Levi didn't mind, if the kiss he gave her was any indication.

The vibe inside Brothers' Pub was light and fun. On both
sides. It was such a strange situation; Jillian couldn't imagine not
speaking to her brothers, or not doing so *while* working with them.

"If you two aren't looking to be this week's gossip, I'd let go
of her hand, Levi Bright," Liam said, walking toward them from
the bar.

His hair was longer than usual, which only meant it wasn't
shaved close to the scalp. He was stocky and tall, a former all-star
football player who'd gone to university on a scholarship before
coming home to open the bar with his twin brother.

He grinned, shook Levi's hand, gave him one of the standard
bro-hugs, then kissed Jilly's cheek.

He clutched his chest with both hands when he pulled back. "I've been asking you out for years, Jilly. And you choose *this* guy?"

She laughed, looked at Levi, who was frowning adorably. She leaned into him. "Can't explain chemistry, I guess."

The wrinkles in Levi's forehead smoothed and his gaze caught hers, setting off little sparklers in her chest.

Liam groaned. "Just what we need; another Keller in love. Something's in the water at Get Lost. I'm going to have to make sure Gray doesn't drink it."

Levi chuckled, squeezed Jilly's hand. "It's good to see you, Liam. The bar business looks like it's treating you well." He gazed at the wall that separated the two halves. He gestured toward Leo's half. "This is new."

Liam's gaze shuttered. "You do what you have to do. If you ever get the chance to go into business with family, run away. Don't walk. Run." Looking at Jilly, he winced. "Unless you're the Kellers. They make it look easy."

"They do," Levi said, clearly confused but letting it go.

Liam smiled at Jilly, but she caught the way his gaze wandered to the partition that separated his half from Leo's. Music from that side sounded like a low bass beat, just enough to feel but not make out the words.

Meeting Levi's gaze again, his friend gestured to his half. "Things are great. Come on, grab a seat. I'll send someone over to take your order."

They walked through the space, which was more crowded than it should be due to each of the brothers squishing tables together to take their own sides. A few people waved; a couple of people Jill recognized by face but not name simply stared. Others ignored them entirely.

Near the back, past the bar, they found an empty two-top table tucked in the corner, giving the illusion of being secluded. Levi helped her with her coat, tucked it over her chair before pulling it out for her to sit.

"Thank you. You're very good at this. Flowers, kisses, taking my coat. Would seventeen-year-old Levi have been this good on a date?"

He laughed, shed his own jacket, and sat across from her, reaching out to take her hand across the table.

"He wouldn't have been allowed to take you to a pub, first off. And no. Probably not."

"I'm dying to know. What would have been a typical date when you were that age?"

Before he could answer, a short-haired, tall woman with knee-high boots and several earrings in her left ear approached them. Levi leaned back, letting go of Jilly's hand.

"Hi. Can I get you a couple drinks to start?"

Levi looked at her, waiting for her to order first. "I'll take a glass of house red, please."

"I'll have the same."

She nodded and left them alone. The song switched to something softer and more soulful and Jilly knew that if she were still writing in a diary, she'd definitely have some things to say about this moment; this night. This man.

Levi reached for her hand again, rubbing his thumb over her knuckles. "No one knows how to date in their teens. Usually, it was hanging out at someone's party after a game. Maybe a dance, though I didn't go to many of them. I think I took Meagan Salcheck to dinner and the movies when we went out in ninth. Saved for weeks to do that." He smiled like he could picture it. "She hated the meal and felt sick from the popcorn."

Jill laughed. "My first date was with Cody Grieggs in seventh.

We held hands all the way to Pete's, had ice cream that he paid for, and he walked me home. The next day, he told everyone Tilly Harper was his new girlfriend."

Levi winced. "Ouch. The wonders of young love."

She didn't even mean to take the opening. "Have you ever been in love?"

She liked that he considered the question, took it seriously. "I think I might have thought I was with you. But you were Beckett and Gray's sister and I was seventeen and leaving. Two years is nothing now but then, it felt wrong, even though I don't think I'd ever wanted to kiss a girl that bad."

Warmth infused her body like she'd sunk into a perfect bath. "And then I tried, and we know how that ended."

He kept holding her hand. "You loved your husband, I'm assuming."

The warmth faded at the mention of Andrew. "I did. Enough to put aside the red flags, push down the warnings, and set my own feelings aside."

"I'm sorry."

She smiled. "It worked out okay."

The waitress brought their drinks, set them down. "You need a few minutes?"

"Just a few," Levi said, smiling politely.

She nodded and went to the next table.

Jillian felt like she needed to sum it all up so it wouldn't be a question between them. "I don't love him anymore."

Levi picked up his drink. "I didn't think you'd be here with me if you still did."

She nodded, took a quick sip of her wine. "I wouldn't. We were over before I ended it. He'd embezzled money not only from his firm but from people we knew. People we called friends. When I found out, they all thought I knew so it was like I'd betrayed them. The life we built together started to crumble before I even knew why. Friends stopped calling, they wouldn't get together with me and Ollie. People talked about us. They'd stop talking when we walked in a room. When it all came out, what he'd done, he didn't try to tell the truth to any of our friends. He let them believe I'd known. That I had supported him."

Levi's jaw tensed, a storm brewing in his dark gaze. He swirled his wine. "If they knew you at all, really knew you, they wouldn't have believed it. I'm sorry it hurt you. Sorry that you went through all of that. I hate it. But I'd like to think what we get through, what we find a way to get over, makes us stronger."

Breathing a sigh of relief that she could put it all out there and not have him look at her differently, she picked up her menu.

"This date is off to a very good start," she said, her lips twitching, her heart beating in quick flashes.

Levi picked up his menu, opened it. "Must be the company."

After they'd ordered burgers—chicken for him and beef for her—they went back to talking, the conversation never lacking or lagging.

"Who was your second date?" Levi asked.

Jilly thought about it. "I don't think I even remember. I went out with Kenny Hicks for two weeks in tenth grade. I don't really have a storied history of relationships."

"How about more recently? No dates that made you want to ask for more?" Levi asked, sipping his wine while he leaned back, gracefully relaxed.

Jilly shook her head. "Nope. I've been out with three men since Andrew. One started the date by asking if I minded if his friends joined us. That in itself seemed off. But when he spent the evening clearly flirting with the other guy's date, I was just happy the night was done. Another asked if I'd mind a long-distance relationship because he was moving the next day. Which he didn't mention prior to that. And then there was the guy who wanted to show me all the disasters he'd matched with on apps."

Levi's wince grew with each example. "I think I would have sworn off dating for good."

Jilly smiled as she lifted her wineglass. "If I had, I wouldn't be here."

He leaned in, smiling widely. "Trust me, tonight won't be like any of those."

She mirrored his pose. "Trust *me*, it's already the best one I've been on." She figured it was wise to protect her heart a little, so she didn't add, *because it's you.*

Levi lifted his glass. "To the first of many."

Letting their glasses touch, she took a swallow of the wine and hoped taking this leap of faith wouldn't end poorly. It was Levi. She had to believe it wouldn't.

Twenty

Levi had had one drink all night; that first glass of red wine. But he felt drunk all the same. Drunk on the scent of Jillian's hair, the way she tipped her head back when she laughed, the way she fidgeted with the strap of her purse as he drove through the quiet streets of Smile.

He reached over, put his hand over hers, stilling it. "Do you want me to take you back to your place?"

Her head whipped toward him. "What? No. Why?"

Laughing at her tone, he kept his eyes on the road. "You seem nervous."

Turning her hand so their fingers linked together, she ran the fingers of her other hand over his knuckles.

"I don't want the night to end." She said it like it was a secret she was scared to admit. He had no doubts about his feelings for this woman—they were snowballing in his chest so quickly, he worried they'd come tumbling out of his mouth.

"How about some pie?"

She looked over at him. "That sounds perfect."

He hadn't been to Petal's Pie Palace since prom. They'd had the event at a hotel in Mackinaw City, and when the bus brought them back to Smile, all of them had been too restless and amped up to end the evening.

Holding the door for Jilly, he was grateful that the shop hadn't changed much and it was relatively quiet. The overhead lighting felt harsh against the night sky through the windows. A couple of teens sat at a booth in a corner, the waitress chatting with them.

"You can sit anywhere," she called.

He and Jilly moved toward the back of the shop, settled into the aging vinyl seats. He liked sitting across from her like this; had pictured it more than once as a teenager.

The waitress, with her short hair pulled back from her face in flower clips, brought over waters then pulled a one-page menu out of her apron. "These are our newest pies. They're on special. Hey, you're the three pieces lady."

Jilly's face scrunched. "I shared them."

Levi laughed. "Do you have a closet pie addiction?"

"I'll give you a minute," the waitress said as she'd already started walking away.

Jilly picked up the menu, gave him an adorably haughty look over top of it. "Sometimes it's hard to choose."

Leaning back in the booth, he nodded. "I'm not arguing. Why don't we get two different ones and share?"

They settled on peanut butter cream and French vanilla, both of which looked and tasted delicious. Levi took another bite of the vanilla.

"Hard to say," he said, pointing his fork at the other one. "That one is a bit too sweet for me, though."

Jilly scooped up a bite. "Rookie. You need to up your sugar tolerance, that's all."

Laughing again, he realized he'd done a lot of that since he got back.

"What happened with Liam and Leo?" Seeing the bar split in two had struck a chord in him. A sad one. Like Beckett, he'd gone to school with the twins and they'd been tight for a bit; played sports together, hung out.

Jilly frowned. "No one really knows, honestly. You know them; they've always been more than twins. They were best friends. Brothers' used to be my favorite place to hang out the few times I came back to visit. It had so much energy and such a great vibe. They got into a fight in the middle of the pub, according to what I've heard. I didn't live here when it happened. When I came home, they'd split it in two. Now, I can't visit one side without feeling guilty. Most of the town feels the same, so people who know them make an effort to visit both."

Levi shook his head. "That's a real shame. I can't think of what could come between two people so close."

Jilly shrugged and Levi got lost in thought about his dad. He'd idolized his dad growing up; never could have imagined feeling the way he did now.

He was happy Jilly changed the subject.

"So, you've narrowed it down to three trucks. What's the key difference between them that's making you unsure?"

He liked her business brain as much as her sense of humor. He was beginning to think there was nothing about her he wouldn't like.

A few more people came through the door, laughing on their way to their table, but Jilly held his focus.

"Price and size are the key factors holding me up."

"Are you getting a loan?"

He nodded. "Already did. I have savings as well. Want to come look at them with me?"

She reached over, took a bite of the vanilla, and added some peanut butter cream to her fork. "Maybe. Things are starting to amp up for the lodge. We've got the fitness company's team coming this week. You're still okay to do the food for that?"

"Of course."

"Then we have Ollie's class coming on an overnight trip to celebrate the end of the year."

"Do you have the meals taken care of for that?"

The waitress glided by, not looking at them.

"We still need to talk to Shane about it."

"I can help."

He wanted to help. He wanted to do whatever he could to be with her more. Plus, the lodge had been fun to work at. He wasn't sure if it was the space so much as the people.

"I'll let you know, but if you get the truck, you might be pretty busy yourself."

He nodded. They chatted about what foods he would serve, he told her about his dad and finding Anderson helping him out. She listened when he talked, her gaze holding his, like she not only cared about what he said, but felt what he felt.

He pushed his plate away, took a large drink of water.

She smiled at him across the table, her gaze lifting through lowered lashes. His chest tightened just from looking at her. Wanting her. She pushed her plate away. "Tell me something I don't know."

He leaned back against the padded seat. "Okay. Hmm. The fast-food industry generates over five hundred billion dollars of revenue a year."

Her expression went blank and then she laughed, picked up her napkin, and tossed it at him. "Not what I meant. Something about *you*. Something I wouldn't know from when you were younger."

He paused, thought about whether or not what he was about

to say would be embarrassing or endearing. "I once wrote out a mini speech on a cue card to read to Beckett. It was so I could ask you out."

Her mouth dropped open. "You did not."

Laughing, he reached out, took her hand, stroked his thumb over her skin, enjoying the warmth that filled her gaze. "I did. Then I found out I'd gotten the scholarship and was leaving."

The look on her face was one that would forever be in his memory. "I love knowing that."

She ducked her gaze, bit her lip, and he had to fight back a groan. When she looked up, her expression was so sweet it made his heart ache. "Lainey and I used to pass notes back and forth about our crushes. Your name was always in mine."

His chest felt full. He reached out, grabbed her other hand across the table. "Oh yeah? One of those ones with 'do you like him? yes or no'?"

She nodded. "Those too. Some of them were: 'who's cuter?,' then your name, Liam's, Leo's, and sometimes if she was being irritating, she'd put my brothers'."

He laughed. "Bet you crossed those ones out. Did you ever *not* check my name? Did you ever choose Liam and Leo over me?"

She shook her head. "Never."

He inhaled deeply, looked around for the waitress, and asked for the check. "Let's go for a walk."

Once they paid, they left his mom's car in the lot and took one of the trails that led to the water. The air was cool but he didn't feel it. He pulled Jilly closer, in case she did, and because he liked having her next to him.

The trail through the trees led to an alcove that followed the water. Large, weathered bricks, stacked about waist high, created a wall where people often sat, stood, or leaned to gaze out or make out. He smiled, thinking about how they'd once called this area Kissing Cove.

They stopped at the wall and Levi turned Jillian toward him. Leaning down, he kissed her, his mouth lingering, his heart waiting for that hitch in her breath.

"Tell me more."

He'd tell her anything. He smoothed her soft hair back from her face. "What do you want to know?"

"Your favorite color. Song. What you hate to eat. Where you'd go if you could travel anywhere. What you love most about being back in Smile. Your favorite thing to do on a lazy Sunday."

Surprising an adorable squeal from her, he yanked her closer, putting his back to the brick and holding her tight.

"That's a lot of questions." He kissed one cheek, the other, then the tip of her nose. "Okay. Dark blue. You can't go wrong with 'Paradise City.' Jell-O is gross."

Jill laughed and moved her hand up his chest, burrowing closer, making him wish they were at his place. Of course, he might want to actually get some furniture before that happened.

He focused on the questions rather than the way she fit against him perfectly, like the dips and curves, the lines and planes of their bodies were meant to fit together. "I'd like to go to Seattle. Never been. Seems like a cool city. Or Nashville." His brain blanked when her fingers, her nails specifically, traced over the back of his neck. "Um. This. I love being here with you. In Smile. Where we grew up. But being grown-up enough to do this." He kissed her then, crushing her body to his, his arms wrapping around her as he changed the angle of his head to kiss her more. He pulled back, swept her hair back from her face. "Kissing you is my favorite thing to do on a lazy Sunday or any day that ends in *y*. You're killing me, Jillian." His voice came out hoarse like he'd been screaming.

She ran her fingers over his face, like she was memorizing it.

"That's funny. You have the opposite effect on me. You make me feel more alive than I can ever remember feeling."

Levi moved his hands to her hips, one of them sliding to the side of her neck so he could feel the heat of her skin. Her breath shuddered out.

"You're so sexy."

"You make me feel that way," she whispered, that hint of vulnerability, along with the slight pinkening of her cheeks, undoing something inside of him.

"There's something I've sort of always wanted to ask you," he said, whispering even though there was no one else around them.

She leaned back, her hands on his shoulders. "What's that?"

"Will you be my girlfriend, Jillian Keller?"

Her laughter floated around them, echoing off the water and making Levi feel like he'd won the lottery.

"Is this a yes, no, or maybe question?"

He tickled her waist, making her laugh more. "Do you need that many options?"

Her gaze found his, all humor fleeing from it. "No. I don't need that many options. I'd love to be your girlfriend, Levi Bright."

He grinned at her, probably looked like an idiot, but he didn't care. He pulled her close, tightening his hold to swing her in a circle.

When he set her down on her feet again, he pressed his forehead to Jilly's. "What now?"

"Now, you kiss me."

She would absolutely never have to ask him twice.

Twenty-one

Teenaged Jilly had written many diary entries on what it would be like to be teenaged Levi's girlfriend. The way he would look at her, talk to her, how he'd make her feel. Adult Jilly couldn't believe that all of those imaginings and wonderings would have paled in comparison to actually being Levi Bright's girl.

After their amazing date, he found ways to let her know he was thinking about her even with both of them being busy. They also found a way to merge their schedules with him helping out for not one but two events at the lodge. Shane had politely requested he not be on the schedule until June first when the lodge opened, and Grayson asked Levi if he'd be interested in cooking for Ollie's class on their overnight.

Ollie, unsurprisingly, found the presence of another adult in her life perfectly acceptable and fun. Jilly and Levi tried to keep the PDA down to a minimum with her daughter around, but all that did was make her feel desperate in the moments she got Levi alone. Part of her didn't recognize herself. She didn't understand the *craving* to see him and make him laugh.

Standing in the foyer of the lodge, one of her favorite rooms, she pulled in some deep breaths, let them out. Grayson would be staying the night tonight so she could get home for Ollie, but the team from Inspire Fitness was currently en route. She was really doing it.

Levi startled her when he approached from behind, slipping his arms around her waist and nuzzling her neck. She felt like Ollie, amped up and excited, wanting everything all at once.

She tilted her head, inhaling the scent of him and herbs she couldn't identify. "You smell good," she told him as she put her hands on top of his.

"I just took focaccia bread out of the oven. You're smelling the rosemary."

She turned in his arms, pressed her lips to the underside of his jaw. He hadn't shaved in a couple of days. An image of his few days' growth rasping over sensitive skin burned into her brain.

"It's my new favorite," she said, going up on tiptoes.

"You're my favorite," he said, kissing her lightly, his lips nearly ghosting hers as his hold on her tightened. He trailed up to her ear, taking the lobe between his teeth. When his lips found hers again, he swallowed her gasp of pleasure, and she couldn't stop her hands from tunneling into his hair, her fingers from curling around the soft locks.

She pulled back, stepped out of his embrace, her fingers going to her lips. "We need to stop." She pointed at him. "You're too good at that." Smoothing her hands down her shirt did nothing to temper the fire inside of her for this man. "We have people arriving. How the hell do Presley and Beckett work together and get anything done?"

Jilly was talking more to herself than him, so his bark of laugher surprised her. "God, I adore you. You're so freaking sweet and wonderful."

Oh. Her breath whooshed out of her lungs. "See? That right there, along with your lips. You need to go. Back to the kitchen. I have things to do."

He smiled, took a step toward her with an adorable glint in his gaze. She held out her hand, flattening it in a "stop" signal. He held both hands up, still laughing.

"There's snacks in the dining room for guests. Dinner will be ready for seven, which gives you enough time for the team-building activities. I made pastries and muffins for the morning that Gray will put out and I'll head back over with you in the morning to prepare lunch."

Jilly nodded briskly. Good. Right. This was better. On track. He was still laughing when he walked back toward the kitchen. Fresh air. She needed fresh air.

The grounds were in good shape, the cabins were ready, and, unlike last year, all of the rooms were ready to be occupied. She'd updated the online calendar this morning and there were six weeks of the summer that were booked to capacity.

Passing one of the larger, unused outbuildings next to the shed on the right side of the house, Jillian took the little footpath into the area where Grayson, Beckett, and Levi had created a challenge run. Beckett, who owned a small percentage of the sporting goods store in Smile, had a connection to a company that sent them a simple ropes course and a handful of easy-to-implement activities that worked within the insurance they had for guests.

Staring at the thick yellow corded rope stretched low between several trees, she imagined Ollie becoming an expert at this. Taking her phone out, she started to text her mom to send Ollie a picture when her phone rang.

"Hello?"

Noise from the front of the lodge alerted her that the guests were there.

"Jillian," Andrew said.

She sighed. "Not a good time, Andrew. I'm at work."

"I saw on Facebook. Camping? Right? That's your new job? Playing in the woods with your brother?"

She squeezed the bridge of her nose and dug for patience. "Sure. What do you want?"

"I've spent a lot of time thinking and planning and working toward rebuilding our lives, Jillian. What I *want* is to see my wife and daughter."

From the front lawn, Grayson's booming voice gave the introductory spiel, welcoming everyone and telling them what was next.

"I don't have time for this, Andrew. Even if I wasn't actually busy, you gave up the right to have us in your lives years ago and you signed the same papers I did that made me your ex-wife. There's no going back." She started walking toward the front, wondering if she'd have to hang up on him.

"Then let's go forward. I'm in Michigan next week. I can get up to Mackinaw. Meet with me. We'll talk."

She stopped, pulled the phone away from her face, and looked at it in disbelief before putting it back to her ear. "I. Don't. Want. To. See. You."

There'd been a brief period after the anger and hurt of the divorce and everything leading up to it had faded to a bad memory that she thought maybe he'd want something to do with Ollie. But weeks turned to months, then years, and he made no effort.

His heavy sigh sounded through the phone. "Don't make this difficult, Jillian. You always make things more difficult. Meet me next week. I'll send you the details. Better this way than through lawyers. Which I have more than enough money to pay for again. Do you?"

She did hang up. She was impressed she didn't throw her phone at the side of the lodge. How the hell had he rebuilt himself to the point that he could engage in a legal battle with her? He'd lost everything. Some of it unintentionally, some of it because he was shady as hell, and them because he hadn't cared enough to hang on to them.

Slipping her phone into her pocket, she forced herself to go greet their visitors. She wanted to meet Eva, thank her for taking a chance on the lodge, and show her brother that this was a more than viable way to fill in the offseason as well as close income gaps when bookings were low. She needed to focus on that. On her future. Ollie's. Hers and Levi's. Andrew would leave her alone. He was bluffing. He'd had his chance and now, she just needed him to do what he'd done early into their relationship (which she'd been too infatuated to pay attention to): get bored of the pursuit.

When she came around the side of the lodge, Grayson met her gaze with a grateful one. This was more her forte than his.

"And here's my sister, Jillian Keller, who has worked hard to put together a two-day retreat that you guys are going to love. Jilly, come meet everyone."

Walking forward, she met Eva first. They shook hands and Eva took care of introducing her to the rest of her nine-person team. The energy was high and people were eager to get the fun started.

With ten rooms, the lodge was fully packed. The first hour included letting everyone settle in their rooms then have a delicious selection of snacks that Levi had set up. The dining table held an array of meats, cheeses, his delicious bread, dips, and even homemade crackers that Jillian wanted to put aside to have later. Instead of hoarding them for herself, she took pictures for their social media. Levi had done an amazing job. He winked at her when he came out to refill some of the platters.

"It's going well," Grayson said, coming up beside her. "This is one hell of a spread."

She nodded, put her phone away. "He did an amazing job. I'm wondering if we should have him and Shane sit down. I'm not sure how Shane is feeling about the event bookings in addition to regular guests. Levi could share some ideas on how to make it easier, and I bet Shane can get us some deals to make it more cost-effective."

Gray put an arm around Jilly's shoulder, pulled her into a side hug. "I'll chat with Shane. Thanks for this, Jilly. Not just for arranging this and Ollie's camp, but all of it. Believing in the lodge and me. It's bringing me back, financially and personally."

With her arms around his waist, she returned the hug, wishing for one second she could offload all of her new worries, about Andrew and Levi and making all of this work with what already existed at the lodge, on her big brother.

"Jilly?" Eva said from behind her.

Letting Gray go, she turned and greeted the woman, who was about her age. Eva was dressed in outdoor gear that held the company's logo, her dark hair pulled into a ponytail.

"I'm going to check in with Levi," Gray said.

"We have a couple of options for tonight but I wasn't sure how long you wanted to let your team get settled," Jillian said, trying to appear as if she'd done this before.

"This is fantastic. The lodge is beautiful and we can't wait to see the grounds."

Excitement bubbled over. "I'm so glad. Thank you for sending me your schedule. I've arranged all of our activities around your staff brainstorming sessions and virtual meetings."

Eva clasped her hands together. "I was so scared to take the leap. I mean, how many fitness companies are there, right? But these guys are amazing and truly believe in my vision."

Jillian could relate. Her brothers and Presley, and even Levi, Ollie, her parents, and Lainey, were providing the same support for her ideas.

"You need that in your corner. Why don't we get started?"

Eva nodded, turned to address her team. "All right, everyone. Settle down, can I get your attention?"

Everyone quieted, looking toward their boss, some sitting at the table, a few standing in small groups. Eva glanced at Jilly, giving her the green light.

"Again, welcome to Get Lost Lodge. We're so pleased to have you. Eva and I have worked together to make your time here relaxing, competitive, and worthwhile. I've organized several group activities that will break up your staff information sessions, provided by Eva. We have our brand-new ropes course, two different hikes, a boating trip, s'mores by the campfire, and a partner trust activity involving maps and treasure."

Everyone laughed and cheered, and Jillian's worries over Andrew drifted away. She got caught up in the enthusiasm of Eva's team, Grayson's approving nods when he joined them, and Levi's sweet look of admiration when he came to clean up.

Everything was going to work out perfectly. There was no reason to believe otherwise.

Twenty-two

After cleaning up the kitchen and getting everything set for a serve-yourself dinner of lasagna, both vegetarian and meat—neither one of them lazy in any way—Levi found Jillian outside. She was in her element. He'd peeked in on her explaining the team and partner endeavors for the ropes course. Every activity encouraged the guests to trust their partners and teams, to let go of the need to be in complete control.

He, Beckett, and Grayson had set up one of the challenges between three large and sturdy oaks. The cordoned-off area looked like a triangle.

"How'd it go?" Levi leaned against one of those sturdy oaks, the scent of earth in the air.

Jillian turned, giving him that smile that made his heart spin. "It was amazing. They did a bunch of challenges including leading each other blindfolded, and then we used these ones," she said, pointing to two parallel ropes they'd set up that were about one foot off the ground and two feet apart. "Two people stood across from each other on the ropes, leaning forward to make a bridge with their hands and arms, and then other teams had to go through it and create the next bridge."

"Sounds fun. Let's try it." He pushed off the oak tree.

Jillian picked up her clipboard—she'd been taking photos when he came out—and laughed at him. "I'm good, thanks."

He smiled as he moved toward the ropes. "Come on, Jilly. We could all learn to lean on each other a little."

It was surprisingly harder than he'd expected to just stand on the rope without falling off. It was thick, corded, heavy-duty rope. He thought he had better balance. Jillian came closer but just laughed as he wobbled back and forth, holding his hands out.

"This is way harder than I thought," he said, falling forward again.

"Want to know a trick?"

She set her clipboard down on the ground and came to stand in front of him.

His hands immediately went to her waist. "I want to know all of your tricks."

She laughed, pushed at his chest, and stepped back, reaching her arms out. "It's easier to do with two people who have simi-lar strength but let's try." Putting her hands in his so they were palm to palm and up between them, she guided him onto the rope while she moved slowly onto hers. They pushed against each other, wobbling and falling, but eventually, they figured out the push and pull and managed to steady themselves on the ropes, arms in a bridge for a good ten seconds.

He felt like he'd hiked with her again when they jumped off. Scooping her up, he swung her in a circle.

They tried a couple more times and Levi could feel the effort in his core. He really did need to work out more. Jillian walked next to one of the oaks, stepped up onto the rope with her hand on the tree and the other held out wide.

"If you're on your own, start by the tree and then center yourself," she said, slowly dropping her other hand so she balanced on the rope. When she wobbled, he caught her around the waist, loving the way she slid down his body.

Her fingers curled into his hair and he shivered involuntarily. He could become addicted to her touch. His heart beat wildly from even the simplest touch from this woman; a glide of her fingers across his cheek, over his chest, the touch of her mouth to his made him feel weak and powerful at the same time.

With both hands, he smoothed her hair back so he could stare at her beautiful face. Every curve and line was becoming etched in his mind permanently.

He kissed her slow and soft, falling into her in a way he'd never experienced with anyone else. He knew, without a doubt, this was where he was meant to be. When she pulled back, her gaze was bright and full of the same desire he felt in every piece of himself. He wanted to spend the night with her. All the nights. And mornings, too. But he needed to remind himself that he couldn't rush her. He wanted to savor every bit of this; of them.

She pulled back, a dreamy look in her gaze. "After dinner is served, we can head back to Smile. Want to watch a movie later? After Ollie's in bed?"

"That sounds good." It actually sounded perfect.

"It's strange how easy this is. Falling into . . . I don't know what to call it . . . couplehood?"

Laughing, he kissed her again, quick and light. "Cute. Whatever you call it, I'm happy. And I want to make you happy."

She tightened her hold on his waist. "You already do."

Then he'd just keep doing what he was doing and they'd work the rest out. Eventually, his careful Jilly would learn that she could trust him and lean on him, and not just because she was standing on a rope. Because she wanted to.

The next several days kept Levi too busy to go and see the food trucks he was interested in, but two of the three people had agreed to walk him through virtually, which had been really cool. He'd bought a bed and set it up, doing his best not to give Jilly some cheesy line about spending the night. Between the team-building event, which had gone great, Gray asking him to cook for the upcoming kids' camp, sneaking in moments with Jilly, chatting with Pete about possible truck menu ideas, and hanging out with Jilly and Ollie, he fell into bed exhausted each night. The bed was an excellent purchase.

He was still in it when someone knocked on his door way too early for his liking. Shuffling out of bed in his flannel pajama bottoms, he was glad he hadn't opened the door with a grumpy snarl. His mom stood on the tiny platform at the top of the stairs with a leafy green potted plant.

"Hi, honey," she said. She looked around him. "I didn't catch you at a bad time, did I?"

He laughed. "No." Stepping back, he waved her in, shutting the door behind her.

"I was going to bring muffins, but no one makes them as good as you so I thought a plant would be better." She set it down on the counter and looked around. "I should have brought two or three."

He pulled her into a side hug, kissed the top of her head. "It's temporary, Mom. Perfect for what I need for right now. The plant is great. Thank you."

She made the coffee while he used the microwave to warm up some muffins he'd made a couple of days ago. When they had everything, they moved over to the couch. He was toying with the idea of getting a small table and a few chairs in case Jilly and Ollie wanted to come for dinner soon.

As they sat, he looked around himself. "I should grab a bit more furniture, even if it's only temporary."

His mom set her plate on her lap, holding her coffee mug with both hands. "We have a small dining set and a couple of coffee tables and end tables in our storage unit, if you'd like them."

"That'd be great."

"So," she said, holding her plate with one hand while she set her coffee on the floor. She sat back up. "You and Jilly?"

"Did someone write it on the chalkboard?"

She laughed, broke off a piece of her muffin. "No. Her mom asked me if I wanted to help out with the exhibit they're creating for the Founder's Day Festival to honor Gwen and Pete. I went by the museum yesterday and couldn't believe all of the old items he'd kept. Actual booths from thirty years ago."

Levi took a generous sip of his own coffee, silently thanking caffeine for all of its wonders. "Some of it is probably worth a lot but all of it is pretty incredible. You could actually re-create the different eras at Pete's just with what he threw away."

"That's sort of what they're doing. Anyway, Edie and I were talking and she said it was nice to have you hanging around. A little different from when you used to go over just to see Beckett." Her tone was teasing.

Levi grinned. That was true for the most part, until the year before he left when that crush on Jilly felt like it doubled every time he saw her. He'd spent a lot of time at the Kellers' home. Maybe more than his own. Sort of like now. The thought wiped the smile from his face.

"How's Dad? It's been a couple of weeks since the surgery. How's he feeling?"

His mom broke off another piece of muffin, staring at her plate. She didn't eat it, though. When she looked up, her gaze was sad. "He was wrong for how he treated you, Levi. I can't change him. When you love someone, you accept all of them, even the parts of them that wear on your nerves sometimes. I love your dad and I understand him. I get where he's coming from because I missed you like crazy when you were away, too. I don't agree with how he's handled any of it, particularly since you came home."

Levi set his coffee and his plate on the floor, turned his body to give his mom his full attention. "I appreciate that, Mom. I don't want things to be like this."

"Then I'm asking you to reach out. To try even though he should be the one to do it."

"Come on, Mom. I'm just setting myself up if I reach out again. I've tried."

Her lips firmed and she looked around the room, stared at his TV. When she finally looked at him again, he thought he'd won. That she'd drop it.

"I didn't think I'd have this again. My family all within walking distance. I'm so happy you're home. And now you're dating a wonderful woman with an adorable daughter from a family we're friends with. I want that, Levi. I want all of it. I want family dinners and holidays and impromptu dinners. I supported your dream and I'm so proud of you. I supported his when he started his business and I'm so proud of him. But it's my turn. I want my family back. I don't want to miss out on anything, and one of you has to swallow your pride."

He hated the catch in her breath, the break in her voice. "Mom, he said I wasn't good enough for Jillian."

Anger and sadness merged together in her expression. "That's a terrible thing for him to have said. Your father isn't perfect. Not even close. And it's not okay that he said it. But knowing him like I do, I think he was projecting his own worries that you won't stay."

Levi knew that. He'd known it when he said it, but it didn't make it feel any better. Hoping he wasn't overstepping, Levi offered a tiny twig—it wasn't an olive branch yet; he had his own stubborn pride.

"Ollie's class is camping at the lodge this weekend. One of the stations I was going to help with was building birdhouses. Actually, Ollie and Jilly and I had a great time grabbing all of the materials. I'll call Dad and ask if he can come out for a few hours and help."

His mom beamed at him, tears in her gaze. "I love you, Levi."

Laughing, he shook his head. "More since you got your own way?"

She picked up her coffee again. "Absolutely."

Twenty-three

For some people, embarking on a two-day overnight trip with eighteen nine-year-olds, their teacher, and six parent volunteers wouldn't be fun. Jilly wasn't one of those people. She was ready for bad knock-knock jokes, campfires, and sticky s'mores. In fact, in between ordering supplies for the lodge, helping Lainey log her inventory into the new system she'd installed on her computer, and cataloging Pete's memorabilia for the museum, Jilly was ready to head to the lodge and enjoy the fun and frivolity that came with third graders. And Levi. She was almost giddy that he'd decided to spend the night since he wanted to be up early cooking for the kids.

Jill glanced over to where he stood chatting with one of the moms, his arms crossed over his chest in a way that emphasized the muscles of his biceps and the light tan he was already sporting from a few days outside.

"You won't be the only one staring at him all weekend," Allison Shriever, a happily married mom, said, bumping Jilly's shoulder.

Jilly gripped the clipboard she was holding tighter. Grayson stepped off the passenger boat that would carry all of them to Get

Lost. The twenty-foot cruiser wasn't new, but they kept it in good working condition.

Allison sighed. "Speaking of men to stare at."

"We weren't," Jilly muttered.

Allison laughed. "I was. Your brother is gorgeous. Both of them. So is Levi. I love my husband but I'm not blind."

Jill laughed and felt like a fool for wanting to go plant a kiss on Levi's lips and shout "he's all mine." She settled for smiling at him when he looked her way.

"Could I have everyone's attention?" Grayson called to the group.

Gray didn't love speaking to large groups, but he had a great voice for it that commanded attention. As a former general manager for a string of pharmacies, he was more used to overseeing staff, making sure stores were running efficiently, and ensuring that everything added up at the end of the day. Sort of like what he did at the lodge in a much more personal and smaller capacity. One that brought him great joy. It was nice to see her big brother carry less weight on his shoulders.

The kids and parents quieted down and formed a half circle around Grayson on the dock. Gramps was unhooking the rope for their departure and would see them off. Several others milled about farther down this dock and on some of the boats in the harbor. Jilly was so happy that Levi's dad was coming out to build birdhouses with the kids tomorrow. Small steps.

Grayson smiled at all of them. "Anyone ever *not* been on a boat?" He went through the rules and all of the adults worked together to help the kids into life jackets. Jillian arched her brows at Levi when Ollie insisted he help her when one of her classmates asked him. Interesting, since her little girl usually took pride in doing things herself. Looked like she wasn't the only one falling.

When they were loaded onto the boat, everyone sitting, Jilly sat at the back, watching the kids and the parents, excited for what lay ahead. The team-building weekend for Eva had gone so well they'd booked another in the fall. This would be drastically different but give them a really good idea of what they could handle and what they were already naturally set up for. She wanted to fill gaps, add to what already existed, not pile on more work.

Ollie led Levi over by his hand and they sat down beside Jilly, Ollie between them. She glanced at Levi over her daughter's head. His gaze was equal parts lust and affection. She didn't know which appealed to her more.

"Did you make biscuits?" Ollie asked, craning her head to look at him. Her reddish-brown curls could not be contained lately but they'd tried by braiding them down her back.

Levi tapped her nose. "I did. But we'll be baking fresh ones, too."

"Bet the ones you made aren't as good as when we made them together," she said with a grin.

He laughed, stretching his arm across the back of the seat, his fingers touching Jillian's shoulder. "I'll sneak you one and you can let me know."

She liked the easy vibe he seemed to have with Ollie and vice versa. Ollie tended to be more adaptable to new situations than Jillian. Or, at least, it felt that way.

"Are you excited, honey?"

Ollie turned her head toward Jillian. "Yes. I wish you'd tell me what we're doing. I could help set up. Uncle Gray told me about the ropes course. I can't wait to do that!"

Jillian nudged Ollie's leg with her own. "You're a guest camper, not a Keller this weekend. No sneak peeks for you."

She looked back at Levi. "Levi's giving me one."

Levi's mouth dropped open. "Hey. Don't throw me under the bus."

Ollie giggled, making Jillian laugh as well.

"Hmm. You're right. Well, that's because he's a softie. Not me." She poked Ollie in the belly teasingly but kept her tone firm. "And no one goes on the ropes course without adult permission and supervision."

Ollie sighed and sank back against the padded seat, flopping her hands down onto her lap with a dramatic flair. "I know, Mom." The weariness in her tone made Jilly's lips twitch.

When Jilly looked at Levi, his were doing the same. His fingers had drifted up to the side of her neck, and even though the breeze was cool, it wasn't the cause of the shivers running through her. He held her gaze a moment and she realized she'd never had this: a man looking at her like there was nowhere else he'd rather be, with her little girl between them. The quiet sweetness of it was something she hadn't known she was missing until this moment. And she wanted more.

"I'm going to go chat with Gray," Levi said, giving both of them a little wave.

Ollie was quiet for a moment. Jillian almost teased her about it, as her daughter wasn't known for her silence, when Ollie asked, "Is Levi your boyfriend?"

How could one word make her giddy at her age? "Yes." She looked down at Ollie, who was looking at her, a serious expression on her face, a little divot forming between her brows. "Is that okay with you?" She wouldn't let her daughter dictate her choices but she also didn't want her to feel unheard. Nothing, so far, had suggested Ollie had any problem with the way things were going.

She shrugged and turned to stare straight ahead. "I guess so. Is that why you and Levi kiss sometimes?"

Jillian bit the inside of her cheek to keep from laughing. They didn't kiss nearly as much as they wanted to. "It is." This was new territory, but she figured this was one of those less-is-better situations. *Keep it simple.* "It's new. He really likes hanging out with both of us."

The waves rocked them back and forth but everyone seemed to be handling it fine. No seasickness so far. Jilly tried not to fidget as she waited for Ollie to sort her thoughts, decide if she was done with the conversation, or just be.

"Is he going to live with us?"

Ollie was still staring straight ahead and Jillian's heart felt like someone was squeezing it. "Ollie. Look at me."

Ollie turned her head.

Jilly took her hand and she realized Ollie must really want an answer because she let her. She even stayed still. "Nothing huge is going to happen without you and I talking. Levi and I have been friends for a long time and we realized we care about each other as more than friends. No one is moving anywhere." Hopefully that was true. She meant Levi wasn't moving in, but her parents' plans were still on standby.

Ollie nodded. "Okay." Then, like the passing of a sudden summer shower, her smile came back and she sat up. "I'm going to go tell Ginny my mom has a boyfriend."

Before she could suggest that didn't need to be said, her kid was gone to find her friend. It could have been worse. At least she liked Levi and things seemed to be going well. The worry side of her brain, which often felt like it took up more than three-quarters, wanted to say "for now." But she was trying to quiet that part of herself and try something new: letting herself go with the flow and just enjoy. So far, so good.

"Okay, campers," Jillian said once they'd arrived at the spot they were pitching their tents. She looked around the group of energized kids, indulgent parents, and Levi. After he'd unloaded supplies in the kitchen and made the kids a snack of fruit tacos—mixed berries inside of pancakes with a choice of Nutella or Cool Whip as a topping—Ollie asked him to come help. Jillian wasn't the only one surprised by the impromptu request. Gray sent her a questioning glance but Jilly was just happy Ollie was happy and connecting to him.

It'll be fine. She can get attached to a man who has already told you he's not going anywhere.

"We're going to break into teams for our first challenge. There will be three teams. The first team who gets all of their tents up, bedrolls made, and gear stowed, gets to have dinner first tonight." She paused so the kids could cheer and share their own little version of trash talk. "I'm pulling names from this paper bag. Those will be your teams. Being in the wilderness often means relying on the people next to you and acting like a team. If you finish before someone else, your job is to help your team. Parents can offer suggestions and advice but can't physically help unless absolutely necessary."

They'd hiked a short distance to a small clearing that was shaded by tall, gorgeous trees that made Jillian feel like they were lost in the middle of nowhere instead of just over a hundred feet from the lodge. Beckett's small stake in a local sporting goods store came in handy once again. The majority owner, Beckett's former boss, Brian, had offered "kids' camping kits" for publicity and a small fee. It was a great deal and the hoop tents were super easy and portable. Once the kids unzipped the canvas bag, the tent sort of burst to life.

She called the names and was really pleased that none of the kids complained about their group members. This had been a great school year for Ollie. She might not be super close to every kid but they were a good bunch overall.

Each of the groups had two parents helping them. Jillian would oversee and watch the time. Grayson went back to the lodge to work. With the success of the last group they'd hosted, he was growing more intrigued by the possibilities of alternate income. If there were flaws, there were no better critics than kids.

Smiling at the way most of the kids couldn't stand still—some of them literally bouncing on the spot waiting for Jilly to say "go"—she drew out the moment. Ollie stared at her, posed in a runner's lunge.

"Go!"

The campers got started, first with their own tents. In between harried chatter, laughter, and a few surprised sounds when the tents sprang up, the parents cheered them on, giving them instructions.

Jilly took pictures with her phone, laughing at one of the parents who was so invested that she was on her knees, calling out instructions while miming every step with her hands.

When all three teams finished—team two winning the dinner first prize—everyone clapped and stood by their tents. "Great job, everyone. Are you sure you haven't all camped before?"

The kids laughed and started talking about different camping adventures. Levi caught her gaze as Ollie took his hand and showed him her tent, just like her friend Christopher was doing with his dad.

Jilly bit her lip, watched her daughter look up at Levi and smile. Something hitched in her heart. *It's okay.* Why was letting Ollie grow attached to a man Jilly was becoming increasingly attached to scarier than letting her go overnight to sleep at a friend's house or ride a skateboard without Jillian beside her?

"Can we have s'mores?" one of the kids called.

Jilly laughed. "Not until tonight. But don't worry, we have lots more fun in store." The good thing about having so many little guests was she wouldn't have a ton of time to dwell.

Twenty-four

Levi laughed when one of the kids asked if his biscuit was a good shape. The kid—Christopher—had so much flour on his face, he looked like a ghost.

"Looks great. Wait until we put butter on them fresh out of the oven."

"They're so good we can even eat them for breakfast," Ollie said, taking time to gently transfer her biscuits from the counter to the tray.

Levi couldn't believe how many amazing activities the teacher and Jillian had organized for these kids. He was doing dinner with this group of six, breakfast with a second group in the morning, and lunch with a third group before they left. All of them would get a chance to cook, make bracelets with Lainey, who was bringing Levi's dad over, and make birdhouses. That was on top of today's multitude of activities that included a scavenger hunt, relay races, and practice tying knots.

Though they'd sleep outside, they were eating at the lodge, utilizing the long, live-edge wood table that Levi coveted. He definitely needed to grab some furniture from his parents' storage unit and maybe think more seriously about finding a long-term place. Jillian poked her head into the kitchen, and the timing, with him thinking about longevity, made him all too aware of how quickly he was falling. For her and her kid.

"How are we doing on time?" she asked as she came all the way in and took some photos.

"Mom, look!" Ollie held up her tray.

"That looks fantastic," Jillian said.

Levi looked at the clock on the stove. "These biscuits are the last bit. The spaghetti and meatballs are ready and so is the vegetable medley salad."

"We made the salad," Christopher said. The kid swiped a cloth across the counter and forgot to catch the crumbs in his hands.

Jillian smirked as they went all over the floor. Christopher shrugged and went back to circling the dishcloth.

"Glad I'm not on cleanup," she said quietly.

"Unless I tell you no dinner if you don't help," Levi said, grinning at her.

"You have to help, Ms. Keller. It's part of being a team," one of the other kids—remembering all their names was hard—told her.

Jillian laughed right along with Levi. "You're absolutely right. I'll go let the craft station know that it's time to clean up."

He winked at her, wishing he could give her even a quick kiss. Or a longer one. Or something more. He'd have to steal some alone time once the kids were in bed. While the biscuits baked and the kids carted place settings to the dining table, Levi smiled, listening to some rather interesting conversations.

"I don't know why we're setting the table. We're in the wilderness. We should eat with our hands," one of the girls said.

"We should catch our own food," another added.

"I went hunting with my dad but we didn't come home with anything because I didn't like it." This from one of the boys.

"We could just skip the dishes. That's what my dad does when I go to his house on the weekend," another boy said.

Levi covered a laugh with a cough. When the timer went, Levi told the kids to wash up and go get settled. Grayson came into the kitchen with Ollie on his heels.

"Dinner's ready?" he asked.

Ollie pulled on her uncle's hand. "I helped make it!"

He ran a hand over her hair. "I heard. I can't wait to eat it."

"Your timing is perfect," he said, handing each of them some of the food to carry out to the waiting campers.

As they sat around the table, Levi couldn't help stealing glances at Jilly and Ollie as they laughed and redirected the kids, asked questions, and heard so many stories. He hadn't thought about having kids. He'd always just focused on tackling what was in front of him. He'd had his teen/youth years. When it was time for school, he was solely focused on that, and then his career. And now, even though he loved cooking and was excited, full of new ideas, his thoughts consistently returned to Jilly. Ollie. Them. What it might be like to have a family. To be a family.

Grayson raised his plastic cup. "I just want to say thank you to our wonderful chefs for the evening. You all did a great job, and as soon as you're old enough, I'm happy to hire you for summer employment."

Levi laughed along with everyone else as ideas and thoughts crisscrossed in his brain about ways to have it all.

Levi was every bit as invested as the young campers in the ghost story one of the dads—Zane—was telling. Some of the kids were so engrossed, their little mouths hung open, their eyes wide in the campfire light. Zane was an excellent storyteller and a really cool guy. Levi could have easily gone home and come back in the morning, but he wasn't missing a perfect opportunity to hang with Jilly and Ollie. And he was finding that even though he didn't have kids, it was nice to connect with some other Smileys, as Gramps liked to call the locals.

He leaned back on the log, reached for the bag of marshmallows, popping one onto a roasting fork before extending it over the flames. When he looked up, Jilly was looking at him from across the flames. The inky black sky was bursting with shimmery stars, real twinkle lights hovering above the ones Grayson had strung around the trees. Even in the low light, Levi could *feel* Jilly's stare like a touch. One he wanted very much.

"Levi," she said quietly.

His muscles tightened, his hands aching to touch her. "Hmm?"

She grinned, then pointed. "Your marshmallow's on fire."

Shit. He pulled it back, blew on it, and accepted the chocolate graham cookies a kid passed him.

"Well done, Chef," she said with a laugh.

"I'll eat it! I like 'em burnt," Ollie said from across the fire.

Levi glanced at Jillian to make sure that was okay. She nodded. After passing the treat to Ollie, he set the stick down, tried to focus on the new story Zane started. He stared up at the sky, remembering how they used to wish on stars when they were kids. They made millions of wishes because they could always see the stars. He couldn't remember the last time he'd taken a moment just to stare at them. Not exactly something he did a lot in the city. And it just wasn't the same.

Nothing was the same in Smile.

After s'mores and story time, the kids went to the lodge to clean up, use the bathroom, and get ready for bed. Not roughing it entirely, but it was a nice blend of the two. While the other parents took the kids, he stayed behind to help Jillian tidy up the campsite area.

"Zane's an amazing storyteller," Levi said, twisting the bag of marshmallows closed.

Jilly looked up, an unopened bag tucked against her chest. "He's very good. He's actually a successful author. He writes under a pseudonym, but every year, he writes a story featuring all of the kids in Christopher's classes, since preschool."

"Wow. That's really awesome." He picked up the sticks, laid them in the box Jillian had brought out of the kitchen. "I should ask him about helping me with my menu. I like the idea of quirky names and descriptions."

She stepped closer. "Like Get Lost Tacos? Those were delicious."

He played with a lock of her hair just for an excuse to touch her. "You should try my fresh buttermilk pancakes."

"Is that an invitation?"

Leaning in, he nuzzled against her neck, feeling her tremble against him. He pressed a kiss to the soft skin where her neck met her shoulder. He wanted to kiss her everywhere. She sighed against him and he knew they only had a couple of minutes so he pulled back. "I will happily make you breakfast any time. But tomorrow, your invite includes about twenty-five other people."

Her fingers traced over the stitching on the front of his hoodie. "As long as that's not the norm. Though, in the summer, if you visit us here, it might be, sometimes. Not twenty-five, but that dining table gets pretty full."

It made him smile that she was thinking ahead. Sure, only to the summer, but still. Cautious Jilly was starting to trust him. Trust them.

"When the kids are tucked in and everyone is asleep, meet me on the dock."

The chatter of kids and parents came through the trees.

"What?" Jill's gaze widened.

"You heard me. One hour. Everyone will be tucked in and asleep. Gotta love fresh air. One hour, Jilly."

Levi wasn't sure if being with Jillian made him feel like a lovesick teenager because he'd been into her *when* they were teenagers or if this was just how it felt to fall in love. He settled on the scuffed and scarred wooden planks of the dock. Maybe tomorrow his dad could give them an estimate on extending and replacing some of it.

While the parents had tucked the kids in, Levi cleaned up the kitchen and got ready for the morning. When he'd left them to it, he'd laughed, hearing one of the parents tell them the first out of the tents were responsible for getting camp set up for breakfast—which pretty much ensured they'd all try to be last out of the tents. Smart. He hadn't seen Jilly when he came back out to the fire but he'd gotten a chance to speak with Zane, who said he'd be happy to chat with him about putting together some content for a cool menu.

When the hour passed, he'd quietly slipped away, anticipation humming in his blood. Even a few minutes alone with Jilly was enough to look forward to. His feet hung over the edge of the dock, and though he wasn't touching the water, he could feel the cool chill of it rising up into the air. The stars and the moon worked together to cast shadows and beams over the pool of darkness. It seemed infinite.

His entire body was chill, but the second he heard her approach, his heart actually soared. Like it was taking a leap off a high-dive board into the unknown waters below.

She sat down next to him, her feet swinging next to his, her thigh touching his, her scent, floral and fresh, wafting around him with the breeze, wrapping him up. It was both stirring and comforting.

He took her hand, and his smile widened as he ran his fingers over the back of it. "I imagined this when we were younger. Not here but just hanging out by the water with you. Just us."

He turned to see she was already looking at him, her gaze so sweet, he could hardly stand it.

She leaned in, kissed him softly. Everything around them was so still, so quiet, this moment between them felt amplified. "Fifteen-year-old Jilly might have passed out if you'd asked."

He laughed, laced their fingers together. "I'd have waited around until you came to."

She leaned her head on his shoulder. "I think this is better. Back then, I wanted you to kiss me more than I wanted the second Hunger Games to release."

Levi slid an arm around her shoulders. "Wow. You really were into me."

Poking him in the side, she tipped her head back against his shoulder so she was looking at him. "But I wouldn't have known how to process my feelings. And you still would have left. This is better, no matter how much I wanted to make out with you."

Levi sucked in a breath. "There's that past and present colliding again. Wanting to kiss me then and me wanting to kiss you now."

Jilly sighed into the kiss, meeting him somewhere in the middle. The water continued to rock the dock beneath them with a gentle cadence that seemed to complement their own movements. Her sighs and his echoed over the water as his hands memorized her face, stroked over her shoulders, along her back. They turned in to each other, shifted so they could be closer. He was certain it would never be close enough.

As their movements became more frantic, their breaths more erratic, he tried to slow them down. Leaning away, he slid his hand along her jaw, held her hooded gaze, offering only the lightest of touches. It was torture for them both. Exquisite torture like he'd never known, but they were at a camp filled with a bunch of kids and parents. He'd just give them something to look forward to. Something more to anticipate. Levi trailed kisses along her collarbone, up the side of her neck, slowly, sweetly, feeling her soften and all but melt with each one.

When her hand came to his thigh, her fingers curling into the fabric of his jeans and her breath hitching, he moved back to her mouth because he couldn't fight it. His fingers sank into her thick, luxurious hair and he lost himself in the feel and taste of her. The feeling that everything he'd gone through, all of his roads, had led right back here. Home. To Jilly. To happiness.

As they kissed on the dock under the moon and the stars, Levi knew it was more than falling. This feeling, the emotions he had for this woman, were stronger than anything he'd felt before and he knew they'd just keep spinning, keep growing, until she was as much a part of him as his skin, his limbs, his heart. She *was* his heart. This wasn't falling; it was crashing. Crashing headfirst into love with Jillian Keller.

Twenty-five

Jillian's heart beat so fast she wondered if she should be concerned, but she was too wrapped up in Levi to truly process anything but him. The feel of his mouth against hers, the gentle slide of his lips along her skin, his fingers dancing along the hem of her shirt, slipping under and driving her mad. The kids were asleep. Gray was staying in the lodge. Two parents had offered to sleep outside in tents while the others had gone into the lodge for the night.

She and Levi were completely alone on the dock and in this moment. She didn't want it to end, and though a little bubble of logic tried to burst through her desire and her need for him—*Ollie might wake up. Someone might want something*—she ignored it. For the first time in her entire life, Jillian let her feelings rule her entire being.

She pulled back, awed by the look of passion and love in Levi's eyes. It'd been a long time since she'd felt it but she was pretty sure that's what she was seeing in that dark gaze.

She stood up and he quickly joined her. He pulled her close. "I'm sorry. I'm moving too fast. I just . . . I lose my head when I'm with you, Jilly."

Grinning, she took his hand and led him off the dock. "Don't apologize for that."

"Where are we going?"

Hoping the little smile she gave him over her shoulder was more seductive than creepy, she answered, "You'll see."

The cabin that Beckett had stayed in the previous summer was closest to the dock. Jilly led them around the side of the yard because it was closest, through the back gate, and up the few stairs of the back porch.

At the door, she turned to him, pushed her hands up to loop them around his neck. "You're moving at the perfect speed and this cabin is empty. Everyone is asleep. And you don't need to make breakfast until seven A.M."

Levi sucked in a sharp breath and it was like fire flared in his gaze. His hold shifted as he yanked her closer, then one hand grazed up and down her back, bringing their bodies flush, as his other hand moved to the back of her head. Even with the height difference she could feel the steady beat of his heart against the front of her own body.

"Are you sure?" he whispered, earning another little chunk of her heart with his gentle tone.

"So sure. Are you? What do you want?"

The moon wasn't as bright back here but she saw his smile, felt the tension coiled tight in his body. "You. I want you, Jillian. More than I ever thought possible."

Jillian dropped her arms but caught one of his hands in hers, used the other to dig the master key out of her pocket. She unlocked the back door, let them in, then released his hand so she could switch on a lamp next to the door, blinking when it cast its low light over the room.

She set her phone and keys on the counter. Tomorrow didn't exist and yesterday didn't matter. Facing him, she forced herself not to fidget. She hadn't been with a man since Andrew. She'd loved him when she married him, with all the affection and optimism of nineteen-year-olds just discovering themselves. But this was different. For one, it was Levi. Two, she'd never felt this sense of rightness combined with the overwhelming longing for anyone other than Levi. This was more than she ever could have imagined. She clasped her hands together, wanting him even as nerves flared to life inside of her.

"Jilly." Levi's whisper was hoarse, nearly gravelly.

Be brave. Take what you want. She inhaled deeply, held his gaze, because in it, she saw herself the way he saw her: sexy, alluring, desirable. She stepped closer to him, put her hands on his chest, her heart rate ramping up again.

"I'm yours, Levi. Part of me always has been."

Levi growled out something that might have been a swear or a word or just an unintelligible sound. His hands went to her hips, closed around them as he lifted her onto the counter, stepping between her legs before his hands moved up to frame her face again. When he did that, she felt like the heroine in one of the rom-coms Presley loved. Until this moment, she hadn't realized how much she craved being looked at, being needed and wanted the way she was right now. The fact that it was by Levi just magnified everything, making her hyperaware of each second, each touch, whisper, and breath.

No man had ever looked at her the way he was now.

They moved in slow motion, his fingers trailing up her thighs. How could so much sensation happen when she was wearing jeans? She felt him everywhere from just a gentle caress. Jilly scooted forward, bringing them closer together, locked her legs around his waist, reveling in his groan. Her hands cupped his face and his traveled under her shirt, the heat of his palms radiating into her skin.

She ran her thumb over his lip, sucked in a breath when he closed his mouth around it. Nothing else existed and it was both the most terrifying and exhilarating feeling she'd ever experienced. He didn't give her long to dwell on that, though.

He captured her mouth in a demanding kiss that had her arching against him, digging her fingers into his back, needing him closer. When he shifted against her, she moaned softly, then pressed her lips to his neck, loving the sharp hiss of air that left his mouth, the way his hands tightened in her hair. He lowered his chin, his thumb caressing her cheek, his mouth claiming hers again. His kiss was all-consuming, energizing, and nothing short of electric.

Her body was all nerve endings and Levi was lighting every single one of them on fire. The kisses deepened and the feel of his tongue against hers was a detonator. Everything inside of her shattered into a million pieces of want and need.

Tugging at his shirt, desperate to feel his skin on hers, she yanked it up, and he finished the job, throwing it to the floor. She wasted no time pressing her mouth to the hard planes of his chest. Her fingers danced in the light dusting of chest hair as her tongue tasted his skin. Little ribbons of pain radiated when his fingers tightened in her hair but she liked it. It made her want to get closer, to drive him mad the way he did her, to make him want with this untethered urgency she'd never felt.

The urgency would have shocked her if she could have felt anything other than Levi. Finally. After all of these years, she now knew what it was like to be treasured, wanted, and loved by Levi Bright.

He rained kisses over her face as her hands wandered up and down his body, over his hard stomach, as she moved against him, locked her legs tighter. She let her fingers trace the ridges of his abs, her nails trace the thin strip of hair that went from his navel to his jeans.

Levi gripped her wrist with one hand, cupped her cheek with the other, angling her head up.

"You're driving me fucking crazy, Jilly. Slow down." He kissed her, soft and light and so sensually she felt herself melting against him. His lips trailed down to her earlobe. "Slow down, honey. I'm not going anywhere. If you're mine, I'm yours. I want to memorize every single second."

She inhaled sharply, part of her wondering how she'd lived her whole life without knowing this degree of want.

Letting her fingers trail back up, she played with the little hairs at the nape of his neck, kissed him in a way she hoped would convey how much he mattered, how much she would treasure this. No matter what happened next.

Twenty-six

Levi couldn't stop kissing Jillian long enough to actually pull in a full breath, and he didn't care. He'd hyperventilate if that's what it took to keep kissing her. All he could see, feel, and think was wrapped up in touching her, getting as close to her as humanly possible. He was drowning in her and didn't want to be saved. What made it all the more amazing was neither did she. With hurried hands and near-desperate kisses, she made it clear she didn't need air if the option was that or them.

Her fingernails scratched across the back of his neck, sending a full-body shudder through his system. His hands went back to her jean-covered thighs, squeezed even as they moved to her ass, to lift her off the counter. He needed more space to explore every inch of her, to savor and devour her, to cherish her and show her how much she meant to him.

"Bedroom," he ground out, unable to say much more as her lips moved along his neck, up to his ear, and her teeth closed around the lobe. "Jillian."

He felt wild, nearly outside of himself. He'd never felt this way; so completely consumed.

"Far corner, front of the cabin."

His long strides ate up the space between where they were and where he wanted them to be in seconds. He didn't need the light. Whisper-thin beams from the moon flickered through the slats in the blinds. When his knees hit the edge of a mattress, he fell forward, his arms under her to cradle the landing.

She gave a small "oof" followed by a laugh and his heart strained so hard in his chest, he thought she might be able to feel it against hers. He lifted his upper body, or attempted to, but she laughed and held on to his neck tighter, trying to keep him exactly where he was.

"One second. I want to feel your skin against mine," he whispered. "Want" was a mild, entirely too-tame word for the storm of emotion raging inside of him.

She dropped her hands to her sides, stared at him through lowered lids, a sweet, sexy smile curving her lips.

With her legs still locked around him, he couldn't move far, so he slid his hands to her thighs, down her calves, unhooking her ankles from behind him, smoothing his fingers back up, watching her face. The gentle *tick, tick, tick* of a clock on the nightstand was the only sound other than the slide of the linens and their breathing.

His eyes grew accustomed to the dark but he didn't need to see Jilly to *see* her. He could close his eyes and picture her with startling accuracy, like he'd memorized every angle and curve of her face. The way her top lip was a touch thinner than the full bottom one. The way her nose turned up the tiniest bit at the end.

What he felt for her was so much deeper than he'd ever felt for anyone. Had he held back in the other brief relationships he'd had? He didn't think so. Until this moment, until Jillian, he hadn't known he had all of this need, all of this *love*, inside of him to give. Levi moved his hands, up, up over her hips, beneath her sweater, his fingers grazing bare, warm skin. She sucked in a breath as he moved the fabric away, pushed it farther up, her lip slipping between her teeth for a second.

"I never really lost all the baby weight," she said.

Levi met her gaze in the darkness and hoped like hell she could see the honesty in his, the lust and longing he felt in every cell of his body.

"You're the most gorgeous woman I've ever met."

He tugged the shirt up, smiling when she adjusted, lifted, so he could pull it over her head. He tossed it in the direction of the floor then returned his gaze to the woman in front of him. The woman he'd wanted for half of his life.

When she fell back to the bed in just a plain white bra, everything in his body coiled at the sight. He was startlingly aware of every muscle, every breath, every pump of his heart. She was perfect. Her hands went to her stomach.

"Mine came with rolls instead of ridges like yours," she said.

Levi laughed because she was funny and he couldn't help it. But at the same time, he took her hands, held them away from her body, stared down at the softly rounded belly she tried to hide. Pushing her hands to the side, he lowered himself to his knees so he could feather her silky-soft skin with kisses.

She relaxed under his touch, against his mouth as his tongue dipped into her belly button. His name left her lips in a breathless whisper. He levered up, rising over her so he could look her in the eyes. Resting on his side along the length of her body, he kept his hand on her stomach and spoke from his heart.

"You're stunning, Jillian. Everything about you, from your smile to your stomach. Your skin, your eyes, the curve of your waist, your hair." He let his lips move over her jaw, and his hand traced up, along her side, over her breast, up to her shoulder and down her arm until their fingers were linked. The seconds, the frantic pace, slowed, tugging them both under as his mouth trailed light kisses along her collarbone, over the swell of each breast. She shifted beneath him, her breath deepening. He smiled against her skin, felt victorious when her other hand roamed restlessly, trying to touch him wherever she could. Eventually, those fingers sifted through his hair. He continued kissing every inch of skin he'd exposed, taking his time, moving down, lingering along the way, moving from one side of her stomach to the other so she could realize how special she was. How perfect. For him.

"Levi," she whispered in the dark, making his blood heat and his heart soar.

Slowly, intentionally, he popped the button on her jeans, lowered the zipper, the sound all but echoing in the quiet. He continued moving down, letting his feet touch the floor so he could stand up and remove the rest of her clothing. He held her gaze, making sure she was on board with every single second of this. Hooking his fingers in the waistband of her jeans, he waited for her nod.

"Stop stalling," she said.

He hadn't expected to laugh while undressing her, but everything about Jilly was surprisingly and delightfully new. Levi tugged and pulled her jeans down her long legs, revealing them inch by gloriously beautiful inch. He tossed them on the floor, unable to hide the wonder he felt just from looking at her.

When he started to climb back onto the bed, over her, she lifted her knees.

"Uh-uh, Bright. Your shirt, my shirt. My jeans, your jeans."

He'd never felt so turned on and so buoyant in the same moment. Taking his time, he arched his brows, let his fingers hover over the button on his jeans. She bit her bottom lip and he had to stifle a groan.

When he unbuttoned his jeans, she went up on her elbows to watch and he couldn't stop the grin from taking over his face. She laughed when, finally shimmying them down, he kicked them off, sent them sailing.

"Can I come back now?" He waited, letting her stare at him like he had her, tension mounting in every fiber of his being. His body was an elastic band stretched to its very limit, mere seconds from snapping.

"Yes," she whispered, lying back and holding her arms out to him. Welcoming him like they belonged together.

His heart inflated so full it stole his breath, made his ribs *ache*. Jillian Keller, with her gorgeous hair tumbled around her shoulders, her beautiful body laid out in a way he'd never imagined he'd be lucky enough to witness, wanted him, and a piece of him couldn't believe it.

"You fucking humble me, Jillian. You're so beautiful. All of you. Your heart. Your mind. Your body. Every bit of you."

She lowered her gaze and he knew she trusted his words; felt the truth in his touch, his look, his every breath. He wanted to find out every secret she possessed, everything she loved and craved, and he wanted to give her those things. He wanted to give her everything.

Slowly, carefully, he crawled back up over her, framed her face with his hands, doing his best not to crush her body with his.

Her hands went to his waist, slid around to his lower back, her fingers teasing just under the band of his boxers before she used her hands to urge him closer.

"I'm heavy," he warned. He hadn't thought much about the differences in their height and weight but as he held her beneath him, she felt precious and breakable and he didn't want to do anything to hurt her in any way. He felt overwhelmed with the need to cherish her. Protect her. Show her how amazing she was.

"I want that. I want you. All of you."

He'd hear those words in his dreams for the rest of his life. A sense of tranquility washed over him as he gave her what she asked for. Jillian arched up into him, shattering his restraint with a kiss that sent them both spiraling into a haze of pent-up desire that had started, innocently, years ago and become a living, breathing force neither of them could hide or run from.

She whispered his name, their hands never stopping as both of them fought to get closer while feeling like nothing could be close enough. He felt the sheen of sweat on his back, the taste of it on her neck, her shoulder, down her arm as he pressed kisses everywhere he could.

Nothing else existed outside of this woman and the sounds she made, the feel of her heart, and her breaths mingling with his own. Every kiss, every touch, every sigh and whisper spurred them both on, turned them both inside out.

As they came together, his gaze held hers and he knew that no matter what else happened in his life, Jillian Keller was his future.

Twenty-seven

Jillian lay beside Levi, his fingers trailing up and down her arm. The sensation sent tingles along her already tingling skin. They'd moved so their heads were on the pillows. Or, at least, his was. Hers was nestled into the crook of his arm, the heat of his body warding off the chill of the cabin.

She watched his chest rise and fall, her hand moving with it, and the moment didn't feel real. It was like a dream. Nothing in real life could be that good. Except Levi Bright.

"You've got the softest skin ever," he said, his voice a little hoarse.

Tipping her head back, she looked at him, her fingers traveling down to his stomach. "You've got the best everything ever."

Her hand moved with his laughter even as he cupped her cheek, pulled her closer to kiss her. The blanket they'd pulled over them slipped, and though she hadn't turned the heat up, she couldn't be cold wrapped in the warmth of his arms.

His kisses trailed from her mouth, over her cheek, and finally to her forehead. When he leaned back, he stared at her like he felt just as awestruck as she did.

"I hope I'm not showing my hand too much if I tell you you've ruined me for all other women," he said with mock seriousness.

She laughed even as delight filled her. Fair was fair. No other man had or would compare to him in any way.

Pretending to get up, she said, "Then my work here is done."

Levi grabbed her around the waist, making her squeal as he rolled them over on the bed until he was perched above her. "Mine isn't," he whispered as he kissed any thoughts of leaving right out of her.

Tucked in a cocoon of blankets and Levi, Jillian forced her eyes to stay open. Levi snored softly beside her, and even that appealed to her. She realized that she missed some of the little things about sharing a life with someone: laughing, for one. But also things people took for granted, like rolling over in the middle of the night to the feel of a solid presence.

Ollie had asked about Levi moving in and the question shocked Jillian because she hadn't thought about the future in that way. The idea of their lives changing so drastically to where they'd live with another person—even the idea of living with just Ollie— seemed unfathomable. But whether she could fathom it or not, life was changing. They were changing. *She* had changed. She wasn't teenaged Jillian—shy, reserved, and a little uncertain. She wasn't young-adult Jill—navigating the ups and downs of marriage and motherhood. She was Jilly. Still navigating a hell of a lot but she felt like, maybe, she was doing it with a bit more grace. She felt confident about herself as a mother (mostly), a daughter, sister, and employee. But this Jilly was more than those things. Levi made her see herself as a person again. A woman. A desirable, funny, adored one, at that.

He startled awake, his fingers pressing into her arm. "Did I fall asleep?"

She smiled against his skin. "Yes."

"Sorry," he said, brushing a sleepy kiss over the crown of her head.

Oh yeah. I like this Jilly and the life she's living right this second.

Levi turned on his side, trailed his fingers up the center of her body. "Should we head back?"

No part of her wanted to. "If we do, we'll have to sneak into the lodge and into separate bedrooms."

"Or the same one, since we're sneaking anyway." He played with the wayward tendrils of her hair. She was sure it looked completely tousled in a way she wouldn't want to explain if Gray caught her sneaking in.

"How about we just stay here and set an alarm? We'll sneak back before anyone wakes up."

Shifting herself into a seated position, she looked around for her phone. When she realized that she'd left it in the kitchen, she turned to tell him, but he was pushed up on one elbow, grinning at her like a Cheshire cat. A mischievous one.

"Phone in the kitchen? Jump out of bed and grab it," he said, tugging on the blanket she kept held around her.

Jillian gripped the blanket tighter, schooled her features. "A gentlemanly thing to do would be for *you* to go get it."

He pushed up so he was sitting too, his side of the blanket dipping low enough to distract her. With a finger under her chin, he lifted it so their gazes met.

"There's nothing gentlemanly about the things I want to do with you," he said, yanking her close for a kiss that scrambled her senses, her pulse, and her thoughts.

He pulled away just as suddenly, a wide grin on his gorgeous face. "I'll grab your phone. Any chance there's some water in that fridge out there?"

Placing a hand on her chest, she nodded. That kiss had stolen her ability to speak. Which, if his laugh was any indication, he was all too aware of. And quite honestly, she was happy to sit there in her lust-hazed stupor while Levi—wearing absolutely nothing—rolled out of the bed and walked out the bedroom door.

He came back showing not one hint of shyness and passed her her phone. No texts. She wasn't being missed. Once she set the alarm, while he stood beside her guzzling half the water, she set it on the nightstand. Levi passed her the rest of the water. Taking a long drink, she put it down beside her phone, then dropped the blanket and went up on her knees, locking her arms around his neck.

He wasted no time returning her touch, with his hands and his mouth. As they fell back into the bed, lost in each other, he whispered sweet, seductive, and wonderful words in her ear.

As the moonlight shimmered through the blinds, Jillian tucked every word, every sigh, and every caress in her memory and her heart and forgot about absolutely everything else. Levi Bright was magic.

Twenty-eight

Jillian couldn't remember the last time she'd had too much to drink and paid the price the next day. But sitting at the table this morning, after sneaking back to the lodge before the sun even considered rising, she was pretty sure functioning on very little sleep as a thirty-year-old was something akin to a hangover.

As she sipped her coffee, the memory of Levi's kisses kept flashing like the greatest slideshow ever through her brain.

The scent of waffles and pancakes made her stomach growl. The kids were noisily chattering about their sleep and who had heard bears. Jilly laughed when Ollie looked at her and shook her head like a mini adult entertaining her peers' tall tales. Fortunately, she'd snuck back early enough to change, get ready, and set up the activities for the day.

Parents started rolling in, looking bleary-eyed and in need of coffee. Jilly smirked against the rim of her mug, knowing that even though she was tired, it had been so worth it. The kids talked back and forth over the table about what they were doing today.

"Morning, Jilly," Zane said. "How'd you sleep?"

Grayson followed behind him, took a seat at the table, and arched one brow. "I think a better question would be, *did* you sleep?"

Looking at Zane instead of her brother, she smiled. "I slept well, thank you. How about you?"

Zane laughed. "I think there's actually an age where sleeping on the ground just isn't fun anymore."

"What age is that, Dad?" Christopher asked.

Zane ruffled his son's hair. "Mine, apparently."

The six kids helping Levi that morning pushed out a rolling tray with an incredible assortment of breakfast options. Waffles, pancakes, berries, muffins, granola, and yogurt. They set it on the table and kids began helping themselves. The adults dug in as well.

"Mom," Ollie said with a reverent tone.

Jilly looked up from her plate.

"Levi's waffles are almost as good as Pete's."

One of the moms sucked in an audible breath. "I wouldn't tell him that, sweetie."

Jilly laughed. "She's right, but you can tell Levi. I think he'll like that."

Gray, who sat on her right, nudged her elbow. "Guessing by the look of your hair, you know what he likes." He said it completely under his breath and she could see from looking at the others that they hadn't heard, but she still fought the urge to smooth down her hair or poke her brother. With her fork.

She glared at him, but he only smirked and reached across to grab a strawberry off her plate. "Your boyfriend is a hell of a cook."

Before she could respond, Levi swung through the door of the kitchen with a fresh plate of waffles.

His gaze found her immediately. "Who wants more?"

The question brought up memories of last night, and her entire body heated. His eyes darkened, which meant, of course, he noticed. He refilled the platters on the table as some of the kids cleared their plates and one of the moms hustled them outside.

They were so cute, some of them still in their pajamas from

the night before, lining up to scrape their plates. Ollie came over after she scraped her plate, and tapped Levi's arm.

"Hey. How was breakfast?"

Ollie crooked her finger, so he bent at the waist and she whispered in his ear. Gray and Jilly shared an amused glance. A happy kind of pressure tightened her chest.

"Are you serious?" Levi said, leaning back and looking at Ollie.

Ollie, hands on her hips, nodded so fiercely, her ponytail bobbed up and down.

"Might be the best compliment I've ever had."

Ollie grinned. "See you." And she was gone.

Everyone cleared out except Levi, Jilly, Gray, and two kids who were working together to push the dish cart toward the kitchen.

Grayson stood up. "Let me help."

He helped the kids navigate their way through the swinging door.

"She said my waffles were better than Pete's." Levi placed his hand on the back of Jillian's chair, brushed his lips against her cheek. "How was your breakfast?"

"Delicious." After kissing him, she whispered in his ear, "I agree with Ollie."

He cupped her cheek, his forehead touching hers. "You don't have to say that, baby. You already own my heart." Her heart seemed to hug itself with happiness.

Just as Levi's mouth found hers again, Gray yelled through the kitchen door, "That's right, guys! It's time to head outside. Through the dining room." He walked through the swinging door grinning at her and she knew he'd given her a heads-up.

There were two teams of nine kids, three parents on each. They were tucked into a grove of trees just behind the lodge with a bunch of everyday supplies that they'd use to create shelters. There were plenty of branches and rocks to utilize for their makeshift structures. They had ten minutes to form a plan as a team and twenty minutes to build.

As they worked together, some of them sniping at each other, some working wonderfully together, Gray came to her side.

"This has been incredible, Jilly. Better than I imagined. You really think this is a cost-effective way to bring more revenue?"

"I do. And I have more ideas on how we can trim the budget a little more. Levi's food is amazing, but I think I can get that cost down with Shane."

"I wanted to talk to you about that," Grayson said.

The timer buzzed with a warning. "You have two minutes, campers," Jillian said, holding up her stopwatch.

A frenzied finish ensued with both teams rushing around to finalize a shelter that, according to the rules Jilly laid out, would withstand the elements. They hadn't clued the kids into what that meant yet.

Her phone chime rang. "Time. Everyone stop!"

Levi leaned against a tree. "That was stressful. I don't think I could ever watch any of you be on *Survivor*."

Grayson laughed. "You and I should do this challenge, Bright."

"I'd pay to watch that. City Boy versus Lifetime Smiley," Zane said, stepping back from his group's shelter.

"I'll do that challenge if you agree to a cook-off as well," Levi said.

The other parents laughed. Leanne looked at Gray. "He'd have you there. I've eaten your scrambled eggs. You don't stand a chance."

Jillian's brain halted, twisted with the idea of her brother making Leanne Shuke, divorced mom, scrambled eggs. Sometimes she forgot her brothers were men who might have lives out-side of being her brother. Just like they did with her.

Weird.

"Okay. No grown-up challenges, but Captain Gray did bring something that will quickly tell us which team has the strongest shelter. Everyone line up in front of your spots."

The kids lined up, all of them looking tired but proud and excited.

Jilly looked at Gray with a smile. "Ready?"

"Absolutely," he said, backing up. "Hmm. How should I test the durability and strength of these forts?"

"Let me see first," Jilly said while her brother made his way backward. She walked around the "tents," pretending to give marks based on height, size, whether she could actually step in-side, and the organization of their supplies.

She started stepping away, pretending she was unsure about which was stronger, when really, it didn't matter and she and Gray had already decided this would be a fun and funny surprise.

Just as she stepped back, saying, "It's hard to choose a winner. They all *look* sturdy," Grayson stepped closer with a hose in his hands.

"Let's check how they'd face the elements," he said, turning the hose on and aiming it toward the kids and their shelters.

Laughter and screaming quickly ensued. The parents had paid enough attention to Jilly and Grayson's movements to back themselves up and out of the spray but every one of the kids got soaked.

Jillian was laughing along with all of them until Grayson turned to her.

"Don't," she warned. "I have a clipboard." She held it up as a useless shield even as ice-cold water sprayed her from head to toe.

The kids started laughing and chanting, "Get her!"

"What?" Jilly yelled shrilly. "Mutiny! Get *them*, Grayson Keller! We're on the same team."

"I'll save you, Jilly," Levi yelled in a hilariously loud and dramatic voice, grabbing the hose from Grayson and turning it on him. The kids on one team rushed Levi, but the surprise to Jilly was Ollie grabbing Grayson to stop him from responding to Levi's attack. It was clearly only play, but Jillian nearly choked on emotion when she realized that Ollie was *protecting* Levi.

"I surrender!" Grayson fell to the ground and Ollie landed on his chest.

Ollie jumped back and did a victory dance. "We got you, Uncle Gray!"

He laughed, soaked just like the kids and her and Levi. "Yeah, you did. You win."

Levi high-fived each of the kids, including Ollie, but when they clapped hands, her boyfriend leaned down and said, "Thanks for the backup, kiddo."

She threw her arms around his neck, giving him a hard, quick hug. "No problem."

Then she ran off with her friends and Jillian stood there staring at what she hadn't spent any time thinking about: her future.

Twenty-nine

Levi had never spent much time around kids. In the last five years of his career, as he busted his ass to climb the ladder, he hadn't spent much time around anyone who wasn't in his kitchen. Spending time with Ollie and the other kids was eye-opening. What really impressed him was the parents, the teacher, and Jilly, and how they just seemed to know when to shift activities, how to redirect a kid who looked like they might pitch a full-blown fit, and how they resolved petty conflicts as if what the kids were arguing over made any sense at all.

By the time his dad and Lainey showed up to the island with Beckett, Levi was exhausted. Jilly walked beside him, like not sleeping all night and wrangling dozens of people were no big deal.

He covered a yawn and Jilly laughed. "I'd like to believe I'm the reason you're that tired, but I think it's because of the kids."

Said kids were running toward the water, where the other adults were helping unload the boat.

Levi looked down at her, touching his hand to the small of her back. "They never get tired."

Jilly leaned her head toward him. "It does seem unfair that they get the lion's share of energy, doesn't it?"

Beckett put a hand out to help Levi's dad onto the dock. Levi's jaw clenched. Even if he were standing right beside him, he didn't know if his dad would accept his help.

"You okay?" Jilly stopped, put a hand on his arm.

"I don't know how to fix anything."

Her gaze shone with empathy. He liked that she didn't offer platitudes. Instead, she reached up, kissed his cheek, and nudged him forward.

Lainey was an immediate hit, with both arms bedazzled in gorgeous bracelets. He should talk to her about buying one for Jilly.

Everyone said their hellos, the other parents joined, and introductions were made. They had about an hour and a half left before lunch, then they'd head back to Smile. Levi didn't know if ninety minutes could make a difference, especially since he needed to duck out in about forty-five to get lunch ready, but he was willing to try.

"Dad," Levi said. "How are you feeling?"

Conversations and laughter crisscrossed over as everyone wandered back to the lodge, including Levi and his dad.

"Doing pretty good, I think." His dad's gait beside him was back to normal, no more shuffling or wincing, so that was good news. "I've been following doctor's orders. Easier than listening to your mother worry."

Levi laughed, because he wasn't wrong.

"It's nice that you came over to do this today," Levi said. He ran a hand through his hair, staring straight ahead, focusing on Jillian's back to center himself. To remind himself that he could do this.

"Your mother said you need some furniture," his dad said.

Levi glanced over. "Not a lot. I don't think I'll stay at Pete's long." Before his dad could add a snide remark, he continued. "I was thinking of renting an apartment. I got a loan. I'm going to pay for the food truck and I briefly wondered if I should put a down payment on a small house instead, but I can't pay for it without the job." He hadn't meant to share all of that, but his father had a successful business and honestly, Levi could use some guidance.

His dad gave a gruff half-laugh. Or it might have been a heavy exhale. But it wasn't dismissal, so Levi was cautiously optimistic.

"If you got a loan, you obviously have your paperwork in order. Do what you intended. The rest will come in time. Doesn't have to all happen now."

As they approached the long folding tables the adults had set up for stations, Levi wondered if his dad was talking about Levi's future or their relationship.

"I'll help you get set up and started, but then I need to get lunch ready," Levi said, stopping before they reached the group.

His dad stopped as well, looked at him. "What does a fancy chef like you make a bunch of little kids?"

Levi laughed and chose to push away the voice on his shoulder saying his dad was judging him. "Actually, I'm fancying up good old-fashioned hot dogs."

His dad's scowl said it all. "Nothing like a perfectly roasted hot dog. You shouldn't mess with some things."

Maybe not, but being with the kids for three meals was giving him an opportunity to try out some new items to see how they went over with this age group.

"Don't worry. There'll be old-fashioned dogs with nothing but mustard and ketchup," Levi said.

In front of them, Jilly and the parents were splitting the kids into groups.

"With caramelized onions," his dad said, a shadow of a smile on his face.

A memory of them having that for lunch during camping trips when Levi was young hit him hard.

"I'll have them. Just for you." Because he couldn't stop thinking about it when his brain actually found a moment of quiet, Levi said what was on his mind. "Went to Bros' Pub. Pretty sad to see the way Liam and Leo have split the place in half."

His dad's chest lifted with his deep inhale. "It's not right for those two to keep that feud up. No one knows what it's about but I'd bet they've probably forgotten, too."

Whether or not his dad realized why the situation was bugging Levi, he didn't know. But he hoped the message came through.

"I agree. Seems like family ought to find a way past the trouble spots."

His dad's lips flatlined and his gaze drifted past Levi's head like the answer was somewhere behind him. When he looked at him again, he nodded. "You got enough time to help me get some of these kids started?"

Levi's heart clenched. "I do."

For the next thirty minutes, everything was a blur of activity. Lainey, Jilly, Zane, and one of the moms got their group settled around some tables with little plates of beads. Levi overheard Lainey tell them about her shop, how she made some of the beads, and how to make each bracelet special and unique. He glanced at Jillian and saw her listening intently. Definitely needed to ask Lainey about creating something specifically for Jillian.

All of the other adults, including Levi, helped the other half of the kids create simple but sturdy birdhouses that could be painted at a later date. When it was time to switch groups, so everyone went home with one of each thing, Levi started for the lodge.

As he walked away from the table, his dad called out, "Don't forget my onions."

Levi was smiling when he entered the kitchen. The lodge was beautiful and the kitchen was no different. High ceilings, lots of windows letting in light, a little nook off the back that led to a decent-sized laundry and storage area. It could use a bit of updating but the appliances were in good shape and the overall layout was efficient. Levi appreciated efficiency.

Working to prepare a variety of toppings for hot dogs, he started getting everything ready. Beckett and Grayson walked in about ten minutes after he'd started.

Beckett popped a pepper in his mouth.

"Food Safe, dude. Don't touch," Levi said.

"Ha. I'm not an inspector so it's fine," Beckett said.

"Thought you were making hot dogs," Grayson asked, looking at the myriad of toppings on the countertop.

Levi paused in his slicing. "I am. But they'll have some choices. Nacho dogs with homemade corn chips, salsa, peppers, and green onions; veggie dogs, which are an assortment of fresh veggies on a bun with homemade ranch dip; classic with caramelized onions and whatever condiments they want; or the bacon cheese dog."

Beckett grabbed another slice of pepper. "Okay, now I'm really hungry."

Gray gave his brother a playful shove in the shoulder. "Wait for lunch like the kids."

Laughing, Levi pulled the bowl of peppers out of Beck's reach. "Everything going okay out there?"

"I have to hand it to Jilly," Grayson said. "Everything has been smooth sailing. There are some ways to make things cheaper, quicker, and easier, but overall, it's a great plan, filling in the off days with letting other people use the space."

Pride suffused his chest. "Your sister always was smarter than either of you."

Both of them laughed, but he didn't miss the look they exchanged, and his muscles tensed.

Before he could spiral into wondering what the hell was up, Gray spoke.

"You haven't bought a food truck yet," he said.

Levi set the knife down. Everything was just about ready. He picked up his cloth, wiped his fingers. "Haven't had much time. It's my hope for next week. One sold but there's still two solid choices."

Grayson nodded.

Beckett tapped his fingers on the counter, almost like he was nervous. "What if you didn't buy a truck?"

Unsure where this was going, Levi grinned. "There's no McDonald's or other fast food in Smile, so I guess I'd beg Pete for a job?"

Grayson straightened his shoulders. "What Beck means is, what if you could cook whatever you wanted, within a preset budget, and could basically run your own kitchen in a way that wouldn't mean a huge start-up cost and risk?"

Levi's jaw dropped. He stood there, staring at two men he'd known most of his life, and had no idea what to say.

Grayson took that as an opportunity to fill his silence. "We want you to cook for the lodge. You'll have carte blanche to do what you want, but need to keep in mind that we're a fishing lodge so it needs to suit the vibe."

"But you have a chef," Levi said as his brain ran in different directions.

Beckett nodded. "Shane is ready to retire. He had an accident last summer, cut himself pretty bad. He's got almost full mobility in his hand back but he's definitely slowing down. He'd been talking about stopping even before that, though, because his husband retired."

Looking around the kitchen, Levi tried to imagine it. He liked it here. He sure as hell liked the employers, and one specific employee. His gaze found Gray's.

"What about Jillian?"

"What about her?" Beckett asked.

"Is she okay with this?"

Gray shrugged. "I'm pretty positive she will be. Shane was always going to leave. He planned to stick around this summer for us but now he can kind of phase out, which I think he'll love. Having you here is a hell of a lot better than having to find someone and bring them in. I tried to talk to her about it this morning but there wasn't time."

The idea was quickly turning into something he wanted. Badly.

Grayson nodded, shoving his hands in the pockets of his jeans. "We haven't worked everything out. We'd need to all sit down, but the rest of us have to do that anyway. There's only a week until we open for the season."

"What would it look like?" Levi asked.

"The lodge will be open from June to November this year. Next year, we'll start earlier, probably beginning of May. You'd be able to keep catering—Beckett said you're doing some of that—plus cooking for the groups that Jilly brings in to use the space."

He started to pace. He needed to get the grill going for the dogs. With a hand on the back of his neck, he did his thinking out loud. "Zane asked if I'd put together a meal for him and his wife for their tenth anniversary. I said yes, but if I did that on the side as well, sort of like a personal chef here and there, it could all gel together into enough." Right? Would it be enough? Would Jilly want to work with him every day? God, it'd be amazing to see her all the time. They'd still have enough space not to drive each other crazy, but at this moment, he didn't think any amount of time with her would equal enough.

Beckett leaned against the counter, crossed his arms over his chest, his flannel shirt seeming a little snug for the width of his shoulders. "I should get you to make Presley and me a meal. Maybe a picnic."

Gray huffed out a breath that turned into a laugh. "Focus, Beckett. Levi, we have money to pay you a competitive wage. We're in a good place right now, and having a great menu will go a long way toward building the lodge's reputation."

Levi stopped pacing and looked at his two friends. Food truck, lodge, fancy-ass restaurant? He just wanted to cook, develop food that made people smile and connect and want to linger or go back for more. He could do that here. He could fully immerse himself not only in the community but with the people he loved. It was a kind of security that he hadn't realized would be appealing. He'd be part of something.

"You know what? I'm in. If you guys are sure and we can get it all down on paper so I can really see what I'm working with, I'm in. I'd love to be part of what you're building here." He held back from saying he'd eventually like to be part of their family indefinitely. Because, one step at a time. Or at least, one step after making a huge leap.

Thirty

By the time they got the kids back to Smile before dinner and unloaded their own things, Jilly was ready to fall into bed. But she couldn't. Not tonight. Tonight, Beckett and Grayson had called an emergency staff meeting. Which was all kinds of odd since they had a staff meeting set up for the end of next week before the season's official opening.

Andrew hadn't stopped calling and Jillian knew, realistically, her options there were slim. She'd either have to meet up with him or he'd show up.

Tonight's meeting was at her parents' at least. Ollie was officially on summer vacation. She'd wanted to stay overnight at Christopher's but Jillian thought a night of rest was a better idea.

Levi had been in a strange mood on the way back. With packing up, getting the kids ready, chatting with parents, she hadn't had any time to talk to him, but he'd sent her numerous glances on the boat, a small smile playing on his lips. She'd wondered, several times, if he was replaying last night like she was. Like she couldn't stop doing.

Ollie came into Jill's bedroom as she finished changing into sweats and a hoodie. Staff meeting or not, she was tired and in her own home.

Ollie was fresh out of the shower, dressed in her jammies and eating a peanut butter and jam sandwich.

"Hey." Jilly sat down at her vanity table to brush her hair. She watched through the mirror as Ollie sat on the edge of her bed.

"I should be at the meeting. I'm seasonal staff."

She bit back her laugh while running the brush through her hair, wishing she'd had time for a long shower. Ollie was very serious about her "position" at the lodge. "Grown-up staff meeting. You're getting a good night's sleep. Tomorrow, I want to look at a few of the summer camp options with you so that you're not stuck at the lodge all the time."

Ollie stopped eating. "I don't want to go to summer camp. You guys need me at the lodge."

Setting the brush down, Jill turned on her stool. "You were the biggest help last year, honey. Truly. And I love having you there, but we're fully booked and there's a lot of new stuff happening. I don't want your whole summer to be there. I want you to have some fun and be with friends."

Her nose scrunched up even as she finished her sandwich. "I had friends at the lodge last summer. We met Aunt Presley, and Bernie will be back and maybe some of the others. Plus, I told Levi I'd show him around and take him on some easier hikes."

She smiled, loving that her daughter enjoyed the lodge so much and was taking to Levi so well.

She led with that. "I'm glad you like Levi so much. He's special to me. And you're the most special to me so that makes it easier for all of us to hang out."

Ollie looked down at the floor.

"You okay, sweet pea?"

Ollie looked up, pinned her with a gaze just like her own. "How come I don't spend time with my dad?"

Jilly sucked in a breath too quickly and choked. Pressing her hand to her chest, she took a moment, caught her breath, and then went to sit on the bed. "Come here."

Ollie came to stand in front of her. "Ginny's mom and dad are divorced and her mom has a boyfriend but she still goes to her dad's house. And Christopher asked about my dad and Ginny said maybe Levi could be my dad. Then she asked about my dad and I said he doesn't like me."

A tear formed in Jilly's heart. "Ollie. That's not true." He didn't know her. There was a difference. "I want to say nice things and make you feel better, but the truth is, people make choices that we don't agree with. That we wouldn't make for ourselves, and sometimes that really hurts us. Your dad made the choice that he didn't want a wife and kid or a family. I hate that it hurts you but I swear to you, it's not *because* of you. It's because of him. Who he is." And she knew, absolutely, that she couldn't let Andrew back in their daughter's life. He'd walked away from the privilege, and Jilly knew whatever he was looking for now in terms of relationships was fleeting.

Ollie shrugged again. She almost never asked about Andrew. "Will he ever come visit?"

Panic flared in her chest. It was one thing to vow he'd never get near Ollie, but he *was* her dad. It was different if Ollie wanted that, too. Jillian took a deep breath, reaching out to tuck Ollie's curly, slightly damp hair off of her forehead. "I'm not sure. Do you want him to?"

"I don't know." She stared at Jillian, her little-girl features too serious. Lines furrowed her forehead like she was thinking too hard.

Jilly gave her a shaky smile. "That's okay. You don't have to know right now."

"I have Uncle Beck and Uncle Gray."

Nodding, Jilly pulled her closer. "You do. And Grampa." She almost said Levi but stopped herself. It was nice that they were connecting, but she didn't want to fill her daughter with expectations she couldn't see through. She and Levi were new. Wonderful. But new. "You have lots of awesome men who want to be part of your life. Who love you and are grateful for you."

Ollie gave her a quick hug, nestling her face in Jillian's neck for just a second. Just long enough to make her heart squeeze.

"I love you," Jilly whispered.

"I love you."

Jillian ended up pulling her hair back into a ponytail and leaving it at that. Ollie settled on the couch with her grampa, looking at the word game he was playing on his iPad. She pointed out a word almost immediately. Jillian's dad tapped Ollie's nose.

"Smarty-pants," he said.

Ollie's smile and her dad's affection for his granddaughter mended some of the tear, but Jillian still worried. She knew change was part of life, but was it so bad to want everything to stay just like this for a little longer? Everyone she loved, or was falling in love with, to just stay like they were, where they were, until Jillian caught her breath and felt ready for whatever the universe threw at her next?

Jilly's brothers were joking around about something when the doorbell rang. She was sitting at the table, showing Presley some of the photos from the kids' camp, her brows pushed together. She heard Ollie exclaim Levi's name before he walked into the kitchen a minute later.

She was equal parts happy to see him and relieved that Andrew hadn't followed through on his threat of just showing up.

Getting up from the table, she went over to him, loving that his arms opened immediately. "Hi. I didn't know you were coming over. We're actually just about to have a meeting about the lodge."

After he kissed her cheek he sent both of her brothers a strange look she couldn't read.

"Why don't we all sit down," Grayson said.

Jilly took Levi's hand and led him to the table, sitting between him and Presley, who had notebooks out, multiple colored pens, and her iPad.

"Hey, Presley." He set his messenger bag on the floor beside him.

"Hi, Levi."

Beckett sat at the head of the table, next to Presley. Gray sat across from her. If her mom were making cookies and there had been music playing, it almost would have felt like a scene from their teenage years, all gathered around the table, hanging out.

Something felt . . . off, though. Levi squeezed her hand and she looked at him, tried to read his gaze. "We didn't get a chance to talk before now."

She smiled. "It was so busy getting everyone packed up. But this is okay. You're welcome to stay for this."

He ran a hand through his hair, messing it up in a way that made her want to bury her face in his neck and get closer.

"I tried to chat with you this morning, Jillian. This definitely wasn't meant to be a blindside," Gray said seriously, pulling Jilly's attention off of her very attractive boyfriend.

"What's going on?" Presley asked, sitting up straighter. Like Jilly, her hair was in a ponytail and she wore cozy clothes.

"Levi?" Gray looked at him.

He turned his body so he was looking at Jilly. "Your brothers offered me a job at the lodge. It sounds amazing. I'd still get to make the food I want to make, I could be creative, I'd get to work with you and them, and I can cater on the side."

Surprise had her opening and closing her mouth without making any sounds. It took her a second but she got her brain to function. "Oh. Okay." She looked at her brothers. "We probably should have discussed this before." It was Grayson's lodge but they were all invested, emotionally and, in small portions, financially.

Looking back at Levi, she tried to smile as her brain worked out what this could mean. "This is something you're interested in? We could talk about it after this, once we get things ironed out for opening next week?"

Levi's expression blanked. She stared, waiting for him to say something, and then it clicked. Her heart hitched somewhat painfully. "You said yes."

He took her other hand as well, squeezed them both. "It's a chance to do what I love to do without the start-up risks."

Jilly pulled her hands back, turned her head to look at Grayson. She felt Presley shift a little so their shoulders were touching; a silent show of support.

"All right." Jillian clasped her hands together just as Ollie walked into the kitchen.

"Hey, peanut," Beckett said, smiling despite the tension he could obviously see on Jilly's face.

"Hi. Gramma said if I want milk before bed I better get my butt in here to get it."

Jillian forced her smile as Grayson got up and grabbed a glass for Ollie, poured her milk. She thanked him, took a long gulp, and then looked up at him. "Mom wants me to go to summer camp but I told her you need me at the lodge."

Grayson winced, looked at Jilly then back at Ollie. He crouched down. "You're the best worker of all of us, kiddo. But you need to listen to Mom. Don't worry, we'll spend lots of time there together."

Ollie's expression shifted, her lips pulling down, her shoulders drooping.

Jilly didn't mean to blurt it out, but it was in her DNA to try to ease her daughter's sadness. "Levi's going to work with us. When you're there, you could probably help him."

Ollie's face lit up like a carnival at night. "Really?"

Levi looked at Jilly, his gaze uncertain, but he smiled genuinely when he looked at Ollie. "Really. I can't wait. Maybe when there's kids staying, you could help me come up with some food ideas."

Jillian's heart felt like it was being stretched out, pulled in opposite directions. Everyone started talking while she tried to process. This could be so wonderful. It could all work out so beautifully. All of them together. Even their parents, when they wanted to take part. But what if it didn't all work out? What if she and Levi didn't last and they had to see each other day in and day out? Part of what made it easier to get over Andrew was reclaiming her life and her space back in her own hometown.

If something happened with Levi, it was bad enough she'd see him all over Smile. She wouldn't even have work as a refuge. On top of that, Ollie looked like she'd been handed the keys to a toy store with the news, which made Jillian nervous. What if they broke up and Ollie had to see him every day still?

She turned her head, saw Levi watching her, and realized what really concerned her, buried beneath all the rest of it, was the issue of why he hadn't talked to her. They'd been busy, sure, but this was huge. This was a complete pivot in his life plan. The one he said he was committed to, excited about.

He was committed to and excited about them. If he could change his mind so easily about one thing, didn't that mean he could rethink them, too?

Thirty-one

Levi sent up a silent prayer to whoever might be listening, while crossing his fingers, that the window he was about to toss rocks at was still Jillian's. Letting go of the tiny pebble, he winced when the sound of it hitting the glass seemed to echo through the dark quietness of Smile.

Rustling the few stones he had in his hand, he counted to five then tossed up another one. A low light came on through the curtains after the third one.

Please don't be her parents or Ollie. His neck was kinking from looking up at the second story. He heard the latch, the slide of the window, and the flutter of the curtains as they were pushed to the side.

Jilly leaned out the window and looked down. He probably had a stupid grin on his face but he couldn't help it. She was so pretty it made the natural rhythm of his heart go wonky. He'd dreamed of doing this the night he left, stitches still stinging in his chin. He'd imagined getting her to come down and finally taking that first kiss before saying goodbye.

"What are you doing?" Her whisper cut through the quiet.

"I needed to see you," he called back, hoping his voice didn't carry.

Her face was only partially illuminated from the light, so he couldn't fully read her expression. She'd been so quiet for the meeting, taking notes after she'd returned from tucking Ollie in.

She'd held his hand when he'd reached for hers, but it didn't feel like it had when he first showed up. He really should have found a way to talk to her before now.

"At midnight?" she asked, refocusing him.

Shit. He hadn't checked the time. "I'm sorry. I'll go. Go back to bed. I'll talk to you tomorrow."

"No. Wait." The curtain closed.

His nerves spun his stomach like the spin cycle on a washer. What was he thinking, knocking on a grown woman's window in the middle of the night? First, he took part in blindsiding her with her brothers, then showed up at her house for the meeting, and now he was here, again, out of the blue while she was trying to get some much-needed sleep. *You're the reason she didn't sleep last night, too. And her kid might be in there with her.* And her parents were home. Levi groaned.

The front door opened and closed softly. Jillian came down the steps to where he stood under her window in the shadow of the trees.

Her smile was soft, reaching her eyes just enough to smooth his nerves. "Levi Bright knocking on my window. I never even imagined you doing that when I was a teenager."

Levi closed the distance between them, his hands sinking into her hair and his mouth taking hers like they'd been apart weeks rather than hours. Jillian made a seductive sound of agreement, her hands going to his wrists, holding on.

She swayed into him, her hands coming to his chest, twisting in his shirt, pulling a few of the hairs there. He didn't care. All he cared about was kissing her. Being with her. There was nothing else in this world that compared to kissing Jillian Keller.

When they pulled back, their foreheads meeting, both of them were breathing heavily.

"Jesus, Jilly. I think I'm addicted to you. Tell me we're okay. Please? I'm so sorry that I didn't talk to you first."

Her gaze went downward. "It's a big decision to make. I won't say it didn't sting that you didn't even run it by me. A relationship is like a partnership, right?"

God, the vulnerability in her voice shredded him inside. "It is, and we are partners." He lifted her chin, met her gaze. "I should have talked to you, but honestly, I got so excited I just dove in."

"That's what worries me," she said quietly.

Levi frowned, pulled back. When she shivered, he removed his zip-up sweater and wrapped it around her shoulders, holding her close. "What do you mean?"

"You wanted a food truck."

"Yeah?" He waited for more.

"The lodge is not a food truck."

"Still with you."

She gave an annoyed sound, tapped his chest. "I thought your dream was a food truck. You had it narrowed down to two, you took a loan, you were going to buy one next week. And then, just like that, new plan. No looking back. Like the food truck meant nothing. You just changed your mind without a moment of hesitation on something huge. Something that could shape and define your future."

He let the words settle over him and, more than that, he listened to how she said them and heard what was beneath them.

Tightening his hold, he dug for the right words to ease the worries beneath her worry. "Jilly, cooking is my professional dream. The food truck was a really awesome idea I was excited about because it would let me be in charge of a fairly contained kitchen and creative menu. This job gives me exactly that, but not on wheels and not on my dime. I didn't change my dream, just the venue. But Jilly, let me assure you." He paused, slid a hand up her back until it was nestled at the base of her neck, beneath all that soft, gorgeous hair. "It wasn't a whim. It wasn't really even a change in direction. It was an opportunity to do what I love with people I trust and grew up with. With the woman I'm falling in love with."

She sucked in a breath. He held her gaze as the surprise turned to longing, and he thought he'd never wanted anything as much as he wanted to make this woman know, down to her core, that she could trust him. That she could believe in him.

"That could make things trickier," she whispered.

He smiled. Sweet, cautious Jilly. Levi pressed his lips to her eyebrow, kissed her softly, then did the same to the other eyebrow. Leaning back, he told her, "It could. Or it could make things absolutely perfect. It was a leap, I'll admit. But the reason I was able to make it so easily, even though I should have talked to you, was because I knew you'd be standing on the other side when I landed. I knew you'd be there."

Moving her hands up his chest, she gripped his shoulders like she was using him as an anchor. He'd be whatever she needed. "Ollie's getting so attached to you."

"I'm getting so attached to her."

"We don't know what will happen."

"No one ever does. So you do the best you can. It's going to be okay, Jilly. And the parts that aren't, we'll handle them together."

He saw, *felt*, the yearning in her gaze to believe what he said. All he could do was show her time and again that he wouldn't let her down. That when she took the leap, he'd be there, waiting on the other side when she landed.

Letting out a long breath, she wrapped her arms all the way around his neck and went up on tiptoes. "I want this so much it scares me."

He smoothed his hand down the back of her hair. "I want it just as much. But it doesn't scare me, Jilly. It makes me stronger. I'm guessing you've had lots of scary moments that turned out better than you thought they would. Ollie? Coming home? Saying yes to our first date? Taking advantage of me last night?"

Her laugh made all of his pieces click into their proper places.

"Right. I hope you're okay with that last one."

He kissed her, hugged her close. "More than okay, and hoping for a repeat very, very soon."

Standing on the porch, the moonlight washing over them like the cool air, Levi knew that he could kiss Jillian for the rest of his life. He wouldn't tell her that now, because she was already scared, but he knew it in his heart and felt it in the way she kissed him back.

The kiss deepened, Jillian's lips and sighs drowning him, pulling him under even as it buoyed him and made his heart soar.

She whispered his name and he knew they'd be okay. There was no other option. Because Jillian Keller was quickly becoming his everything.

Thirty-two

Jillian should have known by how hopeful she felt and how good everything was going, even with the surprises, that it couldn't last. Because she couldn't push the bad or worrisome things away and expect them not to surface. She knew better. The near perfection lasted for almost two whole days.

Andrew

> I'm at the Best Western in Mackinaw. Do I need to take a ferry over to your little island or are you coming here?

Jilly stared at her screen. She needed to deal with this but she had so much to do today. Pulling up her schedule, she looked at what had to be done today and what could be pushed. Levi was heading over to the lodge to get familiar with the kitchen and meet with Shane, and then later tonight, they were all meeting up at the museum to get everything ready for the Founder's Day celebration.

It'd seemed like such a good idea to open the week before the celebration; lots of fun activities and events for tourists. *Maybe if you hadn't offered to help with setting up for the weekend on top of surprising Pete and Gwen on top of agreeing to train a couple of high school students for summer work at the lodge on top of falling in love with Levi on top of—*

"Mom," Ollie said, hurrying in.

Jilly lowered her phone. "Hey."

"Can I go help Uncle Beck at the bike shop this afternoon? Gramma said I can come help with the museum stuff this morning and then she'll drop me off there."

Ollie would be occupied. She could let her mom take care of Pete and Gwen's surprise with her friends, head over to the mainland, and be back in a few hours.

"Yes. That works perfectly because I'm going to go to Costco and stock up for next week."

Ollie put her hands on her hips, her lips pursing out. Her hair was tucked into a ball cap that said BECKETT'S BIKES. She wore a Get Lost Lodge T-shirt and a pair of bright blue shorts. She was adorable and quirky and Jillian's heart actually ached with how much she loved her daughter.

"What's wrong?"

Ollie shrugged. "Maybe I should come to Costco with you and help."

Her kid was amazing. And deserved a father who would never let her down. Who would be there. Who should have been there for the last five years.

"No. You go do your thing and I'll see you around dinnertime, okay?"

She walked over and, before Ollie could leave, pulled her into a tight hug. "Love you, sweet pea."

Squeezing her back even as she set one foot out, ready to run, Ollie laughed. "Love you, too."

And off she went. It was time to make sure Ollie's future wasn't something Andrew could toy with.

Jillian

> I'll meet you at Cora-Belle's Diner at two. I'll have groceries so you have a half hour max.

If she caught the next ferry, she could do the Costco run first, meet with Andrew, and get home. Her mom was in the kitchen chatting with her dad when Jilly walked in, her purse slung over her body, a sweater wrapped around her waist.

They stopped talking the second she walked in the room.

"Hey." She stared at them, wondering what they'd been talking about.

"Hi, honey," her mom said, pushing the spatula through the scrambled eggs she was making. "Want some breakfast?"

"I have to head out, actually. I'm going to the mainland. I'll be back this afternoon."

"Your mom and I want to talk to you and your brothers," her dad said. He leaned on the counter next to the stove, a cup of coffee in his hand, his legs crossed at the ankles.

Her stomach cramped. She couldn't do this right now, too. One thing at a time. Ollie came first, so that meant Andrew was at the top of the list of things to deal with.

She looked at her watch. "Can we do it tonight? I really have to go."

Her dad's expression shifted, a hint of disappointment crossing his features, but he gave her a small smile. "Big sale at Costco or are you hoping to grab some samples for breakfast?"

Hoping her laugh came through somewhat genuinely, she kissed both of their cheeks and headed out.

During the ferry ride over, Jillian busied herself making lists, answering emails, and responding to group chats with Presley and her brothers, one with just her brothers, and one with her family. She also texted with Levi and Lainey.

When she was sure everything was as organized as it could be, she walked to the back of the large ferry and stared out at the water as Smile faded away. The day she'd left with Andrew had been a hard one, but she'd been filled with so much love and certainty, she pushed down the sadness and focused only on him.

They'd headed straight for the airport, catching a plane to Pittsburgh, where he had a job at a prestigious loan management company. He was older and seemed so sophisticated and charming. In truth, she'd only spent a couple of weeks with him while he was vacationing on a houseboat. She'd naively thought she knew him. That she loved him. By the time they settled in his Pittsburgh bachelor pad, she already had concerns. When she got pregnant with Ollie immediately, marriage seemed like the right thing to do. Her and her stupid optimism and blinders. Never again. Not for him.

The shopping trip seemed endless because Grayson kept texting her and adding things to the list. She kept reminding herself that it was good that they were about to be so busy. Everything would be fine. With her car packed fuller than it'd ever been, trunk, back seats, and passenger seat, she found a spot to park in front of the little café she and Lainey liked to visit when they came over for the odd girls' weekend.

The smell of bacon and eggs turned her already nervous stomach when she pulled the door open. Andrew sat in the first booth, facing the door. His smile widened and looked genuine when he saw her. Jillian clutched her purse with one hand and her keys in the other. He stood as she came to the table.

Jillian froze when he put a hand on her waist and leaned down to kiss her cheek. The familiar scent of his piney, earthy cologne was worse on her stomach than the food smells. Years ago, she'd thought it was so sexy. Now she knew, just like so many other pieces, it was a façade. He didn't love the outdoors like he'd claimed. Didn't love connecting with nature or small towns, hiking, swimming, or any of the things he'd said that summer.

"You've lost the weight you carried after Olivia was born. You look stunning."

The keys dug into the delicate skin of her palm painfully. She moved back, slipped into the opposite side of the booth.

Like he was in a high-end restaurant with maître d's, Andrew lifted his hand to signal for the waitress. She gave him an amused glance and went back to what she was doing.

"I'm so glad you agreed to see me," Andrew said. Jillian took in the changes that had occurred with time. His dark hair was still perfectly styled, despite being a little thinner. His sharp, angular jaw was clean shaven, of course, but there were subtle lines around his eyes, his mouth, and he looked tired. Cocky as hell but worn out.

"You didn't leave me a lot of choice," she said, forcing her fingers to loosen so she could set the keys and her purse down.

"Jillian," he said, his tone nearly chiding. "I know I owe you an apology."

She started to speak but he held up a hand. "No. I know. An apology isn't enough. I owe you more than I could ever say."

Surprise that he'd admit to any wrongdoing wasn't enough to break down her walls. "You owe me nothing. I don't want anything from you."

Hurt flashed in his gaze but Jillian's focus on what was best for Ollie made it easy to ignore.

"I don't want it to be like this between us. I let you down in too many ways to count. But I'm back on my feet and I want a fresh start."

Regardless of Levi, she felt zero desire for this man anymore. Nothing. Not even anger. But she couldn't help being curious.

"Why now? It's been almost five years since I came home." Her phone buzzed in her back pocket.

"I always hated that you continued to call that place home. You never let yourself truly adapt to Pittsburgh. To my world."

Folding her hands on the table, she leaned in, keeping her voice low. The waitress stopped by their table.

"Sorry about that. What can I get you two?"

Andrew gestured to her. She shook her head. "I'm not staying. I don't want anything."

Andrew gave her a patronizingly amused glance then looked at the waitress. "I'll have your brunch special, eggs over easy, multigrain toast, and a coffee, please."

The waitress nodded and walked away. Andrew returned his gaze to Jillian's. She spoke before he could.

"Smile is my home. Even when I was fully immersed in your world, holding dinner parties and having brunch dates with your colleagues' wives while taking online college courses and raising our daughter, it was my home. It's Ollie's home. Who, by the way, since you haven't mentioned her once so far, is doing wonderfully. She's an amazing, kind, wonderful little girl." She waited, a small part of her hoping to see a softening in his features. Didn't he want to see pictures? Know every little thing about her? Didn't he want to know what her favorite book was? Why she hated pistachio ice cream? What she was scared of and all of the things she wanted to be when she grew up?

"So, nothing like me," he said, laughing at his own joke.

"What do you want, Andrew?"

He reached for her hand. She snapped both of hers back, put them in her lap.

"I've reconnected with an old friend. Do you remember Harold Banks?" He didn't wait for her to confirm that she did. "He's running a fairly successful company and is considering bringing me on. It's entry level, somewhat beneath me, but it won't take long to move up. We've been chatting quite a bit. Lunches here and there. He remembers you. Fondly. Remember, we spent many evenings together with him and his wife. She liked you as well. Anyway, he started asking about us all getting together. His wife would like that, and do you want to join her book club, all that sort of thing. You know how it works. The schmoozing and mingling go along with the money-making. He hadn't actually heard about our divorce, which worked in my favor. He's invited us to the Hamptons for a week this month. I told him we'd love to come."

His coffee came but the waitress said nothing as she dropped it off.

Jillian didn't know what to say. She didn't know this man. Maybe because she'd grown up and this Jillian wouldn't have found one thing attractive about him. Young Jilly had been so eager for love and connection—outside her family and all the people who adored her simply for being a Keller—for someone to see past the shy girl who stood on the sidelines. Andrew had made her feel special, wanted. Needed. He didn't like her because she was a Keller or because their families were friends. She'd mistaken his charm, intelligence, and quick wit for something he'd never possess: integrity. She'd mistaken his attraction for her as love.

Jillian grabbed her keys as she slid out of the booth and stood up. He looked up at her, confusion all over his face.

"Where are you going?"

"I'm going *home*. If you want to see Ollie, get that lawyer. Start the paperwork. Because until I have it on paper that I'm legally obligated to share her with you, or she, herself, asks to visit with you, you won't ever see her. I want nothing to do with you, just like you've wanted nothing to do with us for years. I'm not a kid anymore, Andrew. I was so worried about being seen by you, I didn't *see you*. I don't like what I see. You know my parents' address. You can forward all communications there. I'll be blocking you the second I get back on the ferry."

She didn't wait for him to respond or turn when he called her name, loudly, from his seat. She hurried to her car, got in, and pulled out of the parking spot. Pride and sadness warred inside of her. She'd done it. She'd told him what she thought, she'd stood up for herself and her daughter and taken control of her life. Ollie didn't need Andrew. And Jilly sure as hell didn't want him.

On the ferry ride home, she did what she promised and blocked him. Then she looked up a few lawyers just in case. She didn't know how she would pay for it, but that was a worry for another day. By the time she pulled into her parents' driveway, she was exhausted. Which was why she didn't notice the For Sale sign immediately.

When she did, it actually knocked her back a step. She stared at it, her mind spinning, her heart racing. Her parents' car was gone, the lights were out.

Getting back in the car—she needed to get stuff over to the lodge—she went to the bike shop to grab Ollie.

When she went in, Beckett was behind the counter. "Hey, Jilly. Whoa. You okay?" He came around the counter. The space had once been an auto shop, which made it a perfect fit for Beck. They'd even kept the bay door that retracted into the ceiling, and though it was currently closed, the streetlights and rising moon shone through the multi-paneled glass. The outside walls of the building had been painted a pale green while the metal around the window panels on the door were painted white. It was an amazing space with a perfect vibe for what Beckett wanted. Both of her brothers had achieved their dreams. Her parents were finding theirs. And Jilly was having a panic attack over having to move out of her childhood home at thirty. Had she thought she was the mature one of the siblings?

She shook her head, the keys jingling in her shaky hands. "I just saw the For Sale sign in Mom and Dad's yard."

Beckett's lips firmed, his gaze filling with empathy. "I know. I'm sorry."

He knew. It wouldn't impact him. He didn't rely on them, live with them, feel comforted by the fact that they were right there. Despite being thirty years old, she hadn't rushed out of her parents' home because in truth, she loved it there. She loved hanging out with them and living in her childhood home, but more than that, she loved that Ollie got so much time with them. *You knew this was coming.*

Tears burned her eyes. Beckett stepped closer like he might hug her. She held up her hand. "Where's Ollie? I have stuff for the lodge. I need to get over there. Is she ready to go?"

Beckett eyed her warily, concern etched in his dark eyes. "She's already there."

"Oh." Okay. That made it easier.

"She wanted to go over with Levi, so he took her for the day."

Jilly wasn't sure what shifted inside of her but it felt like all of the things she had carefully balanced toppled over and crashed right into her gut.

"What do you mean he *took* her for the day?"

Beckett's brows lifted. "She wanted to spend the day with him at the lodge. He was excited to bring her with him. Gray was already there. I didn't think it would be a big deal."

"Where my kid goes is a big deal to me. Levi is not her father," Jillian said sharply, an acidy taste filling her mouth. She didn't even recognize her own voice.

"What the hell is going on with you, Jill?"

The tears were going to fall without her permission. She couldn't stop them and she couldn't explain them, so instead of answering him, she walked away. She was in charge of her life. And Ollie's. Jillian was done sitting on the sidelines just hoping that everything worked out okay. That wasn't how life worked. Fairy tales weren't real. She knew how to take care of herself and her daughter. No one else got to make decisions for them. Not Andrew. Not Beckett. Not even Levi.

Thirty-three

Levi paid close attention as Ollie showed him how to navigate the list-generating app specifically designed to make meal planning and online shopping easier.

Sitting at the countertop on a stool, holding a bowl of sliced apples drizzled with a cinnamon glaze he'd whipped up, she grinned at him, a large gap in her smile.

"See? Easy. Chef Shane likes to write everything down but this is easier. I showed my gramma and she loves it."

Levi squeezed her shoulder, surprised by the easy surge of affection he felt for this kid. "You're really smart, Ollie. This is going to make my life easier. Thank you."

Before Ollie could respond, Jilly pushed through the dining room door. Speaking of surges, it was like his entire body short-circuited. Fuck. He was so in love with her.

"Mom," Ollie said, hurrying off the stool with a slice of apple. "Try this. Levi made the drizzle overtop. It's so yummy."

When Jillian didn't take it, Ollie took a huge bite. Jilly's smile was tight and nowhere near the wattage she naturally gave her kid. Something was up.

"Hey," he said, walking over to greet her.

Her gaze was shiny and remote. "Ollie, it's time to go. Say goodbye."

"Are we going to the museum?" She hurried over and wrapped her little arms around Levi as much as she could.

Levi returned the mini-hug but couldn't take his attention from the strange way Jillian watched them both.

"See you later, Levi." She hurried through the swinging door.

Levi closed the gap between him and Jillian, pulling her close. "Are you okay?"

He leaned in to kiss her but she turned her face, so he brushed her cheek. Alarm bells went off inside of him, sending a buzz of uncertainty over his skin.

Jilly stepped back.

"What's going on, honey? You're worrying me."

"My parents are selling their house," she said, her tone flat.

"Shit. I'm sorry."

"I went to see Andrew." Her tone was every bit as empty.

"What?" He froze. Even his breath went cold.

"My ex."

What the fuck was going on? "I know who he is, Jillian." The better explanation would be why she went to see him and hadn't said anything.

His tone seemed to snap her out of her strange state. "He wanted to get back together. He's been bugging me for weeks to see Ollie and I went to see him today to tell him it's not going to happen."

Because he needed something to do with his hands, he shoved them in his pockets with so much force he was surprised he didn't rip the seams. "And you didn't think to mention to me that you were taking off for the day to meet up with your *ex-husband*?" Or that he'd been bothering her for weeks while Levi was busy falling in love with her and her kid.

She met his gaze, and for the first time since he'd come home, he couldn't read her thoughts. Jillian was so often an open book with her emotions. It made it easier to fall for her. But now, she was shutting him out completely.

"I didn't think to. I'm sorry. But it doesn't matter. Everything is changing and I don't like things being up in the air."

He didn't like the sound of that. "What's up in the air? You're not getting back together with him." There was no way.

The immediate disgust on her face assured him he was right even before she spoke. "Of course not. I told you I don't love him. I'm not sure I ever really knew him. But no. This isn't about him."

"What's not about him, Jillian?" What was she trying to say? His gut cramped with intuition.

"Everything, all of it, I feel like my life is spinning out of control. It's too much. I think there's too much going on for us to keep going down this road."

Yanking his hands from his pockets, he turned and paced the room, stopping behind the counter and then pinning her with his stare. "Everything is wonderful between us. I told you I was falling in love with you and you didn't say it back but it's there. I know it is. Then you turn around, go see your asshole ex, who, by the way, you most definitely should have told me was bothering you, then you come here and break up with me? What the hell, Jillian?"

Something between anger and sorrow clashed in her eyes. "I can't make it all work, Levi. It's too much. It's too scary and too uncertain. I need to know I'm doing what's best for Ollie. I need to find a place to live. We're going to work together and I can't have her falling deeper for you when we have no idea where this will lead."

He started to interrupt but she took a step closer and cut him off, her gaze so full of sadness it nearly took him out at the knees.

"I was married. That's supposed to be forever and it wasn't, and while I'm happy I didn't stay with him, it's proof that there aren't any guarantees. My job is to protect Ollie, emotionally and physically. She doesn't need the kind of upheaval in her life that would come from us breaking up farther down the line. What if we moved in together and then it happened? It would devastate her. I don't even know how to tell her *we* have to move. It's too much. She cares about you. This way, nothing is jeopardized."

Levi's body shook, tiny little tremors rooting him to the spot. "You're right."

"I am?" She whispered the words, her eyes shining with tears.

He nodded, gripping the edge of the counter with his fingers until his knuckles went white. "Nothing jeopardized. No risk in walking away. Saving *Ollie* from possibly facing disappointment and hurt later in life. Sure. That's one way to look at it. Another is that you're being a coward."

"What?" The color drained from her face.

"You're in love with me. I'm in love with you and I love your kid, Jillian. You can say you're protecting her but what you're doing is showing her that when it comes time to fight for what you really want, you should hide away behind excuses. But guess what? It won't stop Ollie from ever being hurt or disappointed in life. That's going to happen because *that's life.* All it will do is show her that when she had the chance for real happiness, her mom was too afraid to take the leap. Then it'll make her wonder if she should live her life that way."

"Don't you dare tell me about raising a kid. You know nothing about taking care of anyone but yourself. You and Beckett had no right to decide between you where my kid went today. She's not yours. She's mine. My whole life revolves around her and you wouldn't know anything about that. I can't let people pop in and out of her life when they decide it's convenient." Her voice rose and her hand shook when she pointed at him.

"Mom," Ollie yelled, standing in a little gap between the partially opened swinging door. "Why are you yelling at Levi?"

"Why is anyone yelling?" Gray asked, pushing the door open all the way, a hand on Ollie's shoulder. He looked back and forth between Levi and Jill. "What the hell is going on?" Ollie started to speak but Grayson sent her a quick glance, brows arched. "I know I said 'hell,' Ollie. It's warranted." He looked back at them. "Jilly?"

"I can't do this. There's too much to do." Jilly turned and looked at Gray. "My car is at the docks, full of supplies. Ollie and I will walk home." She handed him the keys and tried to push past him.

"I don't want to go home," Ollie said, folding her arms across her chest.

"It's time to go," Jill said.

Grayson took the keys. "Jilly, you shouldn't drive the boat when you're upset like this."

Pushing her hands into her hair, she shook her head in frustration. "Everyone needs to stop making decisions for me. Ollie, it's time to go. *Go.*"

"I don't want to!" Ollie yelled back, tears trickling down her cheeks.

Jilly's back went rigid. "Olivia Anne Keller, move it. *Now.*"

Ollie stomped away. "You're mean."

Jilly started to follow but Grayson grabbed her arm. "I'll drive you."

She shook him off. "I don't need you to."

Grayson stood taller, and though Levi was all for Jillian being independent and doing whatever she needed to do despite what just happened, he was relieved her brother didn't take no for an answer.

"You're not yourself. I'm not asking. I'm driving you. Levi, I'll talk to you later."

With that, both of them left and Levi nearly collapsed onto the countertop. Looking around the kitchen, he couldn't tie together the threads of what just happened. Everything had collapsed like a poorly constructed soufflé but there was absolutely no reason for it. What the hell had just happened? His chest and stomach heaved like waves in a storm. He needed to go after her. There were two boats here, weren't there? Nothing made sense. Grabbing his keys and phone, he hurried out of the lodge, flying through the lobby and out the door. Maybe he could catch them. He couldn't lose her. Them. This shouldn't be happening. He ran down to the dock, but stopped just before it, shocked to see his dad tying his boat up there.

"Hey. Gray asked me to come over and look at the dock. I didn't get a chance the other day and figured a quick boat ride would help me sleep better tonight. What the hell's wrong with you?" His dad walked toward him.

"You can't work on the dock," Levi said. And he couldn't deal with this right now.

His dad's chest puffed up. "Didn't say I was going to. I'm assessing it, and I asked what the hell is wrong with you."

Levi gripped either side of his head, yanking on his own hair. "Everything. Everything is fucking wrong. Jillian just broke up with me and she gave me reasons but it doesn't make sense. There's too much good between us not to work through the hard stuff. I don't know what to do."

His dad moved forward more quickly than Levi expected, pulled on one of his arms until Levi dropped both of them, then squeezed his shoulder. "All right. All right. Just breathe now. You'll figure it out. Come on now. Calm yourself down."

He hadn't even realized he was still shaking or that he'd been yelling. His dad's surprisingly soothing voice shocked the calm into him.

"Dad. I can't lose her. I love her. I love her so much."

His dad nodded. "I know, son. It's going to be okay."

Levi shook his head. "You can't know that. How can you say that?"

His dad stepped closer, put both hands on Levi's shoulders, and met his gaze. "I know it. You'll find a way, Levi. You always do. It'll be okay. Now just take a breath. I've never met anyone who went after what they wanted the way that you do. Give her some space and get yourself sorted. It'll be okay."

He realized he was copying his dad taking deep breaths like when he was a kid and he'd get too worked up over a sporting event. It was one of those tricky parenting things that had you doing what they wanted with no instruction whatsoever.

Levi closed his eyes and let the pain wash over him. When he opened them, his dad dropped his hands but kept looking at him, his gaze steady and sure.

"It'll be okay."

Levi nodded. He didn't know if he believed it, but he wanted to.

"Come on. Let's take a look at this dock. I'll write up an estimate and you can do the work. I'll send one of my guys out to help you. I can spare one."

"I took a full-time job at the lodge," he said, falling into step beside his dad, bracing for his dad's frustration.

"I know. Your mother told me. Guess you better get things sorted with your girl or that's going to be awkward," his dad said.

A bark of laughter burst from Levi painfully. "You're not wrong."

He just had no idea how to do that.

Thirty-four

Ollie wouldn't speak to her. Jillian stood outside of her daughter's bedroom—this was one way to get her to sleep in her own bed—and considered knocking again. Grayson, Beckett, Presley, and her parents were in the kitchen and Jillian didn't want to see any of them. She wanted everyone to go away so she could crawl into bed and cry or smash her fists into her pillow. The memory of Levi's face, the shock and sadness, the hurt and anger, made her feel like she was covered in shards of glass. Every breath felt like her skin was tearing.

Walking up the stairs from the basement, where Ollie had asked to have her room moved earlier that year—which Jillian had said she wouldn't like but her daughter insisted she would—she snuck past the kitchen and into her own bedroom.

She should have known that her mom wouldn't just let her hide. Edie Keller sat on the edge of Jilly's bed. Jillian shut the door, leaned against it, and forced herself to take slow, measured breaths.

"Jilly," her mom said, so much emotion and love in one word that Jillian broke.

Silently, tears streamed down her face, her body shaking.

"Oh, honey." Her mom walked over, pulled her into her arms, and Jillian fell into them just as the final blocks fell and her emotions came crashing down around her.

She cried into her mom's shoulder as her mom whispered, "Shh," in a rhythmic, melodic tone, holding her so tight it was like she thought she could actually absorb her pain.

But she couldn't. It was woven into Jillian's skin. It ran in her blood and had seeped into her bones. It existed in every molecule of her being.

"It's okay, honey. I'm right here. It'll be okay."

The thing about falling apart after she'd already hit rock bottom emotionally once in her life was she knew that it would, actually, be okay. One day. Sure, she'd have to see him and work with him and know what it felt like to be in Levi's arms, to feel his mouth on hers, and his body against her. But she'd be okay. Ollie would be okay. There was no other choice. But it didn't have to happen right this second.

She held tighter to her mom, let the tears come, hoping that when they'd all been cried, some of the sadness would fade and it would be like a cut. It would heal. *She* would heal. There'd be new skin over the hurt. It would be rougher and she'd probably always feel the sting of it if she thought about it too hard. There might even be a scar. But she'd be okay. One day. Just not today. And probably not tomorrow.

She wasn't sure how long she cried but as she came back to herself, she felt empty. Completely devoid of anything. Her mom left and came back with a warm cloth. Jillian tossed all of her Kleenex into the garbage, used the cloth on her sensitive skin, and let out a shuddery breath.

Tossing the cloth into the laundry basket, she sank down onto the side of her bed. "Ollie won't speak to me."

"That won't last," her mom said, sitting beside her.

"I broke up with Levi."

Her mom took her hand. "I hope that won't last either. He makes you happy."

More tears threatened, so Jillian didn't focus on that. "You're selling the house."

"We are. We didn't want to drop it on you like this but it's been busy and it's been hard to get everyone together."

"They're all here now," Jillian said, her voice unrecognizable.

"They are. Feel up to coming out? Grayson is going to wear a hole in my kitchen tile pacing back and forth with worry."

The difference between breaking down as a teenager and now was she didn't have the luxury of hiding away and listening to sad songs on repeat. She had a family, a life. And a hell of a lot of things to get organized and settled.

Taking a deep breath, she clapped both of her hands down onto her thighs, then stood. "Time to face life."

Her mom stood beside her but caught her arm. Jillian looked at her, seeing the depth of her mom's sadness, and understood. When Ollie hurt, Jilly hurt. This was no different, and apparently, it didn't go away just because your kid grew up.

"Everything all at once is too much. But when you face each tiny obstacle, put it behind you, it becomes easier. You're not alone, Jillian. You absolutely never will be. You can't predict the future. I know you wish you could, sweet girl. But it doesn't work like that. You can accept that and embrace the things that make you happy, or you can turn your back on them and fool yourself into thinking that you can protect yourself from anything that hurts."

She followed her mom into the kitchen and waves of embarrassment threatened to pull her under. Everyone was sitting around the table, concern and worry etched into their faces. Grayson came forward immediately and pulled her into a tight hug.

"I don't know what the hell happened. Do I need to kick Bright's ass?"

Jillian's laugh was muffled against his chest because he was holding her so tight. She pushed away from him. "No."

"He probably couldn't anyway, but I could, and will," Beckett said, standing up and coming around the table to hug her. "What's going on, Jilly?"

Her dad hugged her next and it smoothed some of her frayed edges. "Sit down, sweetie. I made you some tea."

They sat around the table, Jilly's hands wrapped around a cup of lukewarm tea, her family watching her with worry and love.

She told them about Andrew and her day and losing it when Beckett said Ollie was with Levi.

"Wow," Presley said, her hands flattening on the table. "That's a lot."

Jillian nodded.

"That asshole won't fight for custody, Jillian. You must know that," Grayson said, his hands clenched on the table.

"Even if he does, we'll help you with legal fees. We want to downsize, Jillian, not abandon our family," her dad said.

"I'm sorry. I fell apart," she said quietly.

"It's understandable," Presley said, scooting closer and leaning her head on Jillian's. "First off, being in love is scary as hell. It's like falling off a cliff and having no idea what surface you'll land on. Dealing with idiot exes is no picnic either. And knowing your childhood home isn't something you'll be able to come back to is something I could never imagine if I had the connection with my childhood memories that you do."

Her mom sat down at the table. "We aren't trying to pull the rug out from under you, and maybe we should have worked harder to get everyone together sooner. We won't be traveling all the time—Smile is our home—but we want something smaller. We put an offer on a two-bedroom in Northwood."

Northwood was at the northern tip of Smile, practically at the other end. It was a small, gated community of retirement homes.

"That way we'll have a room for grandkids to sleep over," her dad added.

"You only have one grandkid," Jillian said, as if that were the focal point. Tears burned her eyes.

"For now," her dad said, smiling at Beckett. "But with your brother getting married eventually, let's hope we get some more."

Beckett just laughed. Presley grinned at him and Jillian's chest loosened. She wasn't losing her family. Things weren't ending. They were changing.

"Ollie won't speak to me."

"I've never heard her yell at you like that," Grayson said.

"She loves Levi," Beckett said, somewhat tentatively.

Jillian nodded.

"So do you," Presley said quietly, and Jillian wondered if she was the only one that heard her. Looking around the table, she knew that Presley wasn't the only one aware of it.

"It's easier to push happiness away than accept it," Beckett said, reaching out to put a hand on Presley's shoulder. "Makes you feel more like you're in control. But the truth is, you can avoid him physically, even working with him . . ."

"Though he hasn't signed his contract yet. We can fire him," Gray said, making her laugh.

Beckett continued, ". . . but it won't stop you from loving him, Jilly. It won't keep you from being hurt. You're hurting now."

He was right. They were all right, and she knew it, but she needed time to wrap her head around all of it, and all of it felt like so much in this moment. She *was* hurting, and she'd hurt Levi. He'd called her a coward and that hurt too. Especially when she considered the fact that he might be absolutely right.

Thirty-five

Levi was going stir-crazy. Locking the door behind him, he headed down the stairs on the side of Pete's garage, not expecting to nearly run into the guy when he rounded the corner. Pete was staring at the near-empty garage. In between everything else, the Kellers, his mom and her friends, and Levi had carted items to the dump, the museum, Goodwill; wherever it needed to go.

"I forgot how big this space is," Pete said, looking over. "You look like shit."

Levi laughed. Because what else could he do? "Thanks."

"Heard about you and Jillian." Pete turned to face him.

They hadn't been together long, but this was Smile, after all, so Levi didn't know if the cook meant them being a couple or ending it. "Which part?"

Pete shrugged. "It's Smile. Heard you were together and that she broke up with you. Women are hard to read. Even when you know them well."

Levi stuffed his hands in his pockets and stared into the distance. Garbage cans were out for pickup in the back alley. Birds circled overhead, hoping to find last-minute morsels. "You're not kidding."

"You find the right one, though? It's worth whatever it takes to find a way to keep them in your life."

Levi stared at him, his chest tight. Fuck. He hated this. "What if they don't want you in their life?"

Pete shook his head. "Jilly's a lot of wonderful things, but she's no actress. That girl's emotions shine like a billboard announcing every feeling. She wants you. You just have to give her time to see it."

Levi appreciated the touch of relief Pete's words brought. "I gotta say, I didn't expect to get words of wisdom from you on something like this."

Pete gave a gruff laugh, reached up to pull the garage door closed. "You've met my wife. She's a hell of a woman and damn sure could have done better than me. I might have learned a thing or two along the way."

Levi would be lucky to experience a relationship half as special as what he'd witnessed between Pete and Gwen. He really believed he and Jilly had what it took to be that kind of couple. The kind that weathered it all. That stood strong no matter how rough the storm. But he couldn't hold them afloat alone. She had to want it too.

"I'm trying to let her come to the conclusion that we belong together on her own. But that doesn't mean I'm not thinking of ways to help it along."

"Knew you were smart. You going to offer anything on behalf of the lodge for Founder's Day?"

Levi smiled, happy for the shift in topic even though he needed to get going. "Yes, actually. I'm going to do a bunch of samples of the summer menu I'm working on."

"Looking forward to it."

Levi nodded. He knew things were coming together for the surprise for Pete and his wife but he hadn't checked in for a bit, and now, he didn't know where to be, because he didn't want to crowd Jillian when she clearly wanted space.

"I'll see you later," Levi said, taking off down the alley to do something he'd meant to do sooner.

Walking through Smile felt both familiar and new. The same buildings and structures existed as when he was a teen but there were subtle changes among the more dramatic ones. New businesses, new homes, a park that hadn't existed before. He knew, no matter how much Smile changed or stayed the same, he was happy to be home. It'd only been two days but he missed Jillian like he'd carved out a piece of himself and left it somewhere. Now, he felt like he was wandering around aimlessly, trying to find it.

It was a longer walk than he remembered to get to Tourist Lane. He probably should have grabbed a ride, but the walk did him good. In the last couple of days, he'd worked remotely from his apartment, chatting via text with Grayson and Shane about menus, options, and the Founder's Day Festival. He couldn't avoid the lodge for good, though. Grayson wouldn't say anything about Jillian other than to give her some space, so he had no idea if she was there on the days he wasn't.

He had a stop to make but then he and his dad were heading over with one of his part-time summer guys to work on the dock. Things had been reasonably okay with his dad. Turned out, getting his heart kicked into his teeth really made his dad feel for Levi. Enough to not give him a hard time about stuff, anyway.

He opened the door to Bracelet Babe and saw Lainey behind the counter. She gave him a warm smile that assured him, even if she knew, which she likely did, Jillian hadn't said anything awful about him. He hadn't been kind about some of the things he said, and even though he felt slighted, he knew he could have done a lot better in his response.

"Hey. How are you doing?" She came around the funky wooden counter with cool little displays of bracelets. It was almost like an apothecary table but all of the spaces were open and angled to reveal unique designs.

He shrugged, unsure of what to say. It occurred to him he ought to connect with some other people—maybe Zane or Leo or Liam. At the moment, everyone he knew was tied tightly to Jillian.

"I'm okay."

She stopped in front of him. He had a couple of inches on her without heels, but right now, she was eye level with him.

"Liar."

"You know." He looked around the tiny space, surprised by the homey, eclectically charming feel of the place.

"Not much. She's pretty wiped out from thinking she has to carry the weight of the world on her own shoulders."

Levi met Lainey's gaze. "You know her well."

"So do you. You know she loves you." Lainey reached out and squeezed his shoulder before going back around the counter.

Levi's throat felt thick. He tried to swallow past the lump lodged in it. "That might not be enough. Not if she can't get past the fear."

Lainey put a small silver cloth bag on the top of the counter, keeping it beneath her fingers as Levi came to stand across from her.

"When someone you love and trust, someone who is supposed to be your person, fails you, on purpose no less, you tend to become wary of trusting in the words of others. Even the people who have never let you down. The people you *know* love you and have your back. You think that if the person who supposedly loved you the most could let you down, then anyone could. It changes you. You start to question your own judgment and believe that you can't count on anyone other than yourself. Having that happen to her by the age of twenty-one left some pretty large scars. Ones she's avoided thinking about until you came home. She's scared. It doesn't mean she doesn't love you."

Levi leaned on the counter, clasped his hands together as he stared into Lainey's emotional eyes. "It sounds like you came by that knowledge through firsthand experience."

Her gaze dropped as she smoothed her fingers over the small bag. "You didn't know my mom. She left enough scars to give me a pretty thorough knowledge base."

Levi hated the hurt in Lainey's tone. He covered her hands with one of his. "I'm sorry, Lainey. Jillian is incredibly lucky to have you as a friend."

Lainey lifted her gaze and smiled, all traces of vulnerability gone. "I tell her that frequently. I hope you like this, and more than that, I hope she does." She handed him the bag.

He untied the little bow at the top and removed a delicate and beautiful bracelet made of tiny yellow and pink beads separated by thin rose-gold spacers, all strung onto a soft, adjustable and sturdy black string.

Lainey pointed at the yellow beads. "The yellow are dots, the pink are dashes."

Levi smiled. When he'd tapped on Jillian's window the other night, he'd started thinking about them feeling like teenagers and how she'd told him she used to write notes with Lainey. He thought about what it would have been like to send her a note, and then had a brief image of one of her brothers trying to kick his ass. And the idea came to him. Even after she'd broken up with him a couple of days ago, he knew he still needed to give it to her.

"I hope I get to give it to her," he said, hating that it wasn't a guarantee.

"You will."

Lainey sounded sure enough for both of them, and since she knew Jillian so well, he took it as a positive sign. Lainey pulled a second bag from the drawer and showed him the second bracelet he'd asked her to make. They were both perfect. If things worked out, he promised himself, he'd get one of his own. So they'd match. *Not if. When.* He hoped. He couldn't spend any more time thinking about it right now, though. He needed to head to work and stop pretending he could do that and give her space at the same time.

He truly thought that if he came to the lodge in the afternoon, he wouldn't get in Jillian's space; that she'd be gone for the day. But as he pulled his dad's boat to a stop, parking next to a boat that read BRIGHT BUILDS, he saw two things: his dad supervising two of his employees, offering suggestions as they worked at the far end of the dock, which was getting widened and strengthened. The second thing was Ollie flying toward him down the green expanse of grass in front of the lodge. His heart spasmed as he stepped off the dock and braced for the impact of her arms going around his waist.

He'd missed her. How the hell had this little girl and her mother wrapped themselves around Levi's heart to the point that it beat steadier when one of them was around?

"Oof. Hey, kiddo. How are you doing?"

He crouched down to be on her level, both of the bracelets he'd purchased digging into him through his pocket.

Ollie put her hands on his shoulders. "I'm sorry my mom broke up with you but we're still friends and I can still cook with you, right?"

Jesus. The sides of his heart squeezed so tight it felt like they met in the middle. "We'll always be friends, Ollie. You matter to me a lot. And you're the best sous-chef I've ever had." She beamed at him and he had to ask. "Is your mom here?"

Ollie shook her head. "No. She's working on the presentation for Mr. Pete and Ms. Gwen."

His knees were cramping in this position but he didn't want to stand up yet. "Is she doing okay?"

Ollie's hands came to his cheeks and she pressed them together as she stared at him like she was trying to figure him out. He would have laughed at the strangeness of it if his heart wasn't fucking strangling him.

"She's sad. My gramma and grampa are moving and she's really sad about that. Plus, I'm not talking to her and I think that makes her sad too."

No. He went with his gut and scooped Ollie up so he could stand but still maintain eye contact. "Ollie. Your mom needs you. You shouldn't stop talking to her."

It both surprised him and healed a little piece of him when Jillian's daughter rested her head on his shoulder, her arms coming around him. "I know. But I'm mad at her."

"I know, sweet pea, but she loves you, and she needs all the people who love her to take care of her right now while she's sad." He started walking toward the lodge, seeing Gray come out the front door.

Ollie lifted her head. "Aren't you sad?"

"I am. I love your mom. But I also don't want to upset her more." He lifted his chin toward Gray. "Hey, man."

"Hey." Grayson stared at the two of them.

"You could win her back," Ollie said.

"Ollie," Gray said with a mild warning in his tone.

Ollie jumped in Levi's arms excitedly. "What? It's what Uncle Beck did with Aunt Presley."

Levi couldn't help but laugh at the kid's enthusiasm. He set her down, charmed even more when she immediately took his hand. "I helped Uncle Beck do Instagram live. I can help you."

"Ollie, this is between your mom and Levi."

Ollie shook her head adamantly. "When Aunt Presley left, you said Uncle Beck was a damn fool, because she was part of our family. Levi's part of our family, too."

Gray ran a hand through his neatly styled hair. "I really wish you'd stop repeating all of my words."

Levi laughed. "If there were something I could do, I would, Ollie. Your mom needs to figure out what she wants."

Grayson sighed. "She's miserable, man. Ollie might be right. Maybe we can figure out a way to get her to get her head out of her a—stop being stubborn."

Ollie giggled. "Grampa says I'm stubborn just like Mom."

"He's not wrong," Grayson said.

Thoughts and ideas flitted through Levi's brain. "Is she going to keep avoiding me?" He looked up at his friend while Ollie, apparently done with the conversation, ran over to the side of the house.

Gray nodded. "Probably. If I know Jilly, she feels embarrassed by what happened, on top of every other emotion she's struggling with. She likes to take care of others. She's not so great with others trying to do the same for her."

Ollie came running back to them with a clutch of colorful blooms in her hand. "You could give her flowers. And she wants a pearla." She held out the flowers.

"A pearl?" He took the flowers, studying them while wondering if he shouldn't have gotten her the bracelet.

Gray laughed and came down the stairs. "A pergola."

Levi looked up. "Oh. Where?"

Ollie took her uncle's hand and Levi followed them around the side of the house between the outbuilding, the shed, and the paths through the trees, one of which led to the ropes course.

"Right here." Gray pointed. "She said if we ever host a small outdoor wedding we could decorate it with flowers and twinkle lights, and if we don't, the guests can just sit and enjoy it."

Ideas spun in his head. Ollie looked up at him. "Can you build one?"

He could. And so could his dad. But how would they get it done without Jillian knowing? She worked here and didn't want him there at the same time.

"I can, but it would take a bit and there's already so much going on. How would I pull it off?"

He was more asking himself, so when his dad joined them, his employee at his side, he startled out of his own thoughts.

"You bring in professionals," his dad said, slapping him on the back hard enough to knock him forward a step.

Levi smiled. The bracelets sat in his pocket, waiting for the perfect moment, and now, maybe, he had a plan on how to make that moment happen. He grinned down at Ollie. Thanks to a nine-year-old kid, he might finally get the girl.

Thirty-six

There was no time to dwell on how spectacularly she'd screwed things up. That's what Jillian told herself, but the truth was, she purposely threw herself into every single second of work so that she didn't have to think, breathe, or feel. Because every one of those things led her straight back to Levi. To the anger in Ollie's gaze and the disappointment in her mom's. To the ache in Levi's. Energy hummed in the air at the lodge, like it knew it was opening for business in one day.

The restless feeling coursing through her made her feel like she was trying to hold her balance on the ropes course. She'd braced herself for the impact of seeing Levi today, but so far it hadn't happened. She'd managed to avoid him even though she knew he was working, at least one of the days, in the kitchen. Heat washed over her skin when she remembered the things she'd said to him. How she'd behaved. How would she fix that? Did she want to? Her fears weren't gone but she missed him so much it felt like a wound that wouldn't close. At least Ollie had started talking to her again, even coming to work with her today. Though, she'd kept herself busy as Gray's sidekick instead of hanging with Jilly. And still, no Levi. She found herself listening to see if she could hear his voice, but the lodge was loud with other sounds today, making it hard to concentrate. Gray was doing some construction on the outbuilding next to the lodge, making it more useful, he'd said.

Emmy, who would be with them for the summer, tapped the computer and lifted her hands with a flourish. "There! I did it. It's booked."

Jillian tried to smile at the teen's enthusiasm. She'd been walking her through the reservation booking system and other front desk duties for most of the morning. Emmy's dark hair hung over one shoulder in a long, thick braid. It nearly took Jillian out when Emmy swung her head toward Jill with excitement.

"That's so fun."

Jill could only nod. "The online system does a cross-check with our calendar, but sometimes there are glitches so I try to check it at least once a day."

"Okay. What if a guest has special instructions, like they need a room on the ground floor?"

Jilly leaned around Emmy and pressed another button. "It'll come through here on the screen and we transfer it into the notebook as well and onto the calendar."

"Okay. What's next?" Emmy clapped her hands together and Jillian envied the teen's optimism and excitement.

"We have a messaging system set up so if a guest needs something and we're not at the front desk, they can text," Jill said, pulling her phone from her pocket.

She held out her phone to show Emmy. "If I get a text and you're not at the front desk, I'll text you. Just make sure you have your ringer on when you leave the desk."

Walking Emmy through a few more things, Jilly was confident that the young woman would be a helpful addition to their summer team. "You can help Mateo with stocking up all bathrooms and making sure each room has two extra pillows and a spare blanket. He'll show you where the laundry is and explain how we reset the room. Our first guests will be here at noon for check-in tomorrow. By midweek, the lodge and cabins will be full."

"Okay. I'll go find him. Thanks, Ms. Keller."

Now she just felt old. This week had aged her. "Jilly is fine."

When the girl walked away, toward the kitchen, Jilly felt like a high schooler, wanting to ask her to see if Levi was working in the kitchen. *Pass her a note that says "Is Levi here? 'Yes' or 'No.'"* Jilly cringed at her own thoughts. She really needed to pull on her big girl pants and talk to him. He deserved that and so much more.

Ollie came through the door with Grayson just as Jilly was rounding the counter, working up her nerve to act like an adult.

"Hey, Mom." Her tone was back to normal, though her smile wasn't quite as bright as usual.

Jillian probably overexaggerated her own in response. "Hi, sweetie."

Ollie looked up at Grayson, who gave a very subtle nod. What were these two up to?

Before she could ask, Ollie pulled a slip of paper out of her pocket and handed it to Jilly.

"What's this?"

"Open it," Ollie said.

Jilly's hands shook as she unfolded the long, thin piece of paper she recognized as lodge stationery. On it, handwritten, was a message:

Jilly,

I have to tell you something. Can you please meet me at the side of the lodge where the forest leads to the ropes course? I'll be waiting.

Levi

She looked at her daughter, who was holding her brother's hand. Both of them had strange smiles on their faces.

"What's this?"

Grayson tutted teasingly. "Come on, Jilly. Are you so old you don't remember passing notes?"

"It's a note from Levi, Mom. You have to go."

Her daughter's gaze was filled with so much hope and happiness, it infused Jillian with bravery. She inhaled shakily, let it out. Teenaged Jilly burst to life inside of her. *A note from Levi Bright.* Her fully adult self realized that this moment mattered. She needed to apologize to the man she loved and take ownership of what she'd done. It's what she would want her daughter to do. One of the things that kept eating at her this week was Levi's comment about what she was teaching Ollie. There was no way to protect anyone from hurt. It was part of life. But she could teach her to be accountable, to try her best, and not let go of something wonderful just because she was scared.

Jillian crouched down to meet Ollie's gaze with a startling realization. Ollie taught her that last one. Now, she was giving her the go-ahead and the courage to grab on to something special.

"I love you," she said.

Ollie wrapped her arms around Jilly's neck. "I love you, too."

When she stood up, she pressed a hand to her stomach like that could steady her nerves. The paper crinkled in her grasp.

"You deserve happiness, Jilly," Grayson said quietly.

"So do you," she whispered as she passed him.

Walking through the lobby, out the door, and down the stairs, her steps slowed. What if Levi wanted to tell her that he needed to leave? That he couldn't be here anymore? That she'd made her choice and it wasn't him, so he wouldn't stay?

She stopped herself before rounding the corner of the lodge. Standing still, she pulled in a deep breath, closed her eyes, and held it for a few seconds. The sounds of birds in the distance and her heavy heartbeat were all she could hear. Exhaling, she opened her eyes and took a step toward the unknown, believing that no matter what happened, wherever this took her, loving Levi Bright was worth the journey. And the risk. Now, if she could just get him to forgive her and take her back.

Thirty-seven

Levi wiped his hands on his jeans. He hadn't felt this sweaty or nervous since . . . never. Absolutely never had he ever felt like there'd been more on the line. And then Jillian rounded the corner and it was like looking into a regular mirror after staring into a fun house one. Everything that was distorted came into focus. Only, instead of looking at himself, he was looking at her; his future. His heart revved like an engine and his pulse went haywire.

She looked at him, their gazes locking for one heated second before she saw where he was standing. He'd argued more than once with his dad when the finishing touches were happening. Steven wasn't satisfied with just instructing—he'd wanted a physical hand in securing the pergola in place and, all in all, it'd turned out stunning.

His dad had called in a favor to get the concrete to anchor the footings securely the very night they came up with the plan. From there, his dad had the precut, pretreated wood shipped over early the next morning, and his guys had created the crisscross top quickly. Once the posts were secured and the top was attached, Levi and Gray had carefully strung hundreds of twinkle lights through, over, and around, with Ollie kindly pointing out when they'd missed a spot.

Jillian's hands flew to her mouth with a gasp and she hurried forward, dropping her hands as she looked up and turned around. "What is this? How did this get here?"

Laughing softly, some of his nerves easing, he stepped closer. "We built it. For you."

She whipped her head toward his with another sharp inhale. "What do you mean you built it for me?"

When he went to take her hands, he saw she still had the paper. He smiled, tried to take it. She wouldn't let it go. Holding on to it with her, he asked, "What are you doing?"

She tugged it back. "You're not taking the first and only note I've ever received from Levi Bright. It's mine."

His heart melted and then re-formed stronger than ever, with a new owner. It was Jillian's. As long as *he* was, too, he was okay with that. He opted for one of her hands for now and held it tight, loving the feel of her skin against his in any way he could get it.

"I'll write you notes every day if you want me to. If you'll let me."

Tears filled her gaze. "Levi," she whispered.

"Just," he said, surprised by the lump in his throat, the need in his veins, "let me get this out, okay?"

She nodded, her gaze soft, her lips pressed together. For the first time in almost a week, Levi felt like the life he wanted, the life he now imagined, was attainable. It was, literally, within his grasp.

"Actually, I need a minute. I really need to kiss you, Jilly. I feel like part of me is missing without you and I just—"

She leaned in, went up on her tiptoes, cutting off his words. He had a speech all worked out, but he needed this more than words or air. His arms closed around her waist as hers came around his neck, the paper crinkling in her grasp.

Their mouths came together and they both fell into a kiss that pushed away the last of his uncertainty. The way her lips moved against his, eager and sure, was proof that they were meant to be together. His hands moved up to cup her face, tilt it so he could kiss her deeper and longer. He could kiss her forever and it wouldn't come close to quenching his desire for this woman.

When he pulled away, just a little, so he could see her face, she was breathing every bit as hard as he was. Her lips were red from his mouth, her cheeks painted with a soft blush that made him smile. Her eyes were hooded and sparkling with something so much more than like or lust.

"I didn't break your face," she whispered.

He laughed, hugged her tighter. "No." When he leaned away, he ran a hand over his chin. "Not then and not now. Even if you had, it would have been worth it. You're worth it, Jilly. You're everything. I'm so in love with you, I can't breathe without you. I know I said things that hurt you. I was shocked and crushed and I didn't handle it well. You're an amazing mother and a beautiful person inside and out. I need you, Jillian. In my life, by my side. I want to be a family; you and me and Ollie. Forever. When it's easy, when it's hard, no matter what."

He caught her tears with his thumbs. "I think, in the most innocent of ways, you really were my first love," he told her, the honesty coming so easily.

"I think you were mine, too," she said softly.

His heart was a helium balloon with no string attached. "I want to be your last. At seventeen, I didn't know what it meant to be in love. I do now. It isn't always perfect and it's definitely not always easy, but when you're with the right person, that doesn't matter as much, because no matter what happens, you know you can lean on them. Trust them. I want to be the person you trust, who you know won't ever let you down. I won't break your trust, Jilly. I won't break your heart. I'll cherish it. For as long as you'll let me. For the rest of my life and then some. Please don't let us be over."

Jillian's hands trailed along his hairline and he wondered if it was nervous movement. "I'm sorry I walked away. That I pushed you away and then stayed away. I was so overwhelmed. I'm sorry I didn't tell you about Andrew, that I didn't talk to you. That I didn't lean on you. That wasn't fair. I was so scared by everything I felt for you and how all of the things in my life seemed to be changing."

His precious, cautious Jillian. "Change can be good, honey. It brought me home, to you. It brought me here, to the lodge. It brought *you* here to the lodge. The good thing about coming together at this stage in our lives, we know ourselves better. I love you, Jillian. In a way that I've never loved anyone else. I know it's hard for you to take a leap, but I promise you, I'll always be here when you land. I'm happy to sign a legal document any time in the future, but, for now, it's a promise. A promise to be honest and open with you. To work through hard times and enjoy the good. To walk by your side and hold your hand. To make you laugh and hold you when you cry. I love you so much it feels impossible to explain it, but then I look at you and I know you understand."

She nodded, slowly, her eyes filling with new tears. "I do. I love you, too, Levi. I feel like, in some ways, I've loved you for half of my life. I want to spend the rest of it showing you how much."

Her words settled his pulse and his breath came easier. "Tell me again. It doesn't feel real," he whispered, pulling her closer.

The twinkle lights seemed brighter in the shadows of the trees. "It's so real. I love you, Levi. So much more than I ever imagined possible. And trust me, I imagined it a lot."

"You're my home, Jilly. My heart. You and Ollie. I don't need anything else." He pulled back, dug in his pocket for her gift, and pulled it out, passing her the bag with a smile. "Unless, you know, you want to give Ollie brothers and sisters."

Her mouth formed a little O.

"Uncle Gray says sisters are bossy," Ollie called from the side of the house.

Levi and Jilly both looked over to where Ollie was peering around the side of the house. Grayson gave a sheepish shrug. "Sorry. She wanted to make sure you guys were okay."

Levi laughed as he held out his hand. "Come here, Ollie."

Grayson looked at him with a smile that seemed like approval and then left the three of them alone. Ollie stopped in front of him, her mother standing beside her. He crouched down, the other little bag in his hand. "I love your mom, Ollie. Is that okay with you?"

Ollie's grin, missing teeth and all, filled him with a unique kind of happiness. "Gramma says you can't help who you love."

Jillian laughed. "No. You can't, but when you make a promise to them, you can do everything in your power to keep it. Even when you're scared. I love Levi, too, Ollie, but that won't ever change how much I love you."

Ollie looked up at her mom, her nose scrunching. "I know. Why would you do that? I love Levi, too, and now we can all be together."

God, his heart might burst apart in his chest. He gave Ollie the gift, stood up so both of his girls could open them.

Their dual gasps were so cute. They both ran their fingers over the beads. Ollie's were purple and lime green because Lainey said those were her favorite colors.

"It's such a unique pattern," Jilly said even as Ollie asked, "Did Lainey make them?"

Levi nodded, meeting Jillian's gaze. He might never stop looking at her. "She made them. And the pattern is actually Morse code. It says 'I love you.'"

More tears filled Jillian's gaze but he cleared his throat and continued. "I wanted you both to have something that reminded you that I do. No matter what."

"It's so cool. Thanks, Levi," Ollie said, hugging him.

He leaned down, hugged her back. "Thank *you*, Ollie. For making me step up and be brave."

She patted his cheek. "Uncle Becks said being brave is hard but it's usually worth it."

His laughter merged with Jillian's. "He's right about that."

Grayson came around the corner again and Levi moved closer to Jilly, putting his arm around her shoulder.

"All good here?" he asked, staring at his sister.

"Yeah. We're good." She leaned into Levi, her arm slipping around his waist.

"Look, Uncle Gray. It means 'I love you,'" Ollie said, holding up her wrist.

Gray took her hand and looked at it. "That's beautiful. Lots of people love you and your mom." He looked at Jillian again, like he was reminding her.

"We're very lucky," she said.

"Speaking of which, I'm going to take Ollie home. We've got guests arriving at noon tomorrow. Staff shows up at ten. That should give you two enough time to reset room six before anyone is here."

Before Ollie could ask a question, Gray picked her up, tickling her and making her laugh. "Let's go, peanut. We'll stop and get ice cream on the way home."

"Yay! Bye, Mom. Bye, Levi." She waved over Grayson's shoulder where he'd hoisted her.

"Bye, honey."

Levi grinned as they walked away. "See you tomorrow, Ollie."

When they were out of sight, Levi turned back to Jillian. "I had a lot of hope going into tonight. I honestly wasn't sure if it would work out how I wanted, but on the chance that it did, I may have pulled some favors and had the best room in the lodge put aside for us for tonight. If you want."

Lifting her gaze from her bracelet, which she'd slipped on immediately, she smiled. "I want. Very much. I hope Grayson gave you the friends-and-family rate."

Curling her fingers into his shirt, she pulled him close, kissed him in a way that imprinted everything about her into his heart and soul. Grayson and Ollie were the last to leave, other than them, so he didn't worry about privacy when he scooped her up into his arms. She laughed, arms going around his neck.

"What are you doing?" Her pitch went high like Ollie's but her eyes danced with laughter.

"Carrying you romantically up to the room."

She pressed her lips together on the ride to the front porch. He made it all the way into the lodge then stopped at the base of the stairs. He could sense her fighting back laughter.

"What's wrong, Casanova? Too many stairs?"

He turned his head to look at her. "Think you're funny? I thought teenaged Jilly would want this. I want to make all of her teenage fantasies and your adult ones come true." He sighed deeply, mustering his strength. He really needed to get back into working out, or at least add more cardio to his routine. "I love you, sweetheart."

Jillian kissed his cheek as he took the first step, then shifted in his hold.

He stopped. "What are you doing?" He set her down one stair up so she was a little taller than him.

"You've already made me happier than you could ever imagine,

Levi. You see me, you love me. You love Ollie. You fought for me, you built me a pergola with twinkle lights. You make me laugh and you're an amazing cook. I love you. So much. And I really want to enjoy room six. It has a soaker tub and a fireplace. I'd like you to not put your back out on the way up there. You *are* a couple years older than me." With that, she laughed, turned, and hurried up the stairs with him on her heels, chasing her, making her laugh harder.

They might not know the future, but he knew what was about to happen, and he knew he was the luckiest man on earth. Definitely, in all of Smile.

Thirty-eight

Room six was her favorite in the whole lodge. Because of where it was located, there was a view of the lake and the mountains from the two wide windows that merged in the corner. The king-sized four-poster bed looked like an antique but actually came from Pottery Barn. Jillian had spent extra time on this room, imagining it for a couples' weekend getaway or a honeymoon suite.

Standing in the doorway, Levi's body pressed against her back, his arms wrapped around her waist, she fought the urge to cry again. The room was filled with flowers. Vases and vases of gorgeous blooms in a rainbow of colors covered every surface—along the mantel of the fireplace, on the small table by the window, and on both of the nightstands.

"Levi," she said, because words escaped her. She had no vocabulary. Just feelings on top of feelings.

"Ollie said to give you flowers," he whispered. "I want to give you everything."

She turned in his arms, moving backward as he stepped into the room, closing the door behind them. This time, when he picked her up, she didn't laugh. She wrapped her arms around his neck and fused her mouth to his with an urgency she'd never experienced in her life.

A low growl from the back of Levi's throat let her know he was every bit as serious and focused as she was. They hadn't been apart one full week, but it was enough to know that she never wanted to be without him again.

He set her next to the bed, his gaze full of a hunger she knew matched her own. The sky had grown darker, traces of the sun fading into the water. Enough natural light filled the room for them to see each other.

One of his hands curled around the back of her neck while the other cupped her cheek. He was moving too slow. Adrenaline coursed through her, making her feel like a sprinter off the starting block, just wanting to *go*. She reached out, grabbed the hem of his sweater. A smile spread over his lips as he stepped back, pulled the sweater and the T-shirt underneath over his head, whipped them away. Then he was back, standing so close they shared the same air.

"I missed you, Jilly."

Her gaze locked on his chest, her hands traced over his skin, down the length of each muscled arm and back to the center, then down, her fingers dipping into the ridges of his well-toned stomach. He shuddered under her touch and caught both of her wrists.

"Your turn, Keller. My shirt, your shirt."

She laughed even as her fingers went to the buttons on her dress shirt. One by one, she slipped them open, anticipation setting her skin on fire as Levi's gaze grew darker and more intense.

Pulling the bottom of the blouse free, she tossed it in the same direction as his. He reached out, his calloused fingers tracing over her sensitive skin, along the swell of one breast, down and up over the other until he tugged at the strap of her bra.

"This, too," he said, his voice low and raspy.

As she reached around to undo the clasp, Levi's admirable

but not necessary patience finally snapped and he yanked her against him. Her arms immediately locked around his neck as he brought them both down to the bed.

He kissed her hard as his body pressed hers into the mattress, and it was like neither of them could see or feel anything but each other. The outside world ceased to exist. There was just them, their skin turning slick as they moved together, their breaths sawing in and out as they both whispered words of affection and love and passion. Their mouths met over and over again like a perfect song that had no ending.

When at last there was absolutely nothing between them, Levi stopped, his gaze finding hers. Both of their hearts pounded against each other.

"I love you, Jilly. My dreams have always been about my work. It wasn't until I came home, until you, that I realized how big dreams could get. Now I dream of spending my life with you, waking up with you every single day, crawling into bed beside you every single night." He smoothed her hair back from her face, pressed his lips to hers with a dreamy sort of tenderness. "I want to build a life and a home and a family with you. My dream is to make all of yours come true."

She reached up, cupped his jaw, and pulled him down, stopping just before their lips touched. "You already did."

Moonlight washed through the window, casting a glow that perfectly complemented the serenity Jilly felt. Levi had turned the gas fireplace on and the flames flickered in the hearth, adding a warmth that wrapped around them. Nestled in the crook of his arm, definitely her favorite place to be, she felt her brain finally stop buzzing with what-ifs and if-onlys. Instead, she listened to the steady hum of their breathing, the little snaps of the fireplace, and their hearts calming. His fingers slid up her bare arm and down, a soothing motion that nearly put her to sleep.

"You awake?"

"Barely," she murmured, turning to snuggle deeper into his embrace. She brushed her lips against his chest.

His fingers kept tracing that calming rhythm. "I talked to your mom and dad this week."

Jilly lifted up on her elbow so she could see his face. "Levi Bright, did you ask for my hand in marriage like some 1950s hero in a romance book?"

He laughed. "No. Not quite."

When she settled her hand on his chest, he covered it with his. "I have a pretty big loan for a food truck I'm not going to buy."

She continued to stare.

"I have it on pretty good authority that you really like the house they're selling," he said, closing his fingers around hers.

Jilly's thoughts scrambled like her pulse. "What?"

"You love that house, don't you?"

Could he feel her heartbeat galloping? "I do. But, Levi—"

He didn't let her finish. He reversed their positions so he was poised over her, staring down into her eyes. Her fingers curled around the back of his neck and she wondered if he could feel her awe. This man was more than a dream come true. He was everything.

"No buts, Jilly. I mean it. I want a life with you. Pete's place is cool but I really want a full kitchen. And I didn't mean to go behind your back or anything and everything is up for discussion and I'm fine with whatever you want to do as long as I get to be part of your future but your parents and I got to talking." He took a deep breath, let it out.

Once again, her patience paled in comparison to his. "About?"

"There's four bedrooms without the basement. Two floors, good-sized kitchen, and a den. We wouldn't really need the basement. It's already got a bathroom. My dad's company can do the work to make it a great suite for your parents. Then they're close, they don't have to move. And we make the rest of the house ours. We could renovate a bit. Update some things? You really seem to like that tub." He tilted his head in the direction of the soaker tub.

It felt like something heavy was sitting on top of her lungs. She couldn't pull in a full breath. Taking baby breaths, she held his gaze until she could gather her words.

"Is that what you *want*?"

Levi grinned at her in a way that had stolen her breath as a teenager and did exactly the same thing now. He'd only gotten better at making her stomach and her brain spin.

"I want *you*. We can live there, at Pete's, here. Hell, I'll buy the food truck and we can live in that but it'll be crowded."

She laughed with him, surprise and excitement creating a kind of hopefulness inside of her that she barely recognized.

"Their house really is great for raising a family."

"Turns out I have one of those now," Levi said, his fingers trailing down her neck, along her collarbone. "One beautiful, funny, incredibly smart, and cautious woman, and an adorable, quick-witted, smart-as-hell nine-year-old."

Laughing, she leaned up to kiss him. "Don't forget two loud, opinionated brothers and a sweet and persuasive soon-to-be sister-in-law who will all undoubtably be up in our business all of the time."

Pressing a soft kiss to her mouth, he brushed his lips over her cheek, trailed to her ear. "That sounds perfect."

Jillian hugged him close. "I'd rather have real than perfect. I love you, Levi."

He pulled back, smiled at her so brightly, it lit her up inside.

"This is as real as it gets, Jilly. I love you." Then he kissed her again, more demandingly, urging her closer before he turned them so she lay on top of him. "I apologize in advance."

Her heart hiccuped. "For what?"

He cupped her cheeks with both of his hands, his smile a mix of teasing and sexy. "Because you're going to be so tired on your first full day back tomorrow."

Laughing her way into the kiss, she whispered, "Totally worth it."

Thirty-nine

It was all hands on deck—or, more specifically, luggage—the next day as the lodge opened for the season. Levi shouldn't have been surprised by the efficiency and hospitality of the Keller family, but he was. They moved like a well-oiled unit, checking guests in, showing them around, organizing activities and events. For his part, Levi pitched in where he could and kept things running in the kitchen with Chef Shane. They'd chatted a fair amount and the older man was looking forward to this being his last summer at the lodge. Though, he did say he might bring his husband for a couple of weekend getaways.

Levi and Jilly had woken early this morning, and after greeting the day in a way that felt more like a dream than reality, they'd re-dressed the room and made it to the staff meeting with time to spare.

The lodge was fully booked for the entire first week and many of the weeks after that, with check-ins and check-outs overlapping each other. Mr. Keller and Grayson took care of ferrying guests over while Jilly and Ollie got everyone to their rooms. Mrs. Keller helped one of their high school students answer phones and work the front desk. Mateo, who seemed to do a little of everything, helped bring dishes in from the dining room after the lunch service.

Levi thanked him as the kid switched gears to take a group on a short hike. Ideas swirled in his head for how to streamline what they offered for each of the three meals and snacks. Shane was making him a list of suppliers that he currently used.

"Busy day," Shane said. "Once those muffins come out of the oven, we'll put them aside for snacks. Between those, your granola, and the individual snacks Jilly picked up, there'll be enough for guests who get hungry in between."

"This place is amazing," Levi said, tossing a cloth over his shoulder. They'd served an easy lunch of sandwiches on homemade bread with an assortment of salads that were packed with protein for those heading on the hike.

"There's no stopping the Keller siblings when they set their minds to something," Shane said with a pseudo-fatherly pride.

"It's pretty inspiring," Levi commented, starting to clean the counter. They'd do a family-style dinner of spaghetti and meatballs with salad and garlic bread, and apple turnovers for dessert. He had a lot to learn about creating larger quantities while still putting his own twist on things. He'd cooked for more people at one time—one of the dining rooms he'd worked at sat 150 people—but this was different. People wanted hearty, solid meals that provided comfort and tasted delicious.

Not wanting to get in Chef's way as he took the muffins out of the oven, Levi took the hallway down to the laundry room. He had a load of dishcloths in the dryer. Once that was folded and put away, he'd see if he could help in another capacity, since he was prepped for dinner. He was changing a few things in the small office off of the kitchen that Shane used, making it his own. If no one needed help, he might take a look at the suppliers and vendors. A few changes could cut costs and make things more locally sourced. A lot of what they used could be ordered online, so he wanted to set up accounts. Shane was old school, preferring to head to the mainland, but Levi didn't want that time commitment.

Unloading the dryer contents onto the makeshift countertop over the appliances, he began folding as Jilly walked in.

She stopped when she saw him, laundry basket in hand. "Hi."

His heart did a weird little two-step. "Hi." He stepped over to her, took the laundry basket, set it down in front of the washer.

She laughed, and though he knew she was tired, he also knew neither of them was sorry for it. He hooked an arm around her waist and pulled her close, kissing the laughter out of her. She kissed him back, her hands moving to his hips, then slipping under his shirt so her fingers could dance over his skin and drive him nuts.

He couldn't stop the little growl that left his throat when she pushed into him, sending him back a step into the washer. His fingers tightened on her hips and he considered lifting her up, barely remembering that it wasn't the right time or place when a loud beeping startled them both.

Jillian jumped back. "What is that?"

Keeping one hand on her waist, he turned, saw he'd run into the buttons on the washer and activated the midcycle pause button. He pressed it off, turned back to Jillian.

"Everything okay?" Shane called from the kitchen.

Jillian covered her mouth with one hand, laughter shining in her gaze.

"All good. Sorry. Wrong button," Levi called. He pulled Jilly close again, brushing her hair away from her face. She looked so pretty with it down around her shoulders. The pale pink Get Lost Lodge crewneck sweater was a little baggy on her frame. The humor in her gaze was enough to brighten up the dimness of the laundry room.

He poked her arm playfully. "What are you laughing at? If my boss catches me in here making out with his sister, I could get fired."

She put her hands on his chest, went up on her tiptoes, and kissed his cheek. "No way. You've blended in seamlessly. The guests are raving about the food already. I think he's stuck with you."

Levi hugged her tight. "You're stuck with me, too."

He was pretty sure both of their grins bordered on being silly, like they couldn't believe what they had between them was real.

"I like being stuck with you," she whispered into another kiss. It was too short for his liking. "I'm going to take Ollie home, much to her disappointment. She's going to help my mom start sorting through old boxes in the basement to clear space. Do you want a ride back to Smile with me? I'll be back before dinner."

"Yes, please. I'll be ready to go in about twenty minutes. Just want to get the dishcloths and towels put away."

"Okay. Ollie is out working on an herb garden with my mom. I'll tell them we'll be ready to go shortly."

He stepped aside, because if he wanted things to work, he should actually *work* while he was supposed to. Folding the laundry as she started her load of towels, he glanced over at her.

"My dad wanted to go over some ideas for the basement with your parents, but I know everyone is busy so I thought I could meet with him tonight. I chatted with them for a while last week and have an idea of what they want. If his preliminary sketches are guided by that, it might make things move quicker."

Jilly started the washer and smiled at him. "That sounds perfect. I'm glad things are going better with you and your dad."

"Me, too. It's not perfect, but what is?" He said the words out loud but answered them in his own head. *You. You're perfect for me, Jillian Keller.*

"We're going to grab a beer at Bros' after I'm done here tonight. If we can sort through ten years of misunderstandings, maybe those two can as well."

"Let's hope so," Jillian said thoughtfully. He liked her thinking face. He liked everything about her. She picked up one of the cloths, folded it, and set it on the pile he'd started. "I think we each get wrapped up in our versions of how we expect things to go, and then when others don't fall in line, we feel a disappointment we shouldn't."

Levi set the cloth down, focused only on her. "What do you mean?"

Jillian met his gaze. "With your dad, he obviously thought you'd grow up and work alongside him. When you didn't, he wasn't disappointed in *you* but the loss of what he'd imagined. I don't know what happened between Leo and Liam but I would imagine it's similar. And when I fell apart last week, I was thinking about how I owed it to Ollie to make choices that would lead to the least amount of conflict."

"I don't have experience as a parent but I can understand why you'd want to save her heartache and pain."

Jillian stepped closer. "I think that's true when you care about anyone, but it's not realistic. Instead, I realized I need to show her how to embrace life and all it offers, and that includes learning to pick up the pieces if it falls apart."

With a hand on her waist, he pulled her close, bent his knees so he could stare into her beautiful eyes and so she could see the truth in his. "We won't fall apart, Jilly. I love you too much to let that happen."

"I know. I realized that, too. I feel so lucky that I can believe in that and in you. Loving you and letting you love me back makes me stronger, and it makes me sure that there's nothing we can't do together."

Levi grinned, happiness like a vibration running through him. "There's so much I want to do *together*." He kissed her, backed her up to the dryer with his hands gripping her hips.

"You get lost back there, Bright?" Shane's loud voice called from the kitchen.

Levi pulled away and stared into Jillian's eyes. "Be right there," he called back, pulling Jillian into his arms again. There was no one on earth he'd rather get lost in, or with.

Forty

FOUNDER'S DAY, ONE WEEK LATER

Everyone she loved was standing somewhere in this crowd, mixed in with strangers, people she sort of knew, and ones she'd known her whole life. Most of the guests from the lodge had been eager to join in on the two-day celebration that started today. A few of them had opted to remain at the lodge for downtime. With all of the rooms opened and streamlined activities, the first week had felt much easier than last summer. They had their feet under them now. Every day posed new challenges, but all of them were okay with that because it felt like, together, they were making it work. Mr. Dayton was due to arrive later today and the entire Keller family was excited to see him, especially Ollie.

As everyone congregated on the front lawn of the museum, the double doors open, a podium set up on the wide stone porch, energy hummed through the air.

Gramps walked to the podium. "Look at this beautiful crowd."

Everyone cheered and clapped. He waited until they quieted down. "I've lived in Smile for seventy-three years. My whole life. I've watched it grow and change. I've seen people come and go.

I've been other places and always come home. We have a special community here and it's growing every day. I'm grateful to live here with all of you."

Toying with the bracelet Lainey had given her for Levi today, Jill scanned the crowd looking for him. He'd been serving up samples of lodge fare and connecting with tourists and locals. Like he'd sensed her missing him, his hand slipped around her waist, his face dipping next to hers. "I love you," he whispered.

A full-body shiver went through her as she tipped her head back to look at him. "I love you."

He kissed her, and she marveled at how surreal it all felt to be standing here with him, like this. That this was her life.

Gramps continued after stopping briefly for the murmuring. "As I was saying, we're more than a community. We're a family. And one of the biggest influences for all of us in our family and in this community are Pete and Gwen Reid."

Jillian looked over to where Pete stood a head above several others. She couldn't see Gwen but had no doubt she was next to him.

"What are you doing?" Pete called out.

"Don't interrupt and I'll tell you," Gramps shouted back.

Even Pete laughed.

"Sometimes we don't realize the impact people have on us until we really sit down and think about it. Or, until they get someone to clean out their garage and those kids, who I guess really aren't kids anymore, end up on a trip down memory lane. Pete, it started with Levi needing a place to stay, which turned into the Keller siblings jumping on board. Then it trickled down and out because you've touched so many hearts and lives with your waffles and Gwen's kind heart. Some spring cleaning took on new meaning. Pete, Gwen, we decided to honor you and all you've done for our community by doing a retrospective of sorts in the museum."

The crowd, including Levi, Jillian, her brothers, and Presley, who had found their way to standing together, started clapping.

Gramps looked out at Pete. "You matter. You watched half the people in this crowd grow up."

"Because I'm old," Pete yelled, his gruffness tinted with humor.

"That you are. But that just means you've got more history here. People have so many great memories of the place you've held in our community. Thank you, Pete and Gwen, for being leaders in the community. For being part of our family."

Huge cheers and whistles filled the air. Pete, on the urging of Gramps and probably Gwen, came up to the podium.

He looked out into the crowd. "Get up here, Gwennie. I've never done this alone and I'm not starting now.

"Who did this?" Pete demanded of the crowd, his voice cracking just a little. "What's in there?" He hooked a thumb over his shoulder toward the museum as Gwen joined him on the stage. "If it makes me cry I'll be putting chili flakes in your waffles for a month."

Gwen wrapped her arms around one of his, leaning into him. Pete leaned down and kissed the top of his wife's head.

Pete looked out at the crowd. "All I ever wanted was to live in this town, marry Gwennie, and have our girl. I know I can be a grumpy bas—"

Gwen tugged on his arm.

Pete frowned. "A *grump*. But you all come to my diner all the time and let me do exactly what I want to wake up and do every day. The fact that you'd honor me and Gwennie for the privilege of living here and being part of your lives is too much. But we appreciate you. All of you."

Everyone clapped. Pete and Gwen hugged Gramps and each other. Then Gramps led them forward into the exhibit. People

dispersed, some to get to their booths and tents, others to visit
the museum, and still others to set up on the shore with picnic
spots.

It would be a long and wonderful day, and there was absolutely
nowhere else in the world Jillian could imagine being happier.

As the day slipped into night, a band played a slow song. The moon
rose in the sky, sharing the space with thousands of stars. Jillian
had eaten way too much food, bought too many things, and given
out every last one of her Get Lost Lodge business cards. Grayson
would be returning to the lodge shortly. Shane had already gone
over to make sure the few guests who remained on the island had
dinner.

She saw Ollie moving through the crowd with her parents following behind. She carried a mostly eaten swirl of cotton candy.

There'd be no sleeping again tonight with all that sugar.
Leaning into Levi's embrace, she wasn't sorry. Life was too wonderful in this moment to worry about sleep. She didn't want to
miss a thing.

Reaching into her pocket, she pulled out the thin black leather
bracelet that she'd had Lainey make. It had dark and light blue
beads with silver spacers.

"What? You got me one?" He stared at it, his eyes shimmering
with the kind of love she not only recognized but felt in her bones.

"Lainey mentioned you wanted to match. I'm guessing you
know what it says?"

He laughed as he slipped it on. "I love you."

Pushing her hands up to curl them around his neck, she
sighed into a kiss before whispering the words back to him.

As she and Levi swayed, not really dancing since he moved

behind her, her parents and Ollie joined them. Grayson found them at the edge of the makeshift dance floor. Levi's parents were dancing slowly over by the gazebo. As she continued to hold Levi close, Ollie right there, she scanned the crowd until one sight made her brows arch. Lainey was dancing with Graham. He held her close and they moved together like there was no one else around them. *Hmm. Maybe everyone will get a happily-ever-after.* She'd be asking her friend about that later.

"Excellent crowd," Grayson said. "Our guests are having a great time."

"Why wouldn't they?" Ollie asked, pulling off another hunk of cotton candy. "This is awesome."

Everyone laughed, and Jillian saw Beckett and Presley right in front of them. Her brother was twirling Presley, whose head was tipped back as she laughed at something he said.

When she looked at him, Jilly felt the love Beckett had for her emanating off of him, in his gaze, his stance. Maybe it was easier to recognize because of the man behind her. The one who made her believe she'd have what Presley and Beckett were headed for.

As the band switched to a more upbeat number, Presley and Beckett joined the family.

"You two," her mother said, staring at them with love and hope in her gaze.

"This is so much fun. I love it here," Presley said. Her eyes were shining with happiness, and Jilly felt so much gratitude that she'd dropped into their lives last summer, then decided to stay. No one would have predicted it, but Beckett and Presley were a perfect fit.

Tilting her own head back on Levi's shoulder, she looked at him, smiling as he gazed down at her.

"I love you, Presley," Beckett said. He was probably loud to

make sure she heard him over the music, but standing as close as
they all were, it felt like he'd shouted it.

Presley's eyes opened comically wide. "I love you, too, Beckett.
Is there a reason you're declaring that in this particular moment?"

Beckett nodded, planting himself in front of Presley, taking both of her hands. Jilly's heart seized in her chest. She stood
straight.

Beckett's voice was a little shaky but his gaze was sure. "Like
Gramps said, life is short. I don't want regrets. I've never loved anyone in my life the way I love you, and I've been racking my brain
trying to plan the perfect engagement. One that would make it impossible for you to say no to spending your life with me. But there's
no perfect. Life is hard and messy and there are no guarantees."

He dropped to one knee and Jilly gasped. She wasn't the only
one.

Grayson muttered under his breath. "Holy shit."

Presley had one hand covering her mouth, the other in Beckett's. With his free hand, he dug in his pocket and pulled out a
small black box.

Letting go of her hand while she stared down at him, her eyes
glassy, he opened the box to reveal a sparkling princess-cut diamond ring with a thin band of tiny diamonds surrounding it.

"I love you, Presley. Now, tomorrow, for the rest of my life.
You're the best thing that ever happened to me. I want to marry
you. I want to spend every single day showing you how much I
love you. We'll fight and mess up but I'll always work to show you
how much you matter. You'll never be lonely because you'll always
have me and the rest of these guys hanging around." He gestured
to his family standing around him, watching with happiness and
love and excitement.

Beckett looked back up at Presley. "Marry me?"

Presley nodded, tears slipping down her cheeks as she went down on her knees and Beckett slipped the ring on her finger. She hugged him with so much force he went back on his knees and fell to his butt, taking her with him. She sat in his lap, kissing his face repeatedly, making everyone laugh as she kept saying, "Yes, yes, yes, yes."

Jillian swiped at her own tears, leaning into Levi. Ollie leaned into their side, sort of between them.

Beckett helped Presley to her feet, keeping her close as everyone moved in to congratulate them.

When Jilly stepped back from hugging them both, she tripped over someone's foot. Levi was right there, catching her in his arms. She wrapped hers around him and closed her eyes as his breath warmed the shell of her ear.

"I've got you, Jilly," he whispered into her ear, his hand moving up to her shoulders and squeezing. "Always."

When she gazed into his eyes, she both saw and felt the truth of it.

"Same," she whispered.

Hugging him tight, Jillian tried to commit the happiness she felt to memory. It would remind her, in hard times, that he was someone she could believe in. They were in this together. For good.

Epilogue

Jillian curled up on the couch in the living room, a cup of hot chocolate warming her hands as the lights of the Christmas tree warmed the room. Bing Crosby played softly through the Bluetooth and she smiled at the memory of learning, when moving in his record collection, that Levi had a soft spot for the classics. For his birthday in October, Ollie had insisted they get him a new retro-style turntable, and he'd loved it.

For Jilly, it felt sort of surreal to listen to music her mom had loved, in the house her parents raised her in, while dancing around the living room with her own daughter and the man she'd loved for the better part of her life. The past and the present had done a lot of merging in the months that followed their making up.

Levi came down the hallway, his gaze and smile competing for brightness against the backdrop of the tree.

"Ollie's asleep. I don't know why she wanted me to read 'Twas the Night Before Christmas. She had the entire thing memorized," he said with a laugh, sitting down next to her, careful of her hot drink.

Jillian leaned her head on his shoulder. "It's a family favorite."

Slipping his hand over her thigh, he sat with her listening to the music, the softness of the lights and the crackle of the fire adding an air of romance to the mood. Or maybe that was Levi. Everything felt more romantic, more *right*, now that he was in her life.

"Will it be strange for you if your parents don't come up first thing in the morning?" Levi asked.

Jillian set her mug on the coffee table she and Levi had debated over for far longer than they should have needed to. Turned out, no matter how compatible a couple was, they could still have entirely different furniture tastes when redecorating.

They'd chosen the style he wanted—wide planked with barn-style doors on each side—in the color she wanted—a faded, somewhat distressed-looking blue.

Turning into him, she smiled when his arm came around her, pulling her closer.

"I want us to start our own traditions. Waking up with just you and Ollie is new and I want to enjoy that. They'll be up for brunch, and everyone else will join then, too."

Levi tapped her nose with his finger, then kissed her. "I know the plan. I made it with you. I asked if it'll be strange for you."

She shrugged. "I guess. Different, for sure. Just like it will be for you. How many years has it been since you had Christmas dinner with your parents?"

His fingers trailed over the sensitive skin of her neck. "Too many. I'm looking forward to it. They really adore Ollie. And you."

"Believe it or not, your dad really adores you, too. I overheard him telling Ollie about when you were a kid at Christmas. I can't imagine, as a mom, what it would be like to have Ollie move so far away. When we're doing it ourselves, like you, me, Beckett, and Grayson did, it feels natural, like that's how it's supposed to be. It's strange to be on this side of it now, knowing Ollie may live her adult life far away. It would definitely be hard to wrap my head around."

Things weren't always smooth between Levi and his dad, but for the most part, they'd both let go of whatever expectations they'd had of each other and started to accept who the other was in the here and now. As for her parents, Levi's dad had done a wonderful job with the suite downstairs. They had their own entrance around the back, making it feel like two completely separate homes.

"You never know, she could go and then come home and move in with you again."

Jillian laughed. "Let's hope not. I love her, but something tells me she might get bossier. She'll need her own space to be in charge of. It's hard enough compromising with you."

He stretched his foot out to tap the coffee table. "You love this thing. You know you do."

She'd wanted one with no storage underneath so they weren't tempted to just collect things they didn't need. Levi insisted having storage would make her less irritated by the number of food magazines he purchased because then they'd have a place to hide.

"I love you. I know that." She tipped her head back and looked at him. She really did. More each day, and what truly made her wake up every day in awe was knowing, in her heart and her mind, that he loved her back. The words were powerful and she cherished them but, with Levi, it was more about what he did; how he *showed* his love.

Levi leaned in, kissing her soft and slow, drowning her in gentleness. She was sinking into it, her bones melting with the sensuousness of his mouth moving against hers, when that admirable patience of his seemed to snap. As he pulled her onto his lap, his kisses grew rougher, like he couldn't fight his need for her and like it still surprised him. Jillian loved that; loved knowing he craved her touch, her nearness, the same way she did his. It was one thing to love, but being loved back was something she'd never take for granted. She'd never understood the magic of knowing how much she mattered to someone who mattered so much to her.

His fingers were buried in her hair, her legs on either side of his waist, when he leaned away, his head against the back of the couch. "Superbolts."

Dazed and still lost in him, she blinked. "What?"

He smiled, his thumb tracing over her lower lip. "They're stronger than lightning and rare, less expected. I never saw you coming. And every time I'm with you, touching you, kissing you, or just looking at you, I feel like my entire body is a live wire."

"Superbolts," she repeated softly.

He nodded. "Yup. You literally light me up inside, Jillian."

Pressing both of her hands to his face, she squeezed it gently. "You're already perfect for me. When you say things like that, it's almost too much."

He gave her one of his classic Levi grins. The one that said he wasn't sorry at all and knew exactly how into him she was. "Want me to stop saying things like that?"

Jillian gave him a noisy kiss. "Don't you dare."

His hands wandered down to her hips. "Want one of your presents?"

"Now?" She let her gaze roam over him in his gray Henley that stretched over his chest, then followed with her hands.

With little effort, Levi lifted her and plopped her down beside him. Sliding one of the mini barn doors open on the coffee table, he pulled out an oddly shaped, somewhat messily wrapped gift. It was about the length of her hand and very narrow.

Handing it to her, he scooted back a bit on the couch. She took the gift. It was stiff, with a little ridge. When she looked up at him through lowered lashes he was smiling, but there was tension, or maybe nerves, peeking through as well.

"Unwrap it," he urged.

Focusing on the present, Jillian tore at the holiday wrap to find a standard black pen, much like the ones she used at the lodge. This one, however, had a thin strip of paper wrapped around it.

"I am always running out of pens," she teased.

Levi laughed, eased a little farther back, while Jillian picked at the tape carefully to unroll the paper.

Using both hands, Jillian held on to the pen while opening the curled paper.

WILL YOU MARRY ME?

Yes ☐
Obviously ☐
Absolutely ☐

Jillian's hand flew to her mouth automatically, covering her gasp. She dropped the pen and looked up at the same time to see Levi had slipped off the couch cushion to one knee. He held a stunning diamond solitaire on a thin platinum band between his thumb and index finger. His gaze was steady even though his hand shook just a little.

"You'll need the pen. The note says it all but just in case you need to hear it, I love you, Jillian Keller. Nothing would make me happier than being your husband. I want to stand up in front of all of our friends and family and vow to spend the rest of my days loving you and sharing your life. Our life. I want to watch Ollie grow up with you, maybe have some more kids, travel, any of it, all of it. I want it all with you, Jillian. Will you be my wife?"

How was he talking? She couldn't make words leave her mouth, so she nodded. Emphatically, her gaze jumping back and forth between the ring in his hand and *him*.

"Use the pen, Jilly."

She gave a watery laugh and picked it up off the floor, quickly putting large checkmarks in each one of the boxes.

Levi laughed and she tossed the pen and paper down, held out her hand.

"I love you," he whispered as the ring slid perfectly onto her finger.

"I love you," she said. "I can't wait to marry you."

He leaned up at the same time she leaned down, like they'd synchronized their movements.

Between kisses and laughter, some tears, and more laughter, he kept telling her how much she mattered, how much she meant. She said the same to him, marveling at the fact that, in some ways, her life hadn't changed at all. She was in the living room she'd grown up in; the one she'd spent most of her Christmases in, in the small town she'd always considered home. But in other ways, absolutely everything was different. The familiarity mixed with the newness of it all was a kind of magic Jillian had never known. Levi Bright was the boy she'd loved and the man she'd marry. And while she'd learned the hard way that fairy tales weren't real, she also knew the reality of spending every day with him was better than anything she could have ever imagined.

IT'S NEVER REALLY THE END.

Acknowledgments

If you go to the acknowledgments page in any of my books, you'll see a lot of repetition. The reason for this is because I'm lucky enough to have so many constants in my life. I sort of crave those (like Jilly). So, first, thank you, readers, because this book is for you. And thank you, SMP (there are SO many people who take part in getting a book from idea to shelf—from commas to cover), and, in particular, my team, who are always looking for the best ways to help me keep writing books. I'm very grateful. Alex. You're simply the best. Thank you, as well, to Cassidy. And to Fran; your enthusiasm for my writing keeps me going.

If you're one of those people who reads the acknowledgments (like me), you are probably waiting for me to also thank my wonderful husband, who feeds and indulges me, and my children, who are both unbelievably amazing. I mean, AMAZING. They're so kind and supportive and I love you all so much. My bestie spends a lot of time talking me off ledges, and Stacey and Cole and Sarah keep making sure I believe I can actually do this. Thank you to all the other people who lift me up, including Kim, Addie, Kristyn, Hannah, and so many others who are not just champions for my books but for me. I appreciate you.

You guys, Helena Hunting is reading this book for me and I'm so grateful. Because if you didn't know, she's all kinds of cool and also Canadian. Who else is reading it? Betty Cayouette because she is sweet and so awesome. If you don't follow those two on social media, you should.

I'm grateful for the people who remind me every single day that I belong here, that I'm loved, and that I matter. I think it's all any of us really want.

It bears repeating: thank you, readers, for wanting my words. I hope you love Jilly and Levi.

About the Author

Shelley Bell

Sophie Sullivan (she/her) is a Canadian author as well as a cookie-eating, Diet Pepsi–drinking Disney enthusiast who loves reading and writing romance in almost equal measure. She loves to doodle bookmarks of moments from her favorite books. She's unintentionally funny, geographically challenged, and often late (except for work). But she means well. *Ten Rules for Faking It* and *How to Love Your Neighbor* both received the Canadian Book Club Award for best romance. She's had plenty of practice writing happily-ever-afters as her alter ego, Jody Holford.